"*The German* is a smart and bravely conceived thriller, rich with historical detail that draws readers into its WWII-era story of small-town violence and repressed sexuality. Lee Thomas populates his fictional town with believable, multi-faceted characters, and he shifts perspectives effortlessly to give the most complete view of the story. And at the story's dark heart is the German of the title: a mysterious, seemingly detached narrator whose hypnotic voice reveals layers of complexity as the story unfolds. By the time the book races towards its exciting, agonizing conclusion, readers won't know who the real monsters are."
—NORMAN PRENTISS
Bram Stoker Award Winner, author of *Invisible Fences*

"A worthy successor to Clive Barker, Lee Thomas has a firm grasp of both the epic and intimate aspects of horror fiction."
—BENTLEY LITTLE
author of *The Disappearance*

"...Thomas' prose is an absolute delight, rich in imagery, precise and elegant... [L]ike all the best horror, [he] expands our knowledge—and our fears—about what it means to be human."
—RUE MORGUE MAGAZINE #99
(on *In the Closet, Under the Bed*)

"Lee Thomas is a fantastic writer with a gift for invoking our most intimate fears—and preying on them mercilessly."
—CHRISTOPHER GOLDEN
Bram Stoker Award-winner, author of *The Chamber of Ten*

The German

The German

Lee Thomas

Lethe Press
Maple Shade, NJ

Published in 2011 by LETHE PRESS, INC.
118 Heritage Avenue • Maple Shade, NJ 08052-3018
www.lethepressbooks.com • lethepress@aol.com
ISBN: 1-59021-309-2
ISBN-13: 978-1-59021-309-4

This is a work of fiction. Names, characters, places, and incidents are products of the author's imagination or are used fictitiously.

Set in Warnock and Cloister.
Interior design: Alex Jeffers.
Cover photo: Nadya Lukic.
Cover design: Lee Thomas / execution: Alex Jeffers.
Author photo: Michael J. Hall

Library of Congress Cataloging-in-Publication Data

Thomas, Lee, 1965-
 The German / Lee Thomas.
  p. cm.
 ISBN 978-1-59021-309-4 (alk. paper)
 1. Young men--Crimes against--Fiction. 2. Texas--History--1846-1950--Fiction. 3. Psychological fiction. I. Title.
 PS3620.H6317G47 2011
 813.6--dc22

2010033904

For ED BURLESON, *my first friend in Austin,*
and as always,
JOHN CHARLES PERRY

Acknowledgements

I'd like to thank the early readers of this book for their encouragement and insights. They include Nate Southard, Steve Berman and Howard Morhaim. Thanks guys, much appreciated. For the dark rainbow rising: Jameson Currier, Vince Liaguno, Chad Helder, Paul G. Bens Jr., Michael Rowe, Norman Prentiss, Tom Cardamone, Robert Dunbar, and again, Steve Berman. To the members of *Who Wants Cake?* past and present: a finer bunch you'll not find.

And finally a special acknowledgement to the works of Jack Ketchum, a guy who knows what pain is and how much is required to bend a human being to the monstrous.

"All revolutions devour their own children."
—ERNST RÖHM

"No matter how a man alone ain't got no bloody fucking chance."
—ERNEST HEMINGWAY, from *To Have and Have Not*

Prologue: Munich

Date Unknown – Translated from the German

I remember a hole, deep and dark, with water pooling at the bottom like blood in an open wound. I rub my chest and scabs flake away like bits of autumn leaf, tumbling down to float on the dark water. My thoughts twist tight, wrung like damp linen, each crease made permanent by the wrapping tension.

Gazing along my cold body, clothed only in white drawers, I am disturbed by the hole in the ground and the holes in my torso: three neat apertures from which my blood has poured. But no more. Membranes of skin already seal my muscle and bone from the elements. I can feel the slow knit of flesh. Itching. Burning. That hole. A grave. Meant for me. Rain is in the air, and I observe the sky and the field of granite markers about me as I inhale the scents. Earth. Stone. Grass. From my body a different odor pours. It is foul like the mingling of dirt and rot. Dropping my chin, I again observe the mementos of bullets decorating my chest.

I remember a small cell. It reeks of sweat and tobacco. A man looks at me along the length of his pistol barrel. Outside, a firing squad is being ordered to shoot. The rifle reports fill my cell like thunder roll. The air about me shifts as though disturbed by the gunfire, creating a draft and sending chills over my perspiring body. The man before me is shouting, but I don't remember the words.

Then I am in this cemetery with frigid air running over my bare skin. I shiver against it. Hug myself and wince as I feel my chest contract and the knitting membrane tear so slightly, but I am very, very cold, so I continue the embrace. I have never known such chill. I look skyward and observe an ashen blanket of clouds. The dim light might be that of early morning or late afternoon. I cannot say. I try my voice, whispering a meaning-less prayer. It is rough. My throat feels clogged with dirt. Speaking makes it ache so I stop.

The chill works through my skin. It presses into my wounds painfully like frozen needles. Looking around the cemetery and finding it vacant – save the tall markers – I walk to the east. I was born and raised in this city. A lifetime ago. Bits of that life come back to me as I work my way between the markers toward the eastern wall.

I question the memories flooding me: the faces of so many men. They called me son and soldier and commander. They called me brute and traitor and deviant.

I remember laughter as they marched the accused to the wall.

⫻

While walking I realize the gloom is night's approach, not its retreat. Purple shadow stains the sides of the house before me. Clotheslines run like white veins through the murk connecting the house to the fence at my back. I steal a shirt from the line and a pair of trousers, and then crouch behind a shed. Still I am frozen to the core. My stomach rumbles painfully. Days since my last meal. Base needs conflict with a maddening belief in my own inhumanity. Has the assumption of death reduced me to animal instinct or has it refined my desires, focusing my thoughts on what truly matters, what is irrevocably true? A man must be clothed, must be sheltered, must be fed. All the rest, the aspirations and pride, seem pale and foolish to a man squatting cold and hungry behind a ragged shack in the yard of a stranger.

A lunatic's memories are presented as pantomimes behind my eyes.

I consider entering this house and demanding food. Once I would have commandeered the property and taken what was needed, but the knitting membrane within my wounds reminds me of the tragedy of arrogance. Besides, a friend's home is near by. I can think of few others to trust, and this man has no political affiliation. Our common history explored the intimacies of men not the ideologies.

Hesitantly, I stand. My gaze roams over the yard and the low fence separating this home from its neighbor. Then on I look to the next yard and the next.

A man with black hair stands in the center of this distant yard. He is the friend whose companionship drew me. Tall and slender, he stands motionlessly, dark eyes staring from a pale face. We stand there for uncounted seconds observing one another as if we are the only two men remaining in the world. He cocks his head to the side, a gesture familiar to me. Then his face melts and his mouth opens like a chasm and his eyes stare in dread, and I take his changed expression as a warning, imagining some villain creeping up at my back, but when I turn to face the threat, I find only the shed and the low fence and another yard strung with white drying lines. His fearful expression is for me, and I think it rude and strange that this man I once knew as an intimate should show such revulsion at my face. I lift my hand to wave and indicate I mean no harm, and he flees.

Confounded, I look skyward at the blanket of storm clouds, now black in the late dusk. I remember standing in a cell and a man with the dull countenance of a bull firing his pistol, but I do not remember the shove of bullets or the tearing of my skin, though these things must surely have followed the bright flares from the pistol's mouth if only because of the evidence left on my chest.

And I tell myself this cannot be. I am not dead, nor have I ever been. There is another explanation for the wounds and my waking at the side of a grave, and were I not so cold and hungry my reason would puzzle the situation out, except I am cold and

I am hungrier than I can tolerate, and the baffling perfume of dirt and decay rolls off my skin to fill my nose, and I sense that I am wholly alone for the first time in my life.

Wandering. I steal another shirt to layer with the first and confiscate three pair of socks, but my blood is still ice. Finally the hunger overwhelms me and I break into a house through the back door, and in the kitchen I open the icebox and remove a plate. A hunk of pork sits amid a gray pool of congealed grease and I devour both meat and savory fat. There is a bread box and inside is a half loaf of very brown bread. This too is consumed and my stomach settles, comforted by the meal. I drink water from a jug and then search the house for additional garments as the cold remains in my bones. In a bedroom with walls decorated by prints of purple flowers, an armoire produces a number of suits and a coat, which I quickly take from the hook. The sleeves are too long, and the coat will not close over my chest, but it is wool and heavy, and already traps warmth against my body. I steal a pair of brown leather shoes that are too big for my feet even with the layers of socks. In a small toilet down the hall a teardrop shaped bottle catches my eye. I remove the stopper and the scent of roses wafts from the glass lips. I pour the perfume into a palm and rub it over my cheeks and neck and across my chest beneath the layers of coat and shirts, and my wounds protest the stinging liquid, but the grave scent is masked. I return to the kitchen and drink more water and then leave the house through the door I entered.

Outside I pause with no destination clear in my mind. I dare not seek shelter with friends, because I no longer know who my friends are. Going home could mean further confrontation with those who had me imprisoned, and my face is too well known to allow sufficient anonymity on these streets. The stolen pockets carry no money, and the private resources I might access are secured in a foreign bank. I leave the yard and walk to the darkened road, and I look first to the north and then to the south – uncertain.

Where is a dead man to go if not into flame or earth?

The Barnard Register, D-Day 1944

INVASION!
ALLIED TROOPS BEGIN A SWEEPING CAMPAIGN ACROSS NORTHERN FRANCE

Great invasion is underway in Havre-Cherbourg region.

One: 𝕿im 𝕽andall

We got it wrong. All of it.

Everyone who knew Harold Ashton was convinced he had run off to join the war. It was after all, a patriotic and reasonable thing for young men to do, particularly when the country faced such icons of villainy as Hirohito, Mussolini and Hitler. Many heroes had been born in Barnard, Texas, and now an entire generation of them was noticeably absent from the streets and the shops and the beds of their loved ones. Dozens of Barnard's finest boys were buried in graves across the ocean in Europe – some underneath markers of wood and stone, and others lay anonymously beneath low rises of dirt in nameless fields. Others still fought, like the Richardson brothers, who were somewhere in Normandy, and Delbert Himmelmann who was stationed in the South Pacific. Of course, some men had returned. Ervin "Eagle-eye" Seagle came home the fall before, missing a foot, an ear, and half of his teeth. Stanley "Uncle Stan" Moffat stepped off the train in Austin, looking like the strapping man who had left the city two years before, only to proceed to his house in Barnard and blow a good part of his skull apart with the Parker shotgun his papa had given him. Brett Fletcher returned with a broken back after a mortar turned over the Jeep he was driving. Brett was the first casualty from Barnard, Texas, and he'd been home for a year before the allies landed at Omaha Beach. When asked about his injury, Brett cursed it, not because the doctors had told him he'd never walk again, but because it had taken him away from the cause, the battle, the moral imperative. "I still had me some work to do," he often complained to the groups of boys and girls who frequently visited his farmhouse out on Bennet Road. Harold Marker Ashton was a regular visitor to Fletcher's porch, where he'd looked on in wonder as the man in the wheelchair spun verbal tapestries of heroism. Often enough, Harold told his friends and his mama that he couldn't wait to face off on the Krauts or the Japs and show them what a boy from Barnard, Texas, could really do. So when he went missing on the night of June 7th, folks naturally assumed Harold had tired of waiting, and he'd run away to enlist. He was nearly seventeen years old and big for his age. The flimsiest of lies would have convinced any recruitment officer he was mature enough to fight. His mother sat at the kitchen table on the morning of June 9th and cried. She couldn't have been prouder of her brave son.

Many residents of Barnard felt the same way. Despite grief and fear, it was a good fight. *The* good fight. And the war brought the community together, just as it had the entire nation.

Minor tensions remained in the city of Barnard, certainly. How could they not? Though most residents had never seen an Oriental face outside of a movie theatre or a magazine, nearly one quarter of Barnard's population was of German descent, and petty squabbles became amplified by misunderstanding and doubt. Such uncertainty was to be expected, but rarely had the speculations erupted into overt violence. If anything, it was all treated as a source of humor like the time Cedric Palmer called Old Man Reinhardt a "Goddamn Kraut" for buying the last ham from the butcher one Saturday afternoon. Palmer laughed and slapped his knee. The butcher, who certainly heard the comment – because he was meant to and a German himself – produced a crooked smile in return.

I never noticed this passive animosity on my street. The four-block stretch that ended at Kramer Lake was quiet and peaceful with folks helping their neighbors and smiling politely as they passed on the sidewalks. The houses were of a neat ranch-style design, and all but two were painted white.

Mrs. Reginald Watley had painted her house blue because she'd thought it pleasant, and Ernst Lang owned the yellow house at the end of Dodd adjacent to a broad grassy slope, running to the water's edge.

Mr. Lang had lived on Dodd Street for over seven years, moving to America after fleeing the encroaching rise of the Nazi regime. He made furniture, mostly rocking chairs, that he sold at the hardware store in town. His accent remained strong, but he spoke English very well. Though he mostly kept to himself, Mr. Lang was a respected member of the community and could be counted on by his neighbors to help with the odd chore or errand when asked politely. Even Mildred McDowell, who had lost a son and a husband to the war, tolerated him as a neighbor.

As for me, I looked on the German with a bit of awe. He was not tall, but his brawny build and scarred face gave him an authority that his stature couldn't diminish. Further, he was a good man. He helped me once. He might have even saved my life, but that isn't something I'll ever know for certain.

I will always regret that night in August. What we did to that man was unforgivable.

⫿

The day they found Harold Ashton's body on the far side of Kramer Lake was the first scorcher of the summer. My best friend, Bum, and I had gotten an early start and spent the morning riding our bikes through the city, traveling south toward the fairgrounds and the stockyards and looping up to the east of town. Barnard was shaped like an anvil, with Kramer Lake scalloping the west side and ranchlands pushing in from the east. We pedaled along the smooth gray city roads and their shabbier cousins, the farm roads, to see the factory where my mother worked to support the family while my daddy was overseas, and the greasy stink of the place – an odor that seemed to have worked into my mother's pores and oozed from her every garment – rolled through the hot morning air. In town we walked our bikes over the sidewalks, peeking in windows that revealed the exact same things we'd seen a hundred times before. Sun-baked buildings and windows smeared with glare drew us, and we saw Milton Teague running his barber's razor over a strop and Hattie Barnes adjusting the sapphire-blue hat on a man-nequin's head. We didn't go into any of the shops. Our journey was less about a destination than it was simply to be going and doing and seeing, but as the morning progressed, the beating sun turned up the fire, and Bum complained about feeling like a Sunday roast, and I told him it wasn't so bad, but I was just playing tough. Often enough, Bum and I calibrated the weather by how much lemonade it would take to cool off, and leaning against our bikes in downtown Barnard, we agreed that that sweltering Wednesday in the latter part of June was building up to be a two-galloner — no question in our twelve-year-old minds.

I suggested we stop in at Delrubio's Drug Store for a soda, but Bum wanted the lake, and though I usually won such argu-ments, I had to admit the cool water sounded good to me. Be-sides, a pitcher of tea waited in the icebox at home, and I knew where my mother kept her secret tin of sugar. Rationing had made the sweet crystals valuable and had made me a sneak.

Bum wrestled with his bike until he got the seat under his plump backside, and we set off toward the west side of town.

My best friend was a pudgy kid who had attached to me like metal to a magnet on our first day of school. We'd spent most of the summer together, because Bum didn't like being at home. When he was at home he holed up in his bedroom, read-ing books he'd checked out from the Barnard library to avoid his troublesome family. And yes, Bum was his real name: Bum Craddick. His daddy had a sad sense of humor; so all eight of the Craddick kids were saddled with unfortunate names. The worst was his oldest brother, whose birth certificate read Mud-bug Francis Craddick. Their mama let it happen, but she was slow. Folks around Barnard said she was "touched in the head." My mother said only insanity could explain why such a pretty girl would marry an ox like Clayton Craddick.

There were times I envied Bum's family, having so many brothers and sisters. I didn't have close family to speak of except my mother and her family, and Daddy, of course, but he was off fighting. I wondered what it would be like to share the house with other kids. Then, Bum would come on by with his knees scraped up or an eye blackened – wounds caused by one of his older brothers – and I'd figure things were okay the way they were.

Before the war, my mother was always home. When I woke up, breakfast waited for me on a plate, and after the dishes were done, she swept and dusted and mopped and did laundry, and sometimes she would sit in the kitchen with her best friend Rita Sherman, talking and listening to music drifting in from the RCA console in the living room. She still did all of these things, but now Ma rushed through the chores so that she could accomplish them all before her shift at the factory started. As for my daddy, he had worked as a sales manager at the stockyards before going overseas, and his job required him to take frequent trips to Dallas, Houston, and Austin, and even when his work didn't take him out of town, we didn't see much of him. He liked to spend his evenings at the Longhorn Tavern talking with "the boys" or playing cards over to Deke Williams' house. What little time we had spent together had been on the edge of Kramer Lake where we'd fished for catfish and bass, or up north in the scrublands hunting wild pigs. Those excursions had been rare and had all but dwindled to nothing before he'd been called to service. He gave me my bicycle when I was seven, but didn't have the time to teach me how to ride, so I'd done it myself, leaving a lot of my knee and elbow skin on the street in the process, and for Christmas one year he gave me a baseball glove, but he'd never had the time to toss me a ball. I hated thinking that he'd never get the chance – hated thinking he'd never come home.

The summer had been dry. Too dry, some folks said. The old men who gathered at Milton's Barbershop to play pinochle talked about drought and what it would do to the crops. I didn't know much about that. I just knew the dust was heavy, and the gnats were swarming, and nothing really came into focus no matter what the time of day.

Though eager to get to the cold water, we didn't race across town. We pedaled lazily, knowing relief wasn't too far off.

"The lake's gonna feel good," Bum said. "We ought to just stay out there 'til dark."

"We'd get eaten alive."

"It'd be worth it. Skeeter bites ain't nothing compared to riding around in this. All the dirt sticking to my neck and arms. Feel like I got scabbed over head to toe."

"We'd miss lunch."

"It'll keep. Right now, I about want to spend the whole night up to my neck."

"Don't we have more important things to do tonight?" I asked.

Bum's face lit up with a smile. He arched his eyebrows and said, "Spy Commander?"

"Roger and out," I replied in my best military tone.

Spy Commander was a game we'd built around a cheap tin spyglass Bum had received for his birthday. Whenever the notion hit us, we'd write the name of a neighbor on a scrap of paper, and that was our assignment. Since my mother worked the swing shift and since Bum stayed over at my house more times than not that summer, Bum and I could go out late at night, and we'd carry the spyglass like it was government issue. Then we'd find an advantageous angle – a tree branch, some shrubs, the roof of a shack – and we'd observe whoever's name appeared on our assignment sheet, the glass taking us through windows and into living rooms, kitchens and bedrooms. We didn't know our game was against the law, though I guess we both knew it was wrong. I suppose it wouldn't have been any fun if it weren't.

At home, I reminded Bum to be quiet, because my mother would be asleep for at least another hour, and I fixed us glasses of tea, retrieving the secret sugar tin from my daddy's tackle box, which Ma kept in the pantry. Only a half-inch of sugar covered the bottom of the tin. I showed it to Bum and he shook his

head and I returned it to the pantry, knowing that even a spoon-
ful would likely be missed.

With our glasses empty and placed carefully in the sink,
we crept to my room and changed into our swimming shorts,
and then left the house, wandered down to the field at the lake's
edge. Only a few people lounged on the grass or splashed in
the water. The men that remained in town were at work, and
so were many of the women. Besides, most folks gathered at a
park on the southern edge of the lake for sunbathing and swimming, which made this little patch something of an oasis for the
neighborhood. I saw Little Lenny Elliot talking excitedly with a
bunch of older kids on the right, and Mrs. Lafferty lying on her
back on a plaid blanket in a blue bathing suit that was so tight it
looked like her thighs and chest were attempting to escape like a
butterfly from a chrysalis. I didn't immediately recognize any of
the people in the water, except for my neighbor, the German.

Mr. Lang bobbed with his back to us, looking across the lake
at the finger of land owned by Jerome Blevins. A great mane of
pine and oak rose over the low hills there in the west, sweeping
north and south along the lake's perimeter.

As we approached the water my neighbor turned around.
When he saw us, he lifted his burly arm in a wave.

"Hello, Mr. Lang," I called. Bum echoed me.

"Boys," the German replied.

I always enjoyed seeing my neighbor. Sometimes I thought
he was the only man left in my neighborhood, which more and
more resembled a land of women and children. He pushed
through the water toward the shore and climbed over a narrow beach of rocks to the grass. After yanking a towel from the
limb of a pecan tree, he began scrubbing his face and hair. "The
water's good," he said.

"I bet," Bum said, already peeling off his shirt.

"Are you going back in?" I asked.

"No. No, you boys can have it," he said.

"Maybe you'll come back later."

"Ernst is done for today. I have a chair to finish."

"Another rocker?"

"Yes," he replied. "Hank Carter sold two more of my chairs to a couple from Leander who would like a third for the woman's mother."

"Neat," I said too exuberantly.

Mr. Lang seemed confused by my choice of words, but he smiled and nodded and agreed, "Yes, it is *neat*."

I liked Mr. Lang's voice and frequently found myself searching for topics to keep a conversation going. He didn't sound like the Germans in movies, with their clipped and harsh vibrato delivery. He spoke slowly in a low register that softened the edges of his accent.

"Oh and thanks again for helping Ma with the gutters."

"You are welcome. Now you and your friend enjoy the lake."

"We will."

Then the German wandered away, humming a tune I didn't recognize as he climbed the low rise of grass to the road above, scrubbing his head with the towel like he was trying to put out a fire. As I watched him go, Bum leapt into the water with a great crash.

"Ah," he said upon surfacing. "That takes the rust off."

Eager to get out of the hot day and join my friend, I yanked off my shirt and dropped it next to Bum's, and then I waded in. The morning sweat and dust washed away and the clamp of lethargy at the back of my head loosened, and I began to think Bum's idea of spending both day and night up to our chins in the lake wasn't so bad after all.

We swam a bit but refused any real exertion, preferring to just paddle lazily or float on our backs looking heavenward. Soon enough we stopped this pretext of activity and just stood on the rocks near the shore, the soothing water's surface cutting me across the collarbone while it licked close to Bum's chin.

"Do you think we'll have to go to the war?" Bum asked. He wiped water from his round cheeks and looked at me.

"I don't know," I told him. "If it goes on long enough, I suppose. But it won't last that long. The radio said it would be over before Christmas. We got the Krauts on the run and the Japs won't be far behind."

"Yeah, but they said that last year, before Mudbug got sent to the Pacific, and now Fatty's getting ready to head off to training."

"I bet Fatty doesn't even finish training before it's done."

Bum's brother, Fatty, didn't belong in the service. Like his mama, Fatty's brain moved as slow as a bicycle with flat tires. He'd stopped school just before the sixth grade, because he couldn't keep up with the mathematics. A few years back, he took himself a job out to the paper mill, where he pushed rolls of paper on a cart from the warehouse to the cutting room.

"Fatty's gonna get himself killed," Bum said. "Daddy never let the dummy handle any of his rifles, because he figured Fatty would shoot himself in the head looking to see how fast the bullet came out. The dope can't even wind a wristwatch."

Concern weighed down Bum's face, and I wanted to get his mind off of his brothers, because nothing I told him would stick or help. Bum knew what was what, and I figured he had it pretty much right: if they sent Fatty overseas, he'd probably never see home again. Mudbug on the other hand might just come back a hero. He sure was mean enough. "It'll be over soon," I said.

"I don't know what I'd do if I had to go," Bum said. "I wish I was more like Mudbug or Harold Ashton."

I'd never thought much about true combat. The kids all talked brave – myself included – all of us eager to show the Axis the way real men fought, and during those patriotic bull sessions, I'd felt certain that if someone were to put a rifle in my hands and drop me in Berlin, I'd take out the entire Nazi party in the same time it took Ma to fry up a chicken, but all I knew of fighting came from the movies and the radio and Brett Fletcher, who spun some harrowing yarns from the wheelchair on his porch. War struck me as something involving adults, but Bum didn't see it that way. He had brothers, and one by one the government had requested their services. First Mudbug and then Fatty. It would be Mule's turn next and then Bum. It was like a saboteur's bomb counting down, only instead of ticking off seconds, it had been synchronized to the sons of Clayton and Louise Craddick.

We stood on those rocks for a while and didn't say much. The water didn't feel quite as good as it had, and my feet were starting to ache, toes clamped to the rough wads of stone beneath them. I felt a chill and looked away from Bum.

Across the water I noticed two men standing on the shore at the Blevins place just below the tree line. The glare and distance made it difficult to make the figures out, but one of them wore a hat with a familiar shape.

"What's that all about?" Bum asked.

"Can't tell," I said. "That might be Sheriff Rabbit, but can't see the other man."

"Looks like Sheriff Rabbit," Bum agreed.

"How can you tell?"

"Just think it is."

"Jerome probably caught himself another Mexican," I said.

Jerome Blevins was an old-time moonshiner who owned two hundred acres to the west of Barnard, which hadn't done him a bit of good during the Depression. Though he maintained a good amount of his hill-country cheapness, his lot in life had improved greatly over the last few years. He let the paper folks take some of his trees, and he herded cattle, and while the rest of the country worried about invasion from across the oceans, Jerome had convinced himself the Mexicans were the ones who'd bring the end of civilization with them over the borders.

Bum and I spent another few minutes speculating on the men and their purpose, and then we forgot about them and waded out of the lake to lie down in the tall grass on the shore. Unlike most days, when he would talk about every little thing that crossed his mind, Bum lay quietly, and I knew he was worried about his dim-witted brother, Fatty. I couldn't think of any further words of comfort for my friend, so I tried to distract him with old knock-knock jokes and making funny voices, which he always said I did better than any of the other kids. He laughed a bit, but it wasn't Bum's usual full-throated chuckle.

"Fatty's going to be okay," I finally said. "They'll probably send him out with Mudbug, and you know Mudbug isn't going to let anything happen to him."

"Mr. Fletcher says that if the Germans catch you, they put you in a cage and torture you, and then once you're dead they eat your skin and make furniture from your bones."

"He's just trying to scare the little kids."

"But do you think it's true?" Bum asked.

I told him that I didn't think it was true. People didn't do that to one another, but Bum wasn't convinced, and of course, neither of us knew what they'd found on Jerome Blevins's property while we soaked away the morning in Kramer Lake.

Two: Sheriff Tom Rabbit

Mornings and weekends were the only times Sheriff Tom Rabbit rode his chestnut mare, Pilar. In the pink glow of daybreak, he trotted her through fields of tall tanned grasses, enjoying the peace, the quiet, and the scent of air that wasn't heavy with dust and car fumes. Riding soothed him, from the gentle rocking in the saddle to the rhythmic clop of Pilar's hooves on the hard packed earth as she carried him across the flats north of his home to a squat ridge of hills. At the edge of his property, atop a hillock where the mesquite knotted, creating a tangled fence, Sheriff Rabbit climbed off his mount and looked to the west, gently stroking Pilar's neck as he surveyed the direction a hundred western novels and films made him associate with the future. A string of bruised clouds ran across the horizon, but a sheet of pure radiant blue hung overhead and stretched the innumerable miles to the cumulus. If the clouds intended storm, it would miss Barnard by miles, and though the farmers likely wished for a bit of water after such a dry spring and early summer, Sheriff Rabbit felt just fine with the clouds' decision to pass on by. The streets in Barnard hadn't been poured with an eye toward rain, so when a downpour hit, the water gathered on the roads, a lot of it muddy runoff from the ranchlands to the east, and then got held between the sidewalk curbs, making any travel through town a messy and complicated event. Of course he didn't have to worry about starving if the crops didn't come in.

He fished a sugar cube out of his shirt pocket to feed to Pilar. Then he remounted his horse and turned her nose to the south before clicking his tongue to get her moving.

He felt no urgency to get back to the house and entertained no illusions about his necessity in the office. Things in Barnard had been quiet for months. Nights offered the prerequisite bar brawls and the occasional theft, but no crimes of note had stained the pages of the *Barnard Register* since Molly Jenkins had confessed to the murder of her husband, John, back in '42. The crazy old lady had poisoned her spouse of thirty-five years with arsenic and had called Sheriff Rabbit to "Come on out and pick this bag of manure up off my kitchen floor." With Tom being something less than an expert in the science of poison, old Molly would have gotten away free and clear if she hadn't confessed. John Jenkins had been a sickly old man, coughing like a bad engine, and not a soul would have batted an eye at his demise, but Molly had wanted credit for the killing. After nearly three-dozen years of black eyes and split lips and more egregious injuries which she'd recounted in great detail in her confession, Molly wanted everyone to know that she'd gotten the last word in on the marriage.

As for last words, hers were: "John better watch his tail when I get there," before the state sent the juice through her chair.

But the Molly Jenkinses were rare, and Tom was glad of it. Still he couldn't bring himself to crow about the peaceful state of his city.

The only reason things were so quiet was because of the war, and no matter how much Tom appreciated the ease of his days, he understood that a lot of people were sacrificing themselves for his benefit. Most boys of hell-raising age were overseas or in hospitals or dead. In addition to the abbreviated population, the shadow of war hung over everyone, making imperatives of courtesy and kindness. No one knew which family might have just received a telegram from Washington, DC; bad news traveled fast, but was hardly instantaneous, and most of the petty triggers for arguments were avoided as men and women focused their energies on concern for the welfare of their country and their families. Even the animosity toward the Germans in town had subsided considerably. Early on, folks hadn't easily distinguished expatriates of that nation from the Nazi leaders running it. Suspicions and tempers had run high. Carl Baker had taken a nasty beating at the hands of Burl Jones, who'd spent a night in jail for the assault, and Bruno Gerber got his arm cut with a razor outside of his hardware store by an unknown assailant wearing a potato-sack mask. Miscreants had whitewashed obscenities and accusations on the sides of German-owned shops and homes, and a number of windows had been broken. But that had been early in the war, when patriotism seemed to require retaliation against the kin of Hitler and Goering. Since those early months, a sense of unity had begun to emerge between the lifelong residents of Barnard and their immigrant neighbors.

A pleasant breeze greeted Sheriff Rabbit at the gate to Pilar's corral. He leapt off the horse and untied the rope holding the gate closed, then he led the mare inside to the barn. He unbridled her, removed the saddle, placing it carefully on the sawhorse by her stall. After throwing some hay and oats into a trough, Tom checked her water and decided it was more than enough to get her through the hot day ahead. Then he went inside to see what his housekeeper had prepared for breakfast.

Estella, a small-boned girl with raven black hair and eyes the color of chocolate, met him at the back door with a cup of coffee and while he took his seat at the small table in the corner, she scurried around the kitchen, scraping eggs and potatoes out of skillets and pulling toasted bread from the oven. She dropped everything on a plate and presented it to him with a crock of butter for the toast. He thanked her, and Estella bowed. Then she hurried out of the kitchen to attend to housework, leaving him to eat in peace.

Truth was he wished she'd stay and share the meal with him. Ever since Glynis had died, Tom found himself missing the soothing sounds of a woman's voice. Three years gone now;

he had forgotten what Glynis's voice sounded like and the real-ization disturbed him. He could picture her face well enough, and if his memory failed him in that regard he could peruse the handful of photographs he kept in a tin beside the bed, or the portrait of her he kept framed on the mantle, but even though he could remember a hundred things she'd said to him, he could not remember the way those words had sounded coming from her mouth, and he considered this theft one of time's crueler consequences.

Tom sopped up the butter from his eggs and the grease of his potatoes with a wedge of toast. Meal finished, he drank the rest of his coffee and left the kitchen. At the front door he re-trieved his sheriff's hat from a hook and placed it on his head.

"Goodbye, Estella," he called.

The Mexican girl appeared at the top of the stairs and waved, smiling shyly in farewell. He wished she'd say something, but she rarely did. Estella was embarrassed by her poor English, so more times than not, she gestured her side of a conversation.

Tom left the house and got in the Packard Six the city had given him to do his job. He opened the glove box and reached for the pack of cigarettes he kept there. Lighting up, he pulled out of the drive and headed for the farm road, which would take him into town and what he imagined would be another quiet day.

∭

His deputy, Gilbert Perry, greeted him with the news about Harold Marker Ashton before Tom made it into the office. Limping through the front door at a good clip, Gilbert wore an expression of nervous disbelief and it took him three tries and a terse order to "settle down" from Tom before the deputy managed to say, "Jerome Blevins found the body in the woods between his place and the lake. Said it was murder. Said it was bad."

Though Tom thought to point out to Gilbert that few murders could be called "good," he instead asked, "Why didn't you radio me?"

"The report just came in."

Tom nodded and scratched a mosquito bite on the back of his hand. "What do we know?"

"Jerome said he was out early walking his woods and he found the body just laying there."

"Did he recognize the victim?"

"Lord, yes," Gilbert said. "Jerome says it's Harold Ashton. He's sure of it."

Tom accepted the news with a slow nod of his head, but inside he felt knots tying. He thought about the boy's parents, Charles and Ruth, and how proud they'd been, bragging on about how Harold had enlisted to serve his country. Charles had made quite a show at the Longhorn Tavern about his brave son, and how he'd been a man long before his time. Running off to enlist in the army had simply been the latest example of his boy's maturity and courage.

"Is there any chance Jerome made a mistake?" Tom asked.

"I don't think so, Sheriff. He seemed pretty sure of himself."

"Son of a bitch," Tom whispered.

He cast a glance up and down Main Street. The ease of the morning rituals, performed by people Tom had known his entire life, suddenly looked wrong. Clete Matheson casually swept the sidewalk in front of the drugstore, his round body rocking back and forth with the broom, looking like a buoy on calm waters; Dick Washington climbed out of his Ford and crossed the road to Milton's Barber Shop; Doctor Randolph sat on the wooden bench in front of his office, smoking his pipe and shamelessly eyeing Hattie Barnes washing the window of her dress shop; Carl Baker stood at the window of his bakery, watching the street, his lips pursed as if whistling. By mid-afternoon they'd all be helping the Ashtons mourn and looking to Tom for answers.

"Sheriff?" Gilbert said.

"Yeah," Tom replied, shaking off the reverie. "Who have we got inside?"

"Everyone's in," Gilbert said.

"Send Rex and Don out. We'll drive to Jerome's and take a look. You stay back with Gary and keep an eye on things in town."

Tom couldn't help but notice Gilbert's disappointment at being left behind, and Tom hated doing it to the kid, but he didn't want Gilbert's bum leg to slow them down, and the woods behind the Blevins place could be tricky even under the best of conditions. He knew Gil wanted to prove himself, and he thought the kid made a fine deputy. He'd just had a bit of bad luck involving a speeding car when he was a boy, and the leg had never healed quite right.

"Go ahead," Tom told him. "Have them bring along the evidence kit."

"Yes, Sheriff," Gil said, turning away and limping back into the sheriff's office.

As he waited for his men, Tom returned to the car and lit a second cigarette. Normally he wouldn't have touched another of the things until after lunch, but he figured normal had left town, at least for a few days, and he hoped the smoke would file away the edges on his nerves.

Though premature, he tried to build a suspect list in his head, sorting through names and incidents like flipping through the library's card catalog. By the time Rex Burns and Don Nialls emerged from the office, both wearing white short-sleeved shirts, cream-colored slacks and fat blue ties, Tom hadn't come up with a single viable name. Harold Ashton had been a good kid, a fine student and athlete, and his parents' pride. If he had a taste for causing trouble, Tom knew nothing about it.

"One car, Tom?" Rex asked as he stepped off the sidewalk.

"Should get us there," Tom replied. "Less you've got some friends we need to pick up."

"Nah, sir," Rex said.

Rex climbed into the passenger seat and Don slid in the back, and then Tom pulled away from the curb, made a U-turn in the middle of Main Street, and headed back toward the farm route he'd followed into town. As he drove, Rex and Don fell into their usual banter. The two could talk for hours about absolutely nothing, and they were usually funny as all get out to listen to, like Abbott and Costello with East Texas drawls. Today they kept the conversation respectful and professional, and Tom heard the uneasy timbres of their voices. By the time he'd turned left onto Lakeland Road, his men were sharing their thoughts about the Ashton case.

Don said, "Jerome thinks it's the Mexicans."

Rex snorted and replied, "Jerome thinks everything's the Mexicans. This time he might be right though. Has to be a drifter at any rate. No one in Barnard would hurt a boy like Harold Ashton. I'd eat my hat if that weren't true."

"Did either of you get any details about what was done to the boy?" Tom asked.

"Nah, sir," Rex said. "Just that he was murdered."

"I'd say that's for us to decide," Tom said. "For all we know, Harold went walking in Jerome's woods, fell down and hit his head and coyotes and badgers did the rest."

"All due respect, Sheriff," this from Don in the backseat, "The Ashton boy's been gone for a good two weeks, and Jerome said he'd walked by the place at least a dozen times since then, and he never saw a thing."

"Coyotes'll drag a meal," Tom pointed out.

This silenced his men. Tom knew he hadn't convinced them, though; they just weren't up to arguing with the boss.

After kicking up four miles of dust on Lakeland Road, Tom turned onto the dirt track that led to Jerome Blevins's house. As the house came into view through a thatch of scrub oak, so did four of Jerome's children: three young boys and a little girl who'd recently traded diapers for the graying sundress that had once been robin's egg blue. They stood at the edges of the drive like vagabond orphans eager for a meal.

"Why doesn't Jerome buy his kids some proper clothes?" Don asked. "The lumber company pays him big for the right to cut on his land."

"He's still got his head in the Depression," Rex said. "He had it tough there for a lot of years. It made him cautious. Stingy."

"Those overalls look like they're held together with spider webbing," Don said. "You can about see through the knees. And a little girl like that shouldn't have to wear rags."

"Just keep your mind on why we're here," Tom said. "It's none of our business if Jerome's kids wear potato sacks or silk trousers. Let's just see what he's got to show us."

Tom pulled to a stop before the Blevins house, which looked about as flimsy and cheap as the children's clothing. The porch tilted significantly to the side and the roof above it sagged in the middle like a rope bridge with too little tension; he saw gaps in the boards siding the front of the house, and the glass in the living room window wore a long jagged crack. The oldest boy, whose name Tom couldn't recall, walked up to the side of the car, invited himself onto the running board, and peered in at the three men. Fingers with dirty knuckles clasped on the door and the boy rocked back a bit like he might give tipping the vehicle over a try, and then he spoke.

"Daddy says to take you on back. He didn't want the Mexicans to come and steal Harold's body, so he's a-waiting in the woods and I'm supposed to show you where."

"That'll be fine," Tom said, though he felt it would be anything but. What was Jerome thinking, letting his ten-year-old son walk through the woods to a murder scene?

Tom and his men climbed out of the car and gathered at the nose of the Packard. He checked to make sure Rex had hold of the evidence kit and seeing that he did, he waved at the blond boy, a quick shooing motion that sent Jerome's son to trotting across the drive and between two poplars. They crunched their way through the woods, not speaking. Their pace would have seemed casual to anyone watching their progress. Truth was Tom wasn't eager to see what remained of Harold Ashton, and he rationalized that a few minutes faster or slower wasn't likely to change the boy's circumstances.

After fifteen minutes, the Blevins kid veered to the left, taking the party in the direction of the lake. Light flickered through the treetops, shimmering like the surface of a river at sunset. The air smelled fresh and good, heavily scented by pine and the rich odor of decomposing deadfall. A branch snapped loudly under his heel and Tom reared back, startled.

Eventually they emerged at the water's edge where the land jutted like a finger to the east, and Tom paused. He stared over the peaceful water back toward the small neighborhood south of downtown. Bits of yellow and white siding from the houses on Dodd Street peeked through the trees. A few people already lay out on the grassy shore, and a handful of folks had taken to swimming.

"Almost there," the Blevins boy said.

Tom turned away from the comforting scene and saw that the Blevins kid was hooking back into the tree line. The ground angled upward and a density of fallen tree limbs made the going rough. This was the type of terrain he'd considered when telling Gilbert to stay at the station, and as he tromped up the hillside he knew he'd saved his deputy a lot of physical grief and a bit of embarrassment by keeping him off of this particular hunt.

They neared the top of the hill and Rex said, "There's Jerome."

The man stood at the peak of the hill and to their left. He wore a threadbare cotton shirt over gray trousers. A porkpie hat had been pushed far back on his head. He held a shotgun in his beefy hand, and he turned toward Tom and his men as they approached, looking annoyed.

"He's here," Blevins said, pointing at the ground ahead of him. "Jesse, you stay put. Let the officers of the law come on up."

Tom couldn't see anything but the direction of Blevins's arm. He continued to trudge up the hill and after another three steps, the scene revealed itself clear enough. He suddenly regretted the large breakfast Estella had prepared for him.

"Jesus," Rex hissed at his shoulder.

"Lord have mercy," Don added. Then the deputy raced back down the hillside to relieve his sick stomach.

"Too late for mercy," Blevins said. "Best settle for rest in peace."

The body lay propped against the trunk of an old pine. The boy's legs had been crossed and the hands folded neatly in the lap like a kid sitting on the floor, waiting patiently for his mother to give him a cookie. Flies swarmed the body, thick as a cloud. Tom approached as slowly as he could manage without looking like a coward, swiping his hand through the air to scatter the flies. The terrible expression frozen on Harold Ashton's face came clear in the same moment the reek of his decaying body reached the sheriff's nose. Tom's momma had always told him that dying was a restful thing, like going to sleep, but Tom had seen enough bodies to know that wasn't true. Harold Ashton certainly didn't look like he was napping. The muscles about his mouth had tensed, pulling his upper lip away from his teeth. His eyelids were half open, and the eyes behind them had grayed in death. Tom kept his gaze on the murdered boy's face, because for all of its dreadful composition, it was much easier to deal with than what had been done to his body.

"The Mexicans cleaned him like a deer," Blevins said, seemingly unaffected by the observation. He spoke with all the assurance of a man who'd predicted a hurricane and survived its landing. "That's how they do," he continued.

Rex dropped a hand on Tom's shoulder, startling him and sending his heart to racing. Tom inhaled deeply and pulled away, turned to his deputy, who looked as ill as Tom felt.

"You got a plan?" Rex asked.

"I'm going to talk to Jerome. Once Don gets himself together, you two see what you can make of this."

"I can't make nothing of this, Tom. This isn't right."

"Do your job, Rex. Find what you can find." Tom stepped away from his deputy and approached Blevins. Blevins's full cheeks wore two days of beard, and his forehead gleamed beneath the brim of his hat as if polished. The man appeared so calm and unaffected; Tom didn't know what to make of it. "Jerome, can you tell me what brought you out here this morning?"

"It's my property, Sheriff Rabbit," Blevins said. "I've got the right to walk my own property."

"Yes, you do," Tom agreed. "But this doesn't seem like the most reasonable place to take a stroll, so I'm just wondering why you came out this way."

"That's my business," Blevins said. His eyes hardened and the corners of his mouth ticked down. "Best keep your mind on the Mexicans that done this to Harold Ashton."

Tom knew that Blevins had a history of bootlegging; it was about the only thing that had kept him and his family fed during the hard years. He imagined Jerome maintained a still or two, probably one nearby, and though Tom had absolutely no interest in a shine shop and wasn't going to press for details, he'd need a better answer from Blevins for his report.

"What makes you think Mexicans were involved?"

"No American would do that to a boy."

"Have you seen any strangers on your land recently? In the last few weeks?"

"No, sir, but I got a lot of land. Can't watch it all."

Tom nodded and looked around the woods, the density of trees, the difficulty in navigating the terrain. He cast another glance at the Ashton boy's body and winced. As Blevins had heartlessly noted, Harold had been gutted. From what Tom could see, his killer had completely hollowed him out, leaving ragged lips of skin around a gaping hole just below Harold's rib cage. Rex and Don knelt at the side of the corpse, taking turns swatting flies that insisted on returning for a meal and a place to nest their larva, neither deputy seeming to know what to do with the body but stare.

"What's back that way?" Tom asked, nodding to the west.

"Just more woods."

He looked deep into the forest, then back to the corpse. Harold had been missing for two weeks, but he didn't look to have been dead nearly that long – only a few days, Tom would guess. Considering the summer's heat, it might have been less. There was no blood in the immediate area and no signs of the meaty things the killer had removed, plus he hadn't been gone over by any of the toothier inhabitants of the area, which seemed to indicate that Harold had been murdered elsewhere and then carried out here to Blevins woods to be dumped, but why had the killer gone to so much trouble?

Tom walked away from Jerome and began investigating the path on the far side of the tree where Harold had been left. Blevins hurried to his side and tossed his shotgun into his left hand, grabbing Tom with his right.

"I already been back that way this morning. Ain't nothing to see."

"Maybe you didn't know what you were looking for," Tom said.

"This here is my property, Sheriff, and I say who goes where. You ain't going to find any Mexicans out that way."

Tom spun on Jerome, knocking the man's hand off his shoulder with a violent slap. Anger burned through him, acid in his veins. It came out of nowhere, scorching away his reason.

"I am investigating a crime, Jerome, and you'd better stay out of my way while I do it. I don't give a good goddamn if you've got yourself a still or two hidden in these woods. They aren't my concern. That boy is my concern, and I'll do whatever I have to and go wherever I damn well please to figure out who treated him that way. Now if you keep running your mouth, I just might make those stills my problem and yours on top of it. And I swear to God if you start spreading that Mexicans-killed-him shit in town, I will personally notify the rangers in Austin to come up here and sift through every foot of every acre until they find a reason to be unhappy with you. So move your hairy ass back about ten steps and put a clamp on that pie hole."

Blevins's face burned a beet red, and his mouth hung open. Tom saw the man's grip tighten on the barrel of his shotgun, but the sheriff wasn't worried. He took care of this city, and he didn't think it likely one of its citizens would draw down on him.

"You should be moving back now, Jerome," Tom said to the rigid man.

"Sheriff Rabbit," Don called.

"In a minute," Tom replied. "I said, step on back now, Jerome."

"Sheriff Rabbit," Don insisted. "You're going to want to see this. There's something in his mouth."

Tom walked back to where his men knelt and crouched down himself. Rex already had his fingers in place at the boy's jaw. Gently, the deputy separated the teeth to reveal a small, crimson lacquered box resting on the tongue.

"Looks like a snuff box," Don said, shaking his head and looking more than a little green. "Ain't nothing right about this."

"How do we get that out without messing up fingerprints?" Rex asked.

"You think we're going to be able to get prints off of that?" This from Don.

"Well, it's about the only thing we got to dust, isn't it?"

"He's right, Don," Tom said. "Get me the tweezers and give me your handkerchief."

It took a few tries, but Tom managed to pinch an edge of the lid and remove it from the boy's mouth. The crimson box, hardly larger than a matchbox, had been painted with the portrait of a fat man with bushy sideburns and a waxed mustache. Box in hand, Tom sent Blevins and his son back to the Packard to fetch the canvas bag he kept in the trunk; they would need it to haul the boy's body back to the car.

While they waited, Rex snapped photographs of Harold Ashton and the area surrounding him, and Don dusted the lacquered surfaces but the powder stuck in a uniform film over the whole thing, revealing no telling marks. Tom took the container from his deputy and turned it over a few times. The lid popped off with a gentle flick of his thumb. A folded scrap of paper lay inside, and Tom used the tweezers to lift it free. Grasping the corner tightly with the tweezers, he shook the page until it opened and managed to see someone had left a note. Only a few lines written on a scrap no larger than a piece of cigarette paper. Tom couldn't read the scrawl – not because of the size or clarity of the penmanship, which appeared precise and legible, but because the note had been written in German.

Three: The German

June 25th, 1944 – Translated from the German

They found a dead boy today. His name was Harold.

In the mercantile, after a day at home, I hear Weigle the butcher talking with Errol Ormand, the owner of the store. Weigle is an odd-looking man with a bush of white hair around a pink crown of scalp and eyes so tiny they appear no larger than a baby's, stunted and unchanged since birth. Weigle's accent is still thick, though he's lived in Barnard for more than twenty years. Ormand stands much taller than Weigle, but he is less imposing. The owner of the mercantile has a soft countenance, with a slender nose and a feminine mouth.

The two men ramble on as old men do, spouting suppositions about culprits both familiar and exotic. Weigle blames gypsies, which makes me smile and makes Ormand laugh out loud. The agitated butcher turns angry and insists on being heard, though Ormand is already speaking and neither of them listens to the other. They aren't concerned with solving the mystery of Harold Ashton's death; they just like to hear themselves talk, and their argumentative tone draws others from the back of the store, questioning the cause of their disagreement. A woman squawks at the news. Men mutter.

Listening I come to understand that the boy was quite popular in town and everyone believed he'd run off to join the army. It is a shame that did not happen. The army is a good place for boys. Sometimes I think it is the only place I ever truly belonged. The regimentation and masculine camaraderie are unequaled, and I still find myself longing to return to the conflict, the chaos, and the company of brothers with whom I created the turmoil or quelled it, depending on the needs of the cause. The military was a bastion against political storms, the ignorant rabble, and the cancerous boredom of a tradesman's life, and it is forever denied me now.

I remember being startled from a peaceful sleep. They called me traitor.

New accusations and suppositions as to who could murder such a young, fine boy rise in the crowd, as if they are playing a morbid guessing game. They speak no name but rather invoke labels in conspiratorial voices – Drifters, Niggers, Bean-eaters, Northerners, and Weigle again asserts the guilt of gypsies. Then a plump woman with flat features says that Sheriff Rabbit thinks a German has done this terrible thing. This sends Weigle back a step, and I take it as a petty cruelty on the woman's part, intended to quiet Old Weigle down. Little in the way of valuable information emerges. A boy is dead. His parents and sister are grief-stricken. The sheriff is investigating the crime. I do not know this boy or his family, so I will wait to see what information is printed in the *Register* come morning. But such a crowd has gathered at the counter, I see no way to purchase my few items without being drawn into the discussion, and this sort of conversation has no interest for me. I replace the jar of blackberry preserves on the shelf. At the back of the store I return the bag of flour and the yeast, and then turn for the door.

A man enters. He is handsome with smooth cheeks and finely combed blond hair, slicked back like a movie star's. His name is Jeffrey Irvine. I do not know why he isn't fighting this country's war as he is intelligent and healthy. He is a schoolteacher. He is twenty-eight years old and has a pretty wife named Betty and two little girls. I know this man. We have fucked. When Jeffrey sees me he ducks his head low and hurries past the crowd at the counter to distance himself from me as I continue toward the front door. He remembers following me home from the city park, remembers ejaculating on my thigh the moment my hand wrapped around his cock. He remembers the nights he's come to visit me, rapping quietly on my front door only minutes after full dark has set, and he is ashamed of it.

I reach for the door handle amused by his weakness.

"Nothing today. Ernst?" Errol calls from the counter. He looks at me suspiciously as if he thinks me trying to steal a crock of butter or a can of beans. The rest of the crowd similarly eyes me, and I cannot understand why I should draw such attention unless it is the scars on my face, though these are not new.

"Not today," I reply and leave the mercantile.

I pause on the sidewalk, standing beneath the awning of the store and letting the late afternoon heat work through my muscles as my eyes adjust to the bright light covering the downtown buildings. The oddity of my experience inside the grocery takes hold and I feel a needle of guilt, though I am certain I have nothing to feel guilty for – at least nothing of which these people of Barnard would know. I think to return to Ormand's counter and demand an account of his behavior. The old Ernst would not have allowed such an affront.

The old Ernst is dead, I think. He is buried in Munich in a deep, dark hole.

On the next block, Sheriff Rabbit walks quickly from his office. He crosses the street and greets Doctor Randolph. The two men speak and then disappear into the doctor's office. The woman in the grocery had said the sheriff believed the boy's killer to be German, and I can't help but wonder if there is actual evidence of this – since wounds have no nationality – or if it is simply hysteria like Weigle's belief in Texas gypsies.

I wander down Main Street toward Bennington Road, which will take me south to Dodd Street. As I cross the intersection on the next block, Carl Baker shouts my name. I look up to see him crossing to me, sweeping his eyes from side to side, cautious of traffic. He picks up his pace and says my name again. His face is red and his moustache glistens with sweat.

"Carl."

"Ernst, have you heard?"

I imagine he is talking about the boy. I say I have.

"Terrible, *ja?*"

Though he has been in this country longer than I, he still speaks sloppily. His blunt "*ja*" – so common among my expatriated nationals – strikes me as lazy and insolent. But we are friends, and I know that Carl is – in most things that do not require flour, sugar, lard, yeast, and eggs – something of an idiot. But no, that word is cruel. It is better to say he is naïve. Innocent. He is a good man with pronounced intellectual limitations. He reminds me of a young soldier from Darmstadt I came to know. They share strong, trim bodies and soft eyes and lips. Carl and this boy would be nearly the same age I think, if the boy had not been beaten to death by the Communists.

"Terrible," I agree.

"They say one of us did it," Carl continues. "Gilbert from the sheriff's office came in and told me they have proof."

I ask what kind of proof, and Carl shakes his head frantically. The deputy would not tell him, but Gilbert and Carl are friends, and the young man wanted to warn the baker that there could be trouble. All of this seems to upset Carl greatly and that is to be expected. Soon after America had joined the war a man had taken out his anger on Carl, so my friend understood something of irrational aggression – very little, but something. I do my best to ease his mind, but my words fall like drops of water on a heated skillet. He invites me to join him for supper, stating he thinks it best I not be alone. I decline. Though Carl is a very good person, his wife is not so good. She busies herself in indiscriminate ways while her husband works at the bakery, and though I would never break my friend's heart by exposing her nature, neither would I endure another evening under her hungry gaze, trying my best to ignore her thinly veiled suggestions. I promise to spend time with him at the Independence Day celebration, and would try to visit the bakery soon, and then I say my good evening.

||||

After an early supper I walk outside to sprinkle more grain for the chickens. I feel disgust for the birds. They remind me of the filthy Chicken Farmer with his sharp nose and sinister eyes, made all the more cold and flat by the spectacles he wears. These white hens have done me no wrong and provide welcome fresh eggs, but I hate them still. Ugly creatures.

Once the birds are fed, I cross the yard to retrieve a length of oak from which I will fashion the armrest of a chair, but when I enter the spare room with the plank in hand, I have no desire for cutting. Instead, I sand the spindles for the chair's back, finding some calm in the repetition of movement.

The schoolteacher, Jeffrey, knocks on my door once full dark settles. His arrival is not a surprise. The shameful memories he experienced at the mercantile have warmed him, melting inhibitions into something he can rationalize during the brief span of our meeting. He does not think of the shame just now, only the heat.

I miss home and the honesty of my peers. There is a puritanical oppression in this country, reminding me of my assignment in Bolivia, late in my military career. There the Catholic Church held men's thoughts and cocks in an iron grip of guilt-enforced morality. Even during my brief stays in New York and New Orleans, cities known and celebrated for scandalous behavior, the weight of felony rested on my neck. Companions warned of reprisal should our meetings be discovered, many of them – like this Jeffrey – were so infected with shame, they appeared sick and weathered in the moments it took them to dress and flee my bedroom, and I can't help but wonder what such a weak and frightened existence must feel like, even though the thought of it disgusts me. I would rather die as the man I am than live eternally beneath another man's mask, but for all of the talk of freedom in this country, this Texas, its cries are delivered in harmony with deceit.

Jeffrey hurries across my threshold, and I know that he is eager for me to close the door, so my neighbors do not see him in my home. I imagine his car is parked several streets away and if asked on the stroll back to it where he has been, he will tell the inquisitor he's been to the lake to look at the water, the sky, and the stars.

He wears a nervous grin on his smooth, handsome face, so different from my own scarred visage, and he asks that I turn out the lamp, which I do, and he mutters a rapid apology for not having greeted me properly in the mercantile, to which I simply shrug because I am not concerned with this man's treatment of me, as it has grown from shamed soil, and in my darkened living room he removes his hat and places it on the sofa, and he unbuttons his shirt which he drapes over the hat, and he opens the front of his trousers, and his body is a ghost, floating in the gloom before me. The ritual is familiar, and I do not protest it – despite its cold and precise repetition. He will never fully undress in my presence, nor will he embrace or kiss me, but the blood is in my cock and I unbutton my shirt and unsnap my trousers, and remove my undergarments and stand naked in the middle of the room with my clothes discarded on the sofa beside his hat and shirt. I cross to Jeffrey. When my chest presses against him he takes a shocked step back as if in disgust, but he reaches out to touch my hardening cock. His fingers run over the shaft quickly and he feels all around it before his shaking hand reaches lower to cup my scrotum. Then he returns to my prick, touching it without grace or delicacy like a blind man uncertain of what has been put in his grasp but desperate to know its every contour.

He pulls his own cock through the split in his shorts. It is thick and long and as pale as his shorts. Already his breath comes in rapid gasps.

I step away from his clumsy touch and he asks what is wrong, and I tell him to sit in the rocking chair beside the sofa, and he doesn't understand because this is a new demand and he cannot fathom its meaning, and his fear fills the room like radio static, but I tell him to be calm and sit. In the gloom his expression is difficult to read, but not difficult to know – bravery has many faces, but weakness is singular. With a very calm tone, low yet commanding I tell him again to sit in the chair and he shuffles toward it. Once he has sat down, I approach him and kneel between his legs. I take his cock in my mouth, and he groans and shakes and ejaculates. His trembling stops and he tries to stand to make his embarrassed escape, but I keep him in my mouth and shove his chest with my hand. He is a strapping man, but I am stronger, and the chair works to my favor. Several more times he tries to rise from the chair, but I keep him in place with my palm. He calms and allows me to proceed.

After his third ejaculation and my first I am done with him. When he tries to climb from the chair, I let him. He says nothing but rapidly shoves his prick back into his shorts and yanks up his trousers, and in a minute he is dressed and then he is gone.

His visit frustrates me, reminding me enough of nights in Munich to spark nostalgic longing. But it is only the mechanics that remind me. None of the men in this place bring joy or passion or warmth. There is no union. They accomplish pleasure but it resonates with torment – doubt, regret, and guilt. This thing that brings them such misery is the thing that once gave me greatest peace, and I wonder how two men can perceive the same act so differently. Perhaps it is the difference between digging in the garden to plant a beautiful tree and digging one's own grave.

I pour a glass of whiskey and carry it into the living room, where I dress. Presentable, I switch the lamp back on and carry my drink to the porch. There I sit and listen to the night – frogs, a cricket, a car rumbling many streets away. Across the street, my neighbor Tim and his fat friend are visible through the window of his house. They are alone as Tim's mother works a swing shift at the factory and will not be home for hours. The two boys sit on the sofa talking, perhaps listening to the radio. I turn away and look to the west. At the lake's edge, someone moves, merely a smudge of shadow against the plum-colored surface. Likely a lover sneaking away – though not my lover. Many people meet at the lake after sunset. They kiss behind the shelter of trees, seeking warmth and forgetfulness.

And again my thoughts drift, remembering a hole, deep and dark, with water pooling at the bottom like blood in an open wound.

Four: Tim Randall

The news about Harold Ashton upset Ma. She'd spent the entire afternoon on the phone exclaiming and protesting the information pouring in from her friends all over town. She even considered calling into the factory and taking the night off to stay home to a keep a watchful eye. Bum's parents didn't seem to have the sense to be worried about him, which was okay by me. My mother called Mrs. Craddick and the fuzzy-brained woman was just fine with Bum spending the night at our house, so long as he got home first thing in the morning to help her with chores in the yard. Only slightly comforted that I wouldn't be in the house alone, my mother grabbed her hat and handbag, then she checked the locks on the back door and all of the windows before hurrying out to the factory for her shift.

We messed around in the house until suppertime, and then I fixed Bum and me beef sandwiches and glasses of milk. We wolfed those down before heading to the backyard to play war with sticks, but we quickly tired of the game and ended up sitting on the back steps talking about Harold Ashton and speculating on his killer. With the limited information at our disposal – because my mother had given no details, not even mentioning the note the rest of the city was already talking about – we imagined a number of horrific fates for the older boy (though granted, none as horrific as what had really happened to him).

When it started getting dark we went inside and turned on the radio and settled in for the week's installment of *The Adventures of the Thin Man*. The show never did much for me but Bum liked the way Nick and Nora Charles spoke, the sounds of their voices, so even if the mysteries weren't particularly exciting, he looked forward to the show. I fidgeted throughout, asking questions about the story and the characters and the stuff I was too bored to follow.

Full dark had settled by the time the announcer insisted we tune in next week for the next exciting episode, and I muttered, "No, thank you."

"You're being uncouth," Bum said, doing a terrible impression of Nick Charles.

"So's your butt," I said.

"What's on now?"

"You know, it's dark," I said, ignoring his question and looking at the window as if to prove my point. Across the street, I noticed Mr. Lang sitting in the shadows of his porch, the light from his front window spilled over his shoulders, casting his head in silhouette. My impulse was to wave, but I quelled it and turned away. "We should check our orders and start the assignment."

Bum's mouth dropped open. He shook his head. "Not me," he said. "You want to go out in the dark and get yourself scalped, go on ahead. Besides, we promised your ma we'd stay put, and you just know that some neighbor will see us out there and tell her. I'm not getting tanned just to peek in somebody's window. We never see anything good anyhow."

"The rules of Spy Commander are clear," I said with authority. "We can't refuse a mission, no matter how deadly."

"The rules don't say anything about getting scalped."

"Oh come on, Bum, no one's going to bother us, and what else are we supposed to do?"

"Maybe something good is on the radio now. We'll listen to whatever you want."

"I don't want to sit around all night. We have a mission."

An entire city waited out there like a cave where any manner of treasure might be found. What could we possibly hope
to experience just sitting around my living room? Bum argued
and pouted and even crossed his arms and sat on the floor like a
lump. We played the usual game of dares and double-dares, but
these childhood threats to honor had no effect on my friend. He
remained committed to staying inside, far away from whatever
might prowl the night, so I took a different tack.

"Well, I'm going," I told him.

Bum's face screwed up with concern and then relaxed, calling my bluff. "No, you're not."

I asked for the tin spyglass and Bum pointed to where it
lay by the sofa. I retrieved it and carried it with me through
the living room and into the kitchen. Without pause, I unlocked
the back door, opened it and walked down the steps, stomping
across the backyard. At the low fence, I paused and looked back,
hoping my best friend would be chasing at my heels like a good
dog, but the kitchen doorway was empty. Defiantly, I hopped
the low fence into the Findleys' yard and ran to the corner of
their house. This time when I checked the open kitchen door,
Bum stood on the threshold, looking out. Maybe he saw me, and
maybe he didn't, but I remained perfectly still in the shadows,
thinking that if he decided to follow now, I'd hide and give him
a good scare for being a pain. He didn't come out, though. He
leaned forward, craning his neck to search the yard, and then he
pulled back and closed the door, making it clear he would not be
joining me on the night's mission.

A car passed on Crosby Street ahead, and I pressed hard
against the Findleys' house. Trepidation lit in my veins, and I
heard my mother's scolding voice telling me how important it
was to be responsible with my father gone. I didn't want to go
back and admit defeat to Bum, but neither did I want to walk
the streets of Barnard alone. Even before Harold Ashton's murder, the idea would have unnerved me. Unlike the downtown
streets my neighborhood didn't have arc lamps. Dark houses
like tombs lined the road, and the spaces between them were
filled with thick camouflaging shadows within which any man-

ner of villain might hide. But I'd made such a show for my friend, and pride won out so I left the side of the Findleys' house and walked across their yard to Crosby Street.

As I moved from one shadow to the next, the news of Harold's murder worked deeper into my bones. When I considered meeting his killer in one of the neat backyards or in the alleys between the houses, I imagined myself brave, recalling episodes of *Gang Busters* and *Crime Files*, where a single cop managed to subdue half a dozen crooks with his smarts and a good right hook. The misguided illusion so engulfed me I considered the tin spyglass in my pocket an effective weapon.

Passing onto Worth Street from between two white houses, I made a right and headed for Bennington, which would lead north to town. Only then did it occur to me that I had no destination. Yes, I had written a name on the slip of paper Bum kept in his shirt – though the rules stated it should have been hidden away in a shoe – but I no longer considered the home of Abigail Dougherty a feasible destination.

Abigail lived on the far side of Main Street. Since her husband had been drafted in February, she'd lived alone in a house on Forrester Avenue, and the older boys said she walked by her windows wearing almost nothing at all. They even said that men who worked the same factory shift as my mother stopped by her house when their shifts ended in the middle of the night to mess around with Mrs. Dougherty. Bum had been talking about making her a suspect in our game for weeks, but he'd never managed to build enough courage to write her name on the assignment form. I'd done it for him as a kind of gift. But the idea of sneaking through another fifteen blocks of shadows cowed me.

We'd already investigated most of my neighbors to one degree or another: we'd seen Mr. Klavin washing clothes in his undershirt; we saw Morton Clooney's widow, Mavis, sitting in her living room sobbing into a kerchief, only to laugh hysterically a moment later and point a finger at her Crosley radio as if encouraging what she'd heard there; and Mr. and Mrs. Thrombolt on Worth Street danced in their dining room; and Cleta Ferguson told her children stories around the kitchen table; and

Stella Jackson undressed in her bedroom and lay on her bed in nothing but a slip, fanning herself with a red and gold fan; and Wesley Smalls eagerly picked his nose, sending the snot to the carpet for his dog to eat; and Myrtle Pearlman sat quietly on her sofa knitting a child's sweater, though her only baby had died at birth. These had been the neighbors that had struck Bum and me as interesting. Everyone else was just a neighbor. So where was I supposed to go?

Uncertain and beginning to convince myself that I'd already proved my courage to Bum, I hid between the side of an ugly brown house and a thick shrub, deciding to wait another ten minutes before heading back. I tried to kneel but the tin spyglass dug into my leg, so I removed it from my pocket and set it in my lap once I'd gotten comfortable in the dirt.

After two minutes, I felt restless and eager to get home, but before I managed to get to my feet, voices on Bennington Street stopped me. They began like the whispers of angry ghosts, sounding rough and distant, but the speakers were heading north on Bennington, towards where I sat. The voices came clearer, and though I couldn't see the boys approach, I already knew one of them and my vague fears solidified behind my ribs when I heard Hugo Jones's low, gravelly voice.

"Daddy says it's a German, and he knew it before that swamp-assed Sheriff Tom Rabbit knew it."

A German, I thought. Ma hadn't said anything about that, and I wondered if Hugo's information could be trusted or if it was just more of his hot air.

"Town's crawling with Germans," another boy replied. I thought it might be Ben Livingston talking, because he was always with Hugo, but I couldn't be sure. "How we supposed to know which one did it?"

"Kill 'em all if we have to," a third boy said. This voice I recognized. It belonged to Austin Chitwood, another of Hugo's gang. "Just line 'em up and mow 'em down." He made machine-gun noises and then started cackling like the idiot he was.

"Shut your trap," Hugo snapped. "This ain't no game. Daddy says the Germans have been sending spies over since they lost the Great War. The Nazis trained every one of them and they've just been waiting to attack. And you think it's a coincidence Harold disappeared just after D-Day? No sir. No how."

"Well, if that's true, why'd they wait so long?"

"Because we hit 'em good at Normandy and they want revenge. No reason to expose their spies if they're winning the damn war. Use your head."

The argument played in circles while the boys continued walking down Bennington Avenue. Hugo maintained his confidence that one of the Germans in town had butchered Harold Ashton. Ben Livingston questioned the logic, and Austin expressed his eagerness to kill them all. Again the voices thinned out and became the whispers of violent spirits before the night ate them entirely.

Once I felt certain Hugo and his gang had put sufficient distance between us, I climbed to my feet and worked my way through the bushes and would have headed for home right then, except a car rolled into the intersection at my back, its brakes creaking an alarm as it rolled to a stop. I crouched down again and looked through the bushes to see a black Ford idling dead center in the intersection. The driver had turned off the headlights, or he'd never thought to turn them on. The dark shape of the driver's head was distorted, and I realized he wore a large brimmed hat, a Stetson or Panama, though the former struck me as far more likely. I couldn't make out anything else about the driver, and I again wished the city had spent the money to erect street lamps in my neighborhood to give a face to this mysterious figure.

My first thought was that the driver had been following Hugo, Ben and Austin on their patrol through the streets, but this malicious motive arose and dissipated like smoke. He was probably just lost, trying to decide which direction to turn, except I couldn't convince myself of anything so mundane. The car's presence made me uneasy. I felt as if I hid in a jungle observing a tiger that was waiting for prey. This train of thought gained steam and soon enough, I convinced myself that the Ford had come for me, a precursor to the hearse that would carry me to a final church service. Suddenly, I was drowning in thoughts of Harold Ashton's murder, and panic crackled in my veins hot as electric current. I wanted to flee, but my legs were locked.

Then the Ford rolled forward, slowly crossing the intersection, continuing its prowl down Bennington. Once it was out of sight I ran, retracing my surreptitious path along Worth Street.

Hurrying between two houses, working my way back to Dodd Street, I thought of Ernst Lang, my neighbor, because he shared the killer's nationality. I certainly didn't believe he had murdered Harold Ashton, and I knew he hadn't been the driver of the black Ford because Mr. Lang drove a cream-colored Buick, but his proximity to the important pieces of my life – my house and my mother – made me uneasy.

Why had he chosen to live in my neighborhood instead of on the other side of town where the majority of the German immigrants had taken up residence? Why did he live alone? Where were his wife and children? All grown men had families, but Mr. Lang had never mentioned his, and there was also the issue of the men.

On more than one occasion I'd seen different men visit Mr. Lang's home after sunset, and I'd thought nothing of it. Yet the more I considered these visits, the more their oddity needled me. Often enough, my neighbor would not turn on his porch light to greet his visitors, and soon after they entered his house, the living room lights went dark – sometimes the whole house. Most of the time the visits were brief, hardly the length of a good chat among friends. The recollections of these visits struck me as significantly more peculiar as I made my way through shadows and bushes on my return home.

I was so caught up in my suspicions of Mr. Lang, I nearly ran into him. My neighbor came around the corner of the Ashcroft's front lawn and blocked my path like a bull, and his appearance so startled me, I backpedaled clumsily and fell on my butt.

"Ah, good," he said. I could hear the humor in his voice. "Your friend is worried about you."

He stepped forward and leaned down, reaching out a hand to help me to my feet. At first, I couldn't take the hand.

"Come now," he said. "Your fat friend is very upset. He thinks you've run off and gotten yourself killed."

"W-where is he," I asked.

"In your living room, eating a piece of cake. He came outside to see if you were at the lake, and I told him to go inside and wait until I found you."

I took the German's hand and let him pull me up. He patted my back lightly a single time and then set off down Crosby Street.

"It's quicker if we go between the houses," I said nervously.

"But those aren't your houses, or your yards. It's rude to make a road of a man's property if he hasn't invited you. We will walk around the block like gentlemen. It is a nice night and you are safe, so where is the hurry?"

I didn't respond. When we reached the corner Mr. Lang placed his hand on my shoulder, stopping me.

"Where did you go tonight?"

"Just took a walk."

"A walk?" he asked. The scars on his nose and cheeks seemed more pronounced in the gloom as if the furrows in his skin had no bottom, just openings revealing great, black space beyond the flesh. "You took a walk through bushes and between houses? A walk that upset your friend so much?"

"That's just Bum. He's a scaredy cat."

"Because of that boy who was killed?"

"Yeah."

"But you are not afraid?"

"No," I said, but the lie rang in my own ears so clearly, it must have been obvious to my neighbor. Still, I pushed on, hoping to camouflage my fear with reason. "Why would anyone want to kill me?"

"Why would anyone want to kill that other boy?" he said

"I don't know."

"Yes, good. Enough of this. Let's get you home to your fat friend before he eats all of the cake."

We walked the rest of the way to my house, and at the front door, my neighbor patted me on the back again and said, "Good night."

"Mr. Lang," I said, "are you going to tell my ma about this?"

He chewed on the question a bit and shook his head. "No. Some things are just between men. Go inside now and see your friend."

His comment about men puffed me up. I said good night and strutted into the house as if I had returned from an actual spy assignment, and I teased Bum for an hour, not telling where I was or what had happened, but allowing him to stew in the material of his imagination.

Five: Sheriff Tom Rabbit

Tom sat at his desk, face in his hands. He scrubbed his palms over his cheeks and eyes, trying to erase a bit of the fatigue the long day had left with him. Gilbert Perry remained in the front office but Rex had gone home to develop the crime-scene photos and Don was out to the city hall building a list of suspects from the town's census, focusing on the German population. Tom still believed, or wanted to believe, that the murderer of Harold Ashton had crept into town, done his evil, and then moved on to some new, distant location, but he couldn't count on that. Doc Randolph had done a thorough job with the boy, and noted the cleanliness of the multiple cuts necessary to remove so much material from Harold's torso. Though any number of the city's residents could dress a deer in a few minutes flat, Doc Randolph thought a good place to start would be with butchers, stockyard workers, and surgeons. A preliminary list already sat on Tom's desk, and he'd gone over it a dozen times.

The note they'd found in a lacquered snuffbox in Harold's mouth turned out to be something of a puzzle. Rex suggested they have Brett Fletcher translate the thing, since Brett spoke a little German, but was not part of their community. He'd been trained in the language to work for army intelligence, but had barely been able to put it to use before his Jeep exploded out from under him. Tom agreed with Rex and they'd paid Brett a visit. It took him just under two minutes to decipher the message with the help of a translation dictionary. According to Brett the note read:

One less gun against the Reich.
One more pig for the slaughter.
Did you know he was the third?

Tom had asked Brett to check his findings, and Brett said that was as close as he could come with his limited knowledge and the dictionary. The last line bothered Tom most of all. The third? The third what?

For the time being Tom was keeping the contents of the note quiet, only sharing it with his men and Doctor Randolph, who'd suggested based on the final line of the missive that perhaps the killer had struck before. This possibility needled at the sheriff. Harold Ashton wasn't the only person to disappear from Barnard in the last few months. Dewey Smith's parents had reported him as a runaway just after the start of the new year, and Karen Perry – Gilbert's cousin – had also disappeared, though it was highly suspected she'd eloped with a boy she'd met at a church in Austin. The girl had a history of family troubles, so no one was surprised when she didn't call or write to explain her whereabouts. Still, no word on either of those two kids in months, and those were just the two that immediately sprang to Tom's mind. People of that age often ran off, whether it was to chase love, escape the family, or seek out their dreams in a bigger city. Except for the families, hardly anyone batted an eye.

It had been hard as hell breaking the news to Harold's parents, seeing the collapse of Chuck Ashton's face as his wife fell against his chest, but to have them storm into his office an hour later, infuriated that Tom hadn't revealed his evidence – the German's note – had been impossible. He let them scream and accuse, and he had said nothing until they'd worn themselves out. He calmly explained that the note didn't actually tell them much. The German population of Barnard was enormous: five hundred new residents in the last two years alone, and more than a thousand in the ten years since Hitler had taken power of their homeland. Then there were the second-generation families and third-generation families, many of whom retained a functional knowledge of the language – certainly enough to get through the Lutheran Christmas Mass out to St. David's. Any other foreign language would have whittled down the suspect list considerably, even Spanish, but a note written in German could have come from any one of two thousand different people.

Chuck Ashton demanded that he be kept informed of every scrap of evidence Tom found. Tom declined politely, apologized a third time for the man's loss, and then asked Gilbert to see the Ashtons out of the sheriff's office.

Since their departure, Tom had sat at his desk, reading a short list of names – names of people he knew quite well – and wondered if any of them was capable of the violence he'd seen done to Harold. He didn't think so, but it was his job to check them out.

Doc Randolph knocked on his office door just after sunset, and Tom asked him in. The doctor was a short and narrow man, reed thin from shoulders to toes. He wore a neatly cropped fringe above his ears, which stood only a few steps off pure white, and a pencil-thin mustache cut a line above his all but imperceptible lips. The doctor sat in the wooden chair across from Tom, his face twisted with questions, but he didn't say anything for a very long time. Finally, Tom asked, "Something on your mind?"

"Too many things, I'm afraid."

"I know the feeling," Tom said. "Want to take them one by one?"

"Where was Harold all that time?" the doctor asked in a burst of frustration. "Gone for weeks but he hasn't been dead for more than a day, maybe two. Did he leave and get accosted on his way back into town? Was someone holding him prisoner all that time?"

Logical questions, Tom thought. He'd asked himself those very things a number of times, and his conclusion was, "He didn't run off. If he was going anywhere, then it was to enlist, and we all know if he'd succeeded he wouldn't be back, and if he didn't succeed he'd have been back a whole lot sooner. So

I'd have to guess that he was kidnapped and the murder came later."

"But there was no ransom demand, was there?"

"No, there wasn't," Tom confirmed. "I think we can trust Chuck and Ruth to have let us in on something like that."

"I would rather not consider why someone would hold a boy for that length of time, expecting no external gratification."

Tom didn't understand the comment and he said so.

"Well, this monster must have wanted something, and if it wasn't a ransom or some other stimulus from outside the situation, then he must have been hoping to get something from Harold himself."

"Get something?" Tom asked. "Such as?"

"I don't know," Doc Randolph said. "To the best of my observation I saw no signs of sexual interference, but who can say? So much of the boy is gone."

"Sexual interference?" Tom said, feeling a flush of heat in his cheeks. "What are you talking about?"

"I'm trying to help you find a motive, and the motive may be a pronounced mental illness. If your theory is correct, Harold didn't just stumble into a bad situation to get his throat cut and have his body discarded. There was planning to this, and there was a purpose. I'm suggesting that the killer may be compelled by certain stimuli – and that could be sexual – and if that's the case, then it's likely this will happen again."

"Look, Doc, I know the note said Harold was the third, but we don't have the slightest idea what that means."

"The note is only part of it."

"Then where is all of this coming from?"

"Jack the Ripper," Doc Randolph said. "Albert Fish."

Tom knew about Jack the Ripper, he'd read about the killer in pulp novels and even seen a movie based on his crimes, but he wasn't connecting a murderer of London prostitutes with the death of a local boy. He knew nothing about the other man Doc Randolph had mentioned.

"Fish was a child molester, murderer and cannibal," he said.

"Oh for the love of God," Tom interjected.

"Hear me out," the doctor said. "They executed Fish in New York a few years back. He is known to have killed three children but may have killed many more. The thing is, there are similarities between those cases and this business with Harold Ashton. The most obvious are the mutilations of the bodies and the pieces missing from those bodies, and the killer's need to communicate what he'd done. In this case, the note you found in Harold's mouth."

"How do you know about these cases?" Tom asked, feeling the doctor had more than one-upped him.

"Psychiatric magazines," the doctor said. "I don't buy into a lot of the mumbo jumbo they throw around, but there are some interesting articles on deviant behaviors, and I remember reading about Fish in one of those journals right after he was executed."

"So did the article tell you how we catch this guy?"

"No," the doctor said, "I mean if we knew anything at all about Jack the Ripper, who he was, why he did what he did, or if we knew of other such cases we might be able to make some comparisons, but this Fish character was uniquely insane. For example, he shoved needles in his privates and beat himself with nails."

"Why in the name of God would he do that?"

"He found pain sexually gratifying."

"You're pulling my leg."

"It's not uncommon. Masochism is a well-documented sexual perversion, like pedophilia, homosexuality, bestiality, and necrophilia. Generally it is believed that childhood factors play into the formation of these illnesses, and there are numerous people suffering them, but of course, the taboo nature of the diseases means the afflicted don't go around talking about them."

Tom got the impression Doc Randolph was quoting from one of those magazines he'd mentioned. It sure felt like a classroom lecture to him. Further, he didn't know what good the information would do them. He knew nothing about the diseases the doctor had listed, but a man sick enough to carve up a boy like Harold would have to stand out.

Doc Randolph pulled his pipe and a pouch from the hip pocket of his jacket. He wore a stern expression, like a parent waiting for a child to explain himself. His expression didn't change as he tamped the tobacco into the bowl.

"What else are you thinking?" Tom asked, knowing the doctor wasn't finished showing off.

"You said there was no sign of the boy's organs and no blood."

"None that we could see."

"So you've already guessed the boy was murdered elsewhere and left in that particular place."

"Yes."

"Why in Blevins's woods? Furthermore, why on a trail the killer had to know was frequented?"

"He wanted us to find him. He wanted us to find the note."

"Exactly," Doc Randolph said, striking a match and setting it to his pipe. "He's got more on his mind than just killing. He wants you to know he's doing this for Germany. After all, the note did say, 'One less gun against the Reich.' He can't – for whatever reason – fight for his country *in* his country, so he's decided to do it in ours."

"So I just look around for a swastika or a guy with jack boots and a little mustache, and we're all set."

Doc Randolph shook his head as if frustrated with an obstinate child.

"I see where you're going, Doc, but these people weren't kicked out of Germany; they fled the damn place."

"But when did they flee? And why?" the doctor persisted. "I can think of at least one of our residents who's been with us for a good long time. In fact, he left Germany just about the time the first wave of socialism was crushed. At that point, leaving made a lot more sense than staying. He couldn't know Hitler would emerge from jail a hero – a man of the people."

"Who are you talking about?" Tom asked.

"Gerhardt Weigle," Doc Randolph said before puffing on his pipe and filling the air with a smoky-sweet scent.

"The butcher?" Tom asked.

"Precisely," Doc Randolph said. "Gerhardt Weigle, the butcher. And I'm sure there are a number of others as well."

⠿

Tom sat at the window of his bedroom, gazing south where the sky shone a pale purple from the lights of Barnard. He couldn't see the lights themselves as a ridge obscured the city from his view, but he saw the radiance cast by the lamps and homes miles in the distance covering the town like an ominous dome. The list of suspects – all German names – sat on the table beside him. He knew every man named on it, had drank with several of them and had spoken to them all at one time or another, and he couldn't bring himself to believe that any one of them had murdered the Ashton boy. Even Gerhardt Weigle, who was a difficult man on the best of days, struck Tom as unlikely. Tomorrow, Rex would head up a crew to comb through Blevins's property, looking for signs of a transient's camp, anything to offer hope that Harold Ashton's killer was not a regular at Ormand's Mercantile, or Milton's Barber Shop, or Carl's Bakery. Tom would make calls to Dallas and Austin and the sheriff's departments in between to see if they'd had any recent violence. If it weren't for that damn note he might just have been able to convince himself that Harold's death had been an isolated tragedy, but like the dome of light covering Barnard, Tom felt engulfed in something immense and inescapable.

More than ever he wished Glynis was still with him. His wife had always listened to him talk about the troubles in Barnard, and unlike Doc Randolph, who treated Tom like a babbling infant, Glynis comforted him and allowed him to work through the mysteries. She'd questioned things, had given him new perspectives and even if their talks didn't produce an ironclad solution, she had been there to laugh at his bad jokes and whisper encouragement in his ear. He wondered what she'd make of a case like this one.

The whole thing left a heavy rotten lump in his stomach. He'd seen his share of death, both accidental and planned down to the second – gunshot wounds, knife wounds, poisonings, even a young woman who'd met the angry side of an axe – but this business with Harold Ashton was unlike anything he'd witnessed. Doc Randolph had gone a good ways towards undermining Tom's confidence by spouting off about that Fish character, acting like some small city Sherlock Holmes and treating Tom with no more respect than he'd show a dense ward. And what good did the information do him? Was he supposed to strip every German down to the skin and see if he'd been jabbing his privates with pins?

Gazing through the window, Tom shook his head. Where did monsters like that come from? Was it really just a sickness or something more sinister?

Over the years, he'd watched the power lines go up all over Barnard and as a boy he'd marveled at the endless, steady light the electric bulbs cast through living-room windows. He'd seen the dirt tracks leading in and out of town fall beneath smooth bands of concrete as great veins of road began to spread through the state, and soon after he'd witnessed the laying of the sidewalks which kept his pant cuffs from getting muddy, but scuffed his shoes if he wasn't careful with the curb, and cars replaced horses, and refrigerators replaced iceboxes. Telephones in every home. Radios sending him the beautiful voice of a woman in New York, singing with an orchestra. He'd seen so many things change, and he couldn't help but wonder if man was changing, too.

A board creaked behind him and Tom turned away from the window. Estella stood in the doorway, chin against her chest, peering at Tom through her eyelashes. He waved her into the room and turned out the lamp.

Six: Tim Randall

All I knew of the war came from newsreels, movies and radio broadcasts, but the scope of the conflict never really struck me. I knew my daddy was in Europe. All spring, letters had been coming in, and Ma let me keep the stamps along with the small notes Daddy sent along, specifically for me. If he wrote about the war, he did so in the letters Ma kept, and she almost never read me passages from those notes. She'd tell me where Daddy was currently stationed and that he was just fine. His notes to me were always the same. I kept them in a metal box on my dresser. In late June Ma received a letter, the longest one yet, but the scrap of paper – Daddy's note to me – like a piece of fat ticker tape, was no different than a dozen others:

We're giving them a good run, Timmy. Be sure to behave yourself and mind your mother. Your father, Fred Randall.

I imagined when he returned he'd have a thousand stories to tell, and he'd share them while we fished in the lake or went hunting for wild pigs up north. Before his leaving, these had been quiet excursions with little said between father and son, but he wouldn't keep the war to himself. I felt certain of that.

Seven: The German

July 1, 1944 – Translated from the German

The anniversary.

My face looks no older, but perhaps the fault lies in the mirror. Age is a slow infection working on skin and muscle imperceptibly until one is irrevocably stricken, and the mirror is an easily misread instrument. If I had a photograph of myself from all of those years ago, then perhaps I could refute this strange conviction, but I have no such picture and no one familiar to whom I might pose such a bizarre question. All I have is the mirror and it shows me the same face another did in Bad Wiessee, only the day before the passing.

I have nothing of my previous life but the scars and memories: not entirely trustworthy.

Once the coffee is on the boil, I walk to the front door and pull it open to retrieve my milk and the morning paper. My neighbor Tim stands outside, and his face lights up when he see me, and he lifts his hand to wave, and we both say "good morning," though only his greeting is sincere, and he tries to speak to me, not knowing that this is a miserable anniversary. Lately he has been eager for my company. I am pleasant but impatient to end this morning's conversation, though he does not seem to see this. He chatters about his mother and the lake and about going fishing, and I feel that his every word is another coat of varnish, cutting off oxygen from my lungs and affixing my limbs beneath heavy layers of stain. A clamp tightens at the base of my skull, and I want to ask him if my face has changed at all in the years we have been neighbors, except I know he will not understand the question. He keeps me on the porch as long as he can, but finally he runs out of trifling topics, and he wishes me a good day, and I thank him before escaping back into the house.

The boy's manner is familiar to me, and it concerns me. Men under my command and men in my bed have exhibited similar eagerness for my sanction, and though I recognized the need I similarly felt wholly unqualified to fulfill it. The boy's father is in battle, far away from home, and it is natural for him to seek a male figure to exalt in replacement, except I am no one's father. I have no lesson that could benefit this boy. Soldiers mistook my leadership for paternal guidance; lovers confused dominant affection for some deficit in their childhoods, and these were weaknesses I exploited to fashion better soldiers and better lovers. What do I know of fathers and sons? My own father was nothing but a vile shadow on the walls of my childhood home, a threatening shape that was void of light, darkly insubstantial.

I remember the man who comes to the reeking cell to kill me. He is arrogant and cold as all executioners should be. The gun he places beside me carries a single bullet, and he says there is honor in its use. I refuse this generosity. Let the fuckers erect their own deceit. I have spent a life in service to this fraudulent cause, and if I'm to die for it, my death will be honest. My executioner leaves me alone with the weapon, which remains untouched until his return. Two flashes of light send me to the floor and my executioner peers down into my face, leveling the gun's muzzle at my chest, and then I am cold, standing in grass and staring into a hole.

Holding the coffee pot, my hand trembles. I return it to the stove. My cup remains empty.

I will not leave the house again today, except to feed the chickens. This is a bad day. A terrible day.

Eight: Tim Randall

The scent of frying chicken woke me on the morning of July Fourth. Since she worked so late at the factory, I wasn't used to Ma waking before me, but from the sounds and smells emerging from the kitchen I could tell she'd already been up for a good long while. In the kitchen I found her turning chicken in the skillet. Potatoes for a salad boiled on the stove, and a sheet of cookies sat on the counter waiting to go into the oven. Ma kissed my forehead and retrieved two slices of toast from the oven, which she quickly replaced with the cookie sheet. Sitting me at the table with my toast and a jar of strawberry jam, she returned to her cooking.

Before we left for the celebration at the fairgrounds, the chicken and potato salad had been tucked into a wicker basket and placed in the refrigerator, where it would wait until early evening, accompanying us to the nighttime celebration on the southern edge of Kramer Lake. The fireworks had been cancelled this year, but it was for the war effort so nobody made a fuss, and it was still nice to see so many people.

We walked to the fairgrounds, greeting various neighbors along the way. Rita Sherman caught up with us at Pine Road. Her floral print dress clutched her body so tightly I couldn't imagine how she'd make it through the day's heat. Her face had been powdered heavily and it reminded me of the sugar cookies waiting at home, and her lips were the color of blood. She clasped her church hat to her head and waddled rapidly, talking to Ma a mile a minute about her evening at the Lonestar Tavern and a nice gentleman she was meeting at the lake that evening so they could "trade recipes."

Ma shot me a concerned glance and then smiled at her friend and said, "That will be nice."

The two women spoke, and my mind drifted. I thought about Ma, the way she'd seemed particularly fidgety this morning, how she'd been in constant motion since I'd woken; but mostly I thought about my daddy, walking on ground so far away I had no real understanding of the distance. When I pictured him in battle my mind placed him into scenes from the movies, settings and situations Hollywood had created, so of course I saw him as a hero, the star of the motion picture, not one of the anonymous actors surrounding him, whose characters fell, dramatically clutching their chests as the battle raged on. In my mind war was neat and orderly, played out in shades of gray on vaguely unreal-looking fields. Nameless, faceless actors fell, but the star always lived to see his girl again, and Daddy would too.

By the time we reached the fairgrounds, the field was already swarming with people. Tents framed the north and east sides, and the odors of mesquite smoke, sausages, barbecue sauce and fried dough scented the air. Mr. Carlson's brass band played marching songs from the bandstand, and I saw Bum's uncle Reggie pumping his trombone with gusto as he stomped his foot on the stage. Ma and Rita sat at a bench, but I was eager to find Bum and explore the different tents. She told me to have fun and to stay out of trouble, and I promised before setting off.

Wandering over the hard packed dirt I saw friends from school, and teachers, and neighbors, and everyone smiled. I'd hoped to see Mr. Lang among the crowd, but if he was there I didn't see him. Eventually I found Bum with his family sitting at a bench on the southwest side of the fairgrounds.

Clay Craddick, Bum's daddy, stood behind the bench and several feet away, talking with a group of men that includ-

ed Burl Jones, the barber Harvey Milton, and Deputy Walter
Long. Jones seemed particularly agitated, though all of the men
looked angry and perplexed like cowboys whose herd had suddenly vanished. Bum's ma sat on the bench, holding a small um-
brella above her Sunday bonnet, shielding herself from the sun.
She smiled warmly as if in love with everything that crossed her
line of sight. On the bench next to her, Bum's brother Fatty, as
dull faced as a cow, chomped on a piece of gum. Bum saw me
and leapt from the bench, racing forward to intercept me. He'd
never been proud of his family, and he kept me a good distance
from them whenever he could.

"Morning, Timmy," Mrs. Craddick said, waving languidly.
"Such a nice day."

"Yes, ma'am," I agreed.

Bum grabbed my arm and spun me around, leading me back
into the throng of Barnard's gathered population. Behind us
Burl Jones shouted, "Horseshit," before the other men shushed
him and told him to keep his tone civil.

"Daddy's got himself all worked up," Bum said. "All morning
they've been talking about the men Sheriff Rabbit questioned,
all those Germans, and they're thinking they should do some
questioning of their own."

"You think they will?"

"Nah, it's just hot air," Bum said. "But a lot of folks are talking the same way."

We emerged through a pack of women who had gathered
in the center of the fairgrounds, and I saw Mr. Lang standing
by himself next to a scraggly looking pecan tree which was
wrapped in a red, white, and blue banner. It struck me as odd
that he should be alone with so many people around, so I pulled
Bum to a stop and suggested we go say hello, but my friend
shook his head.

"Daddy told me to stay away from the Germans until they
catch the killer. He told me he'd tan me good if he caught me
talking to any of them, even the kids."

"Jeez, Mr. Lang is okay."

"That's not the point," Bum said earnestly.

"He's always been nice to us," I said.

"Don't matter. Daddy said to stay away, and I'm doing it."

So we continued to the tents along the north side of the fairgrounds and we got ourselves a lemonade, which wasn't sweet enough. Rationing assured that most everything tasted strange – either flour bland or bitter. Still, the drink quenched our thirsts, and we were given a second glass two tents down. Girls giggled and chatted. A group of boys asked if we wanted to play tag, but we were too old for that. A boy and his grandfather flew a kite with little luck, as they failed time and again to lift the kite into the tides of wind. We ran into a gang of older boys from school who were putting together a baseball game, and though Bum wasn't much for sports, we happily agreed to join in because we took some pride in being asked. The game didn't last long. The day had turned sweltering, and most of us wanted to return to the celebration for a cold glass of tea or more lemonade, and then the food started coming out. Bum told me he'd promised his Ma that he'd eat supper with the family. He made a screwy face and a gagging noise at the prospect but promised to catch up with me after, so I returned to Ma and Rita, who hadn't moved since I'd left them. Ma asked if I was having fun and if she could get me a supper plate and I said yes to both.

In the middle of supper, I wiped barbecue sauce from my mouth and asked Ma, "Do you think Daddy is celebrating, too?"

She didn't answer.

"I'll bet he is," I said.

When I looked up at Ma, tears shimmered in her eyes. "I'm sure you're right," she told me.

⫼

I walked all over looking for Bum after supper. It was mid afternoon and the fairgrounds radiated merciless heat. Lethargy seemed to have a good hold on the folks, most of whom had gathered in the tents or beneath patches of shade to shield them from the sun. Hugo Jones sat on a picnic bench, smoking a cigarette. He was a tall wiry boy with veins like maps on his forearms. Thick black hair fought against a sheen of oil and seemed about ready to spring free, and pimples like spider bites swarmed his cheeks and chin. Hugo and his buddies, Ben and Austin, were talking to three girls, and though I thought I recognized Jilly Irvine, whose uncle taught at my school, the other girls weren't familiar at all. Ben Livingston wore a brown Stetson pushed back from his rectangular face, shirt sleeves rolled up past his elbow, and he chewed on a length of straw, looking like a cowboy from a movie: Tim Holt or a young John Wayne. The blond boy, Austin Chitwood, appeared sloppy in a dirty chambray shirt and wrinkled blue jeans. His mouth and eyes moved constantly as if he were a puppet manipulated by a palsied hand. Hugo paused in something he was saying and eyed me through a cloud of smoke, but his interest was passing, and he returned his attention to the girls.

Having all but given up on finding Bum, I followed a voice I recognized to the bandstand, where Brett Fletcher had parked his wheelchair in the shade and was telling stories to a small audience. I was surprised to find Bum sitting near the back of this gathering, as he'd never been fond of Mr. Fletcher's stories, and he only went out to Bennet Road to hear them when I insisted.

Mr. Fletcher threw a sharp glance at me, letting me know I was in his sights. Maybe it was because of the wheelchair, or the authority that thickened his voice, but I always thought of Mr. Fletcher as old. He wasn't. In fact, he was younger than my daddy, but he displayed an air of maturity and confidence that put him well beyond his years. Ma and Miz Rita agreed he was a handsome man. Miz Rita called him "a rugged looker," but she'd used the same description for my neighbor Mr. Lang, and he didn't look a thing like Mr. Fletcher.

I walked around the audience of kids and dropped onto the dirt next to Bum. "I've been looking everywhere for you," I whispered.

"Daddy said I had to hear this."

"You wanna go?"

"Tim Randall, is your story more interesting than mine?" Mr. Fletcher called.

I looked up red-faced. All of the kids had turned to me. Some giggled and others looked surprised.

"N-no, sir," I said. "I don't imagine so."

"Then perhaps you'll let me back to it?"

"Yes, sir."

He set into a new story. I usually liked listening to Mr. Fletcher, because the stories he told were exciting, and he threw himself into their performance, but the day was just too hot and the air too dry for me to get comfortable. As he spun a tale about his unit avenging the deaths of two village girls, who had died at the hands of "Nazi filth," I shifted on the hard-packed dirt but couldn't for the life of me get situated. Bum nudged me to get me to settle down, and I stretched out on my side. Not nearly soon enough, Mr. Fletcher finished his story, assuring his audience that the men who had murdered those two girls got what was coming to them, and then he worked his way into the moral of the story.

"I'm not saying all Germans are Nazis, but you can never tell, so you have to be careful. Right now, we got a boy dead, cut to pieces by a Nazi piece of filth, and I don't want to see a one of you follow in his footsteps."

Mr. Fletcher's warning crawled over my skin as tangible as the day's heat and the sweat it drew from my body. How did you avoid a monster that wore a human face? How did you identify the enemy?

Nine: The German

July 4th 1944 – Translated from the German

The celebration is held at the fairgrounds. It is an ugly patch of field, mostly scabbed dirt and jutting wiry grasses. The train tracks run down the west side of the grounds. Stockyards squat along the southern border and the scent of manure, blood and rending meat mixes with that of locomotive oil. A sun-bleached sky hangs above, nearly white. An untalented brass band comprised of white-haired men plays patriotic noise. Marches and anthems meant to invigorate. Ladies have draped red, white and blue bunting across two tree trunks. These are not healthy trees. Insect-eaten leaves hang from narrow limbs, and their shade is insufficient on this hot day. Tents stand like an army encampment. The air is dry and blows through the tent fabric, and the barbecue pits, and over the jugs of lemonade, the children throwing balls, the women gossiping at one long table, and the men who did not go to battle. The Germans have gathered away from the others. I am a German, but I am neither with them nor separate from them. I sit at a table indifferent to the conversation of those around me. I nod when it strikes me as appropriate and smile when I realize someone has told a joke. I close my eyes when a wave of dust rises from the earth to crest over me. Fifteen meters away, my neighbor Tim is drinking lemonade with his plump friend. They have given up playing ball and instead make a show of wiping sweat from their brows as if to justify quaffing so much bittersweet drink.

Smiles lie over worried and uncomfortable expressions. The Americans are not the only ones who suppose on the identity of this killer. At the celebration, I see Germans assessing their countrymen. I see the whispers and the nods, and the shaking of heads. Such suspicion is disheartening, and while this crime has unified the Americans as such crimes will, it has divided us – from them and each other. I am reminded of Fritz Lang's film *M*, and when I imagine this local criminal I think of a pudgy psychopath whistling a bit of Grieg's *Peer Gynt*. I enjoyed that film very much and took the director's last name when I came to this country, but now the suspicion and fear that film made show of engulfs me. I am similarly reminded of Peter Kürten, and Fritz Haarmann and Karl Grossman, and I can't help but wonder if this brand of cruelty is particular to my nation. We have nurtured this Vampire of Düsseldorf and this Butcher of Hanover and who knows how many others. Do such monsters arise in Spain? In France? In America? I do not know.

I remember a bathhouse and a marble pool in which so much beauty bathed; and splashing in a refreshing lake on an overcast day before taking a strong blond man to my room. I remember full-throated prayers, shouted like orders before the firing squad silenced them.

Are these memories or lies I tell myself?

Another film occurs to me. It is *The Cabinet of Dr. Caligari*, and my mind fills with the flat, harsh scenery and Conrad Veidt's flat, harsh face. Intrigued by the ideas in the film, I found myself viewing it again and again with men from my squad. My companions teased and said that with my scars – still very recent and red – I would make a fine monster for the screen. But now, over two decades later, what I remember about the film is the ending, when the hero emerges from his delusion and finds himself in a lunatic asylum, and the audience realizes that all that has come before was a fiction of his demented mind. I remember this because of the deep, dark hole, and the flakes of blood that fall from my chest like tiny leaves.

I remember this because I should be dead, and if I am not, then perhaps I am mad and nothing I see with my eyes or my memory can be trusted.

No longer comfortable under the hot sun, feeling the scorch on my neck, I cross the dried field to one of the German tents and order a glass of tea from Yvette Wagner, who smiles warmly at me and comments on the depth of my tan. I thank her and pay for the tea and carry it to one of the benches at the back. Soon others will tire of the afternoon sun and fill the various tents, but for now, I share the bench with only a few people. People I recognize as German but do not know by name. We are polite and greet one another, but I leave them to their conversations. In turn, they cast furtive glances at me, perhaps wondering if I am a murderer of children.

Before long the sheriff peeks in. He smiles and says, "Hello," to Yvette and then looks at us sitting on the bench. When his eyes reach me, I know without question he wonders on my guilt, but I take no offense. He is a policeman, investigating a crime. What else would he be thinking?

The sheriff is a fine-looking man. He has the strength of maturity and honest work about him, but he is not a clever man. I see that in his eyes. The way he unsubtly appraises me is both aggressive and apologetic. I keep my eyes on him. Though I have much to hide, the murder of a boy is not among my crimes. He flinches first as I knew he would. He drops his gaze to the hard-packed dirt and then casts a quick smile to Yvette. Before he exits the tent, he allows me a final glance. I nod, and he is gone.

The tea is strong and cooling. I buy a second glass and Yvette says that the third one will be free before she winks at me. She is a pretty girl and will one day make a fine wife for a man who requires such a thing. She imagines I am this sort of man. Greater mistakes have been made.

Carl Baker enters the tent and upon seeing me rushes to the bench.

"Have some tea," I tell him. "It is good."

"Did you hear about Weigle?" Carl asks.

I tell him that I had heard the sheriff and the butcher had spoken.

"It's not just Weigle," Carl continues and he proceeds to list names of men who worked at the stockyard and the two German doctors in Barnard: Reinhardt and Hoffman.

One of the men who had been questioned – the foreman at the stockyards – was familiar to me. He was a greatly muscled but ugly man with a face like a goat. In the bedroom he spoke like a woman, going so far as to affect a falsetto tone and call me "husband." My laughter at his display kept him from returning, and though I regret that my uncontrollable humor over his performance caused him some humiliation, I did not miss his company.

My thoughts have wandered and I do not realize that Carl is addressing me by name. "Ernst," he says. "Ernst."

"Yes, Carl," I reply. "I'm sorry. I was daydreaming."

He insists that this is no time for daydreams. Soon it will be our turn to meet the sheriff and endure his questioning and the prospect makes me smile.

"What have we to fear?" I ask. "I've done nothing wrong. Have you?"

Carl looks as if I'd slapped him. "Or course not," he exclaims.

"Then let the sheriff ask his questions. He will get his answers and then go ask his questions of someone else. Should I worry over something I haven't done and cannot fix?"

"I'm very worried, Ernst."

"I know that. I see that."

"Who could have done such a thing?"

He is working himself into a panic, and I know this will do him no good. He is gentle, this Carl Baker, and I don't know any words that can soothe him. His own son is not much younger than the Ashton boy and his daughter only a year younger than that. I understand his concern for them, but it goes deeper than his fatherly fear of a monster preying on his children. He carries the fear of being seen as a monster by the Americans and dreads their retaliation against him and his family.

I was called a monster many times, but the label means nothing. In politics and in war, monsters are defined by which side of a fight a man claims. He is still a man to those who share his beliefs, perhaps even a hero. To those that oppose his philosophy, he is a beast, a creature, one of a thousand unspeakable demons clashing over an ideal.

With no words to soothe my friend, I tell him that I do not know who could have murdered Harold Ashton. I express my disgust at the crime and voice a hope that the monster will soon be caught and executed.

Peter Lorre strolls through my thoughts, carrying a balloon and whistling from *Peer Gynt*.

My conversation with Carl takes a turn toward the common and he talks about his family, his shop. He comments on the wonderful celebration and taps his fingers in time with the untalented brass band that has resumed banging and honking on the bandstand. Though we discuss many other things, I see the weight of concern on Carl's face, but since there is nothing I can do to relieve it, I pretend it is not there.

Eventually, he excuses himself. He tells me that he must find his wife and his children, and asks if I will be staying for the barbecue because he has baked many pies, and I tell him that I will, and I promise to come visit with his family for a time. I finish my second tea and stand, stretching out my back and feeling a pain beneath my shoulder blade. It is a bullet trapped between my ribs, one of many I carry in my chest, and on cold days they feel like bits of ice lodged in my tissues, but only this one shell brings me discomfort regardless of the weather, and it is my belief this is the bullet that killed me.

As I leave the tent, Yvette reminds me that I can have a third glass of tea free of charge, and I thank her and ask her to keep it for me until I return. Behind the row of tents I take a piss and notice two other men are doing the same. They stare at the stream between their legs as if it is magical and will tell the future. I couldn't care less for the functions of my body and scan the rows of trucks over my shoulder and the wagons laden down with hay for the cows that will soon face the sledgehammer. A train approaches from the south. In the sky above, the sun appears to be melting, spreading out in a vast pool of molten light.

⑈

The barbecue at the celebration is good. Weigle serves bratwursts and frankfurters from his shop. To everyone he serves he tells the story of how the sheriff requested his assistance in solving the murder of Harold Ashton, and I know he is lying, but see no reason to question him when he seems in a rare good mood. Good for you, I tell Weigle. With your help, the sheriff will catch this man in no time. He smiles and nods tersely, proudly, as if I am absolutely right. I eat with Carl and his family. His wife makes inappropriate overtures that Carl laughs off as if this is a common game between them. I attempt smiles of my own, but find the woman's behavior terrible – showing such little respect for Carl.

I am used to flirtation, though I am not a handsome man. Scars make an otherwise unimpressive face fascinating. Long ago, my position and authority assured a quantity of admirers from both genders who found power an efficient aphrodisiac, and while I could have my pick of lovers, never once did I attribute their attentions to any physical quality I possessed, but rather understood it as a benefit of my social stature like good cigars, fine brandy, and convertible motor cars. Now, if I am considered attractive it is simply because I am here – present when so many others are absent. Women see me as strong and available, lacking the emotional obligation of a wife. As for the men of my sort, who can say what they see? In this place I represent all that they loathe in themselves, yet they come to me like starving peasants begging sustenance from a despised baron.

After the sausages and salads and slices of Carl's blackberry pie, fatigue falls over me. It is pleasant in its way, but with the persistent heat it drives me nearly to sleep. Feeling it would be rude to drop my head on the bench while Carl speaks, I excuse myself for a walk around the grounds. Again, I see my neighbor Tim. His fat friend is no longer with him. Instead, Tim sits at a bench with his mother and she speaks to a plump woman with crooked teeth as Tim devours a wedge of watermelon. Pink spots cover the white napkin tucked into his collar and drip to a plate already freckled with black seeds. He doesn't see me pass and I do not stop to say hello but rather continue to the edge of the fairgrounds. As I wander, I carry a vague hope of seeing the teacher, Jeffrey. If he sees me perhaps it will occur to him to visit my house again, and I immediately scold myself for such a pathetic yearning, because I do not enjoy the man's company. He is shamed and weak and brings me little but a few moments of distraction and every moment in his presence diminishes me. But it is company, and suddenly I am aware of how very long it has been since I shared my time with a companion of value.

I think of a man named Richert. He gave me a car I rarely use and offered me a home by the water, though I could have purchased these things myself. We spoke as good friends, but only later did I understand his opinion of me was far lower.

It is this place. A place of freedom shouldn't know such fear, but it clings to these people like flies on the dead.

At the edge of the fairgrounds, I decide it is time to go home. My mood has soured and I find no joy among this population. So I cross the field a final time. Near the bandstand I see a group of children gathered around a man in a wheelchair. He is speaking loudly and waving a hand in the air – his face a twisted mask of mock fury. The children – and there is Tim's fat friend among them – listen rapt by the man who I recognize as Brett Fletcher, the town's first war hero. His eyes are those of a madman, sharp and at the same time focused on things well out of sight. He makes fists of his hands and twists his shoulders back and forth to give the impression of marching and the children laugh, and he raises his arms as if sighting down a rifle and the children gasp, and he makes a stricken face and falls back in his chair and the children applaud and shout. I leave the performance and the fairgrounds behind, and walk home.

On the road into town a car approaches. It is traveling very fast and the driver honks the horn in a staccato flurry. The car swerves across the lane, and I believe it is the driver's intention to hit me. I expect to be afraid, but the feeling never appears. The grill of the car races for me and I look upward searching for the driver's eyes and I see the vehicle is crowded with young people and they all look insane as their faces fly toward me, but I do not move, not so much as a flinch, and I have no explanation for why this is so – it isn't bravery, nor is it death's welcome – but I stand there as if watching an approaching friend and at the last moment the car swerves sending up a spray of dust to cover me as many young voices scream obscenities and call me "Kraut." None of those faces are familiar to me. How they know I am a German simply by my face and my clothes I could not say. Perhaps it is as simple as a predator recognizing its prey.

At home I strip off my clothes and use a damp cloth to scrub the dust and sweat from me. Then I lie down for an inordinately long nap. When I wake, the sweat is thick on me, so I again wipe myself off with the damp rag. Unsatisfied with the rapidly warming moisture on my skin, I retrieve my swimming trunks from the line in back and walk to the lake.

Evening is falling and the mosquitoes dance thickly about me. I wade out until the water covers my shoulders. My feet sink in the spongy foliage at the lake's bottom, and I find a stone on which to stand. I watch the smooth surface as the water works through my skin to cool the muscle and bone beneath, and for a time I am comfortable and calm. Except for the occasional refrain from *Peer Gynt*, my mind is quiet.

Dark falls and I wade out of the lake and I go to my house, and inside I shower to get the lake off of me, and I splash rose water on my palms and massage it into my skin, and I pour myself a whiskey and return to the porch and sit in the hard backed chair and close my eyes. No fireworks tonight. The city is supporting the war effort and conserves the powder for the killing of the Japanese and the German. It is not quiet, though. Men fire their guns into the sky. The reports echo across town, and distant guns fire back – violence summoning violence like animals calling mates. Shouts of appreciation rise and fall as this place celebrates the birth of America. It sounds like battle, and the familiarity of the barrage brings melancholy warmth to my skin.

In the streets of Munich my men and I confront a communist brigade with chair legs and broken bottles, and I smash a man's nose beneath the pine club before slashing his cheek and stomping his throat under my boot. Next to me, another communist meets the blade of my lieutenant's knife. Later the lieutenant recounts the fight over a brandy in my home, and later still, we are in my bed and he is sobbing, and I drift off to sleep as if on the notes of a lullaby.

This life I imagine is impossible, but I have no memories to contest it, and what is a man but an accumulation of memories? He is neither his name, nor the names others call him, but rather a series of events recorded in tissue like scars behind his eyes. A name is meaningless. Names are for the corpse registry and the carvers of stones.

I remember being cold and wiping flakes of blood like bits of dried autumn leaves from my chest. I remember laughter and the sound of a man choking on blood, and that man is me.

I think of Caligari and wonder if these mad memories hold me in black waters, trapping me under ice until I emerge from delusion into the hands of my keepers.

𝕿𝖊𝖓: 𝕾𝖍𝖊𝖗𝖎𝖋𝖋 𝕿𝖔𝖒 𝕽𝖆𝖇𝖇𝖎𝖙

Tom Rabbit also spent his afternoon wandering the dusty fairgrounds. Though solemn, he occasionally forced a smile when greeting friends and neighbors, and he shared moments speaking with them, but never settled into real conversation. Walking among the people he had been charged to protect, Tom was stricken by the uniformly changed demeanor. The Texans had made the city a courtroom with hundreds of jurists already weighing guilt. Tom saw the quiet conversations, the subtle nodding of heads as simple folks with absolutely no evidence passed judgment on their neighbors, and many of them looked at Tom, not as an ally, but as an accomplice to the crime because he had not yet solved it. On the other hand, the Germans wore guises of the accused when Tom spoke to them. Faces became contrite and words crawled from lips in a stilted yet respectful way, all except for Weigle who believed himself somehow above suspicion.

Days had passed since Harold Ashton had been found, and Tom was no closer to identifying the killer than he had been. The snuffbox was of German origin and very common in that country; it could have arrived with any number of families who had chosen this part of the country to settle. No additional evidence presented itself, and he'd received no reports of similar crimes from any of the sheriff's offices he'd contacted. So he was left with a dwindling list of men who needed to be interrogated and all but useless tip-offs from the community. It seemed that every slight against a neighbor had become sufficient cause for suspicion. Phone calls came in day and night. Angry citizens marched into his office certain they knew the identity of the Ashton boy's killer and their convictions were born of evidence that amounted to: he plays his radio too loud; he closes his blinds at three in the afternoon; he parked his car in front of my drive; his son threw a muddy ball into the clean sheets I had drying on a line and all he did was laugh about it. Petty and ridiculous.

He stopped at a tent to share a glass of tea with Doc Randolph, and the doctor asked him how he was feeling, though both of them already knew the answer, and Tom expressed his frustration, but the doctor only added to it with a glare of superiority cast through a fog of pipe smoke. Rex Burns joined them and the three men exchanged ideas, all of which they had exchanged before and the futile redundancy of the exercise fueled Tom's aggravation, because he knew that the crime would remain unsolved unless the killer walked right up to them and confessed, but of course he couldn't say that to anyone except Estella – and only because she could never translate the admission of his failure.

Finally, Tom excused himself and returned to the sun-baked fairgrounds. He walked from tent to tent, hoping to see every face in the city. He thought on the information Doc Randolph had given him about Albert Fish and imagined that such sickness must surely cover a face like warts or boils, and if he looked hard enough, the blemishes of malevolence would show themselves. He strolled to the bandstand and crossed the grounds to the German tents and peeked inside each to find families and young couples and plump, pretty women attempting celebration as the shadow of the Ashton boy's murder hung over them all. They regarded him sheepishly, then looked away like bashful children. In one tent, Tom saw a man sitting alone at a back table. The man wore deep scars like a line from cheekbone to cheekbone, and Tom felt a tickle of unease under the man's gaze so he turned away.

He checked the next tent and the next, and then wandered back across the dusty field, through small groups of playing children and the parents who hovered at the edges of the games, speaking quietly and keeping close eyes on their boys and girls.

He'd shaken a hundred hands before the celebration began to break up. The forced smile had brought an ache to his face, and the greasy food and acidic drinks were working to tear a hole in his stomach. By five o'clock only a handful of people remained. The vendors packed away their supplies and disassembled their tents.

With no fireworks to look forward to, Tom imagined fewer families would gather by the lakeside, swapping flasks and stories as the moon rose over Barnard. But single men would still gather at Mitch's Roadhouse, the Longhorn Tavern, or the Ranger's Lodge for beers and whiskey. The German men would gather at Mueller Beer Hall to the east.

A cold beer sounded good to Tom, and maybe a few shots of whiskey as well. He hadn't had so much as a sip since the morning they'd found the boy in Blevins's woods, but today the call of intoxication was just too loud.

So he left the fairgrounds and drove the Packard back into town. He parked in front of his office. Gil limped across the room, carrying a short stack of papers. Rex had beaten Tom back to the station and sat in a chair, reading over a ledger and shaking his head. Don Nialls would be at home with his family; he'd become obsessive over their protection in the last few days, and Tom didn't blame him in the least. Dick and Walter wouldn't be in for another hour to monitor things on the night shift. Tom had given their dispatcher, Muriel Iverson, the day off so she could attend the Independence Day celebration with her family. Six officers were out on general patrol, so that left Rex and Gil.

The three men exchanged exhausted greetings and Tom nodded at the ledger in Rex's hands.

"Anything useful come in today?"

"Not really. Same old horseshit. Mrs. Reeves over to Fredericks Street thought she saw someone prowling around her neighbor's yard last night. Couldn't describe the guy, except to say he wore a long gray duster and a gray Stetson."

"A duster? In this heat?" Gilbert asked.

"Who's the neighbor?"

"That's the Williams place. Deke and his son David."

"Sure," Tom said, having known Deke Williams since their school days. "Those two can handle themselves just fine. Anything else?"

"A missing cat. Someone else spotted Hugo Jones and his friends walking through the lakeside neighborhood."

"A bunch of donkeys," Tom said. He shook his head and crossed to his office. At the door he paused and said, "Once Dick and Walter get in here, I'm buying a round at the Longhorn for those law enforcement officers interested in joining me."

This brought out a "Whoop" from Rex and a smile from Gil.

"Count me in," the young deputy said.

"Good." Tom turned on his heels and returned to his desk.

The phone rang off and on for twenty minutes, but Tom let his deputies take the calls while he rested his head on his arms. Sleepless nights and a day in the sun had sapped his energy and despite the phone's constant interruptions Tom fell into a deep sleep.

It felt as if he'd just dozed off when a strong hand shook him awake. Rex was saying his name urgently, and Tom shot upright. He rubbed the fog from his eyes and was almost startled to find himself at the office rather than at home.

"Tom," Rex said for the third time. "You need to pick up the phone."

"What's going on?"

Instead of replying, Rex lifted the phone from its cradle and handed it to the still-disoriented sheriff. Tom put the device against his ear and then quickly pulled it away.

Two people were screaming: one was a man insisting Tom come at once; and the other was a woman who made no requests but rather shrieked incoherently like two saws trying to cut each other down. Tom eased the phone back to his ear.

"Who is this?" he asked.

"Sheriff Rabbit," a man shouted. The shrill cries of the woman continued in the background.

"Yes, who is this?"

"This is Mort Grant from the Ranger's Lodge. You have to get over here."

"What's the problem, Mort? Who's making all that racket?"

"It's another boy," Mort said. "Here at the lodge, we got us another dead boy."

The phone began to shake in Tom's hand, so he pressed it tightly to his head to keep the tremors from showing and to keep the plastic cup from rattling against his ear. "At the lodge?" Tom asked, because he could think of nothing else to say.

"Hurry," Mort insisted. The woman screamed again to punctuate the demand.

Tom slammed the phone down and leapt to his feet. "Rex, get the evidence kit." Then he shouted into the station, "Gilbert, you find Doc Randolph and have him meet us at the Ranger's Lodge as soon you can get him there."

He ran around the side of his desk, through the station and into the street. The Ranger's Lodge was a minute's run from the sheriff's office, and he poured on all of his steam in an attempt to cut that time in half.

⫻

Thirty years ago, Theodore Bixby, then mayor of Barnard, had visited his sister in Boston. At the invitation of her husband, Bixby had joined his brother-in-law at a men's club near the harbor. There he found white-haired men in crisp suits lounging in wingback chairs, smoking cigars and pipes, while colored men brought them cocktails on silver trays. Bixby had so enjoyed his time in this establishment that he'd thought to bring the idea with him back to Barnard. Still a man of the West, Bixby had insisted the club speak to the rich culture of Texas, and as a result the lodge owed as much to an old Houston saloon as it did to an Edwardian parlor. A polished walnut bar ran across the back of the room. Three card tables occupied the polished oak flooring on the left of the door and to the right were a number of high-backed leather chairs, which formed a series of conversation areas, leading to a stone hearth against the far wall. Over the years, the membership had remained exclusive and the lodge was frequented mostly by the male heirs of those few men who'd chipped in to have the club built. Mort Grant was not one of those heirs, but his father had managed the Ranger's Lodge for twenty-five years before a heart attack had taken him home to Jesus. His son, who'd apprenticed under his father for eighteen of those years, had assumed the mantle.

Now Mort Grant stood in front of the lodge in his white shirt and black vest. Tom spotted him the moment he took the corner.

He wanted to believe that Mort had made a mistake. He ran with all of his might, but it was an eagerness to refute what the barman had suggested, not confirm it, that drove him.

"This way," Mort said, waving the sheriff to the open front door.

Tom hopped onto the sidewalk and took two steps under the eaves before stopping in his tracks. The room beyond the threshold was dark and Tom was momentarily shadow blind. He blinked and the shape hanging in the middle of the room began to develop and come into focus.

A pudgy young man hung by his neck from a slender rope affixed to one of the ceiling beams. Except for a single black sock, he was naked. The boy wore the same dazed and tense death expression Harold Ashton had worn. His plump tongue stuck from between his lips like a bruised slug. Worse still, Tom knew this boy; he had spoken to his men about him less than an hour ago.

"That's David Williams," he muttered. "Jesus, that's Deke's boy."

"Yes sir," Mort said at his shoulder. "We found him there when we were opening the lodge for the evening."

Once his initial shock at seeing the hanged body receded to a thudding discomfort at his temples, Tom stepped into the lodge. He took a deep breath and then instantly regretted it. The coiled scents of shit and piss stung his nostrils, and though he felt some gratitude that the stench of rot was not similarly entwined with those of waste, it came as minor consolation. Tom took further solace in noting that David hadn't been opened up the way Harold had, but again his sense of relief amounted to a drop of dye in a rushing river. He crossed to the body, which hung high, so that David's privates were at the level of Tom's face.

Rex arrived with the evidence kit and cursed up a storm upon seeing the dead boy's body. He set the kit down and stomped in a circle like a thug who'd lost a bet. Mort Grant remained outside. There was no sign of the woman who'd been screaming so frantically in the background of his call.

"Fuck. Fuck," Rex barked.

"That's enough," Tom said. "Let's get as much information as we can and then get that boy down. I want you to keep that front door closed so we don't put on a show for the whole town, and tell Mort to stick around for questioning. He lives out back doesn't he?"

"Yeah, he and Maggie live in an apartment behind the lodge."

Maggie must have been the source of the screaming, Tom reasoned.

"Okay, have Mort wait for us back there, and make sure he stays away from his phone. We don't want him telling anyone anything until we've had a chance to go through this place. Did Gil get Doc Randolph on the phone?"

"Didn't stick around to find out," Rex said.

"Fair enough. You go on and get Mort settled."

Rex didn't move from his place by the door. He dropped his head and spoke toward the floor. "You think it's the same guy that killed Harold?"

"Don't know," Tom replied. He hoped to God not.

〰

Tom turned on the overhead lights, bathing the room and the corpse in illumination. He checked the beam above and noted the looping rope and thick knot that secured the cord. This struck him as important. The killer hadn't hauled David into the air, using the beam like a pulley, but rather had prepared the noose and somehow managed to get the boy into it – probably at gunpoint. Tom's gaze swung toward the polished walnut bar, and he began to get an impression of what had happened: the killer had made his gallows and then forced the Williams boy onto the bar. He put the rope around the kid's neck and then pushed him off. Gravity and hemp had done the rest.

Satisfied with this explanation, Tom moved through the room, searched for evidence. Except for the waste that had escaped from the corpse, the floor and the bar were spotless, a testament to Mort Grant's dedication to the lodge. The sheriff went to the front door and checked the locks, opening the door only wide enough to get some idea of the jamb's condition. It appeared undamaged, and the locks were in good working order. He continued to the service entrance off of the lodge's kitchen and found the jamb splintered and the hinges bent.

Tom stepped into the sweltering alley. The reek of heated garbage accosted him as he slowly walked between the wood-sided buildings, back to front and back again. He continued on past the building's extension – Mort and Maggie's apartment – and through the alley between Rainey's Tack and Saddle and Purcel's Boots to find himself standing on Santa Anna Avenue. Tom checked both directions, noting the German-owned businesses across the street. There were only two – Gerta's Café, where Tom had on occasion stopped for lunch, and Weigle's Butcher Shop next door.

He returned to the lodge and found Doc Randolph standing beside the hanged boy. Gilbert, who looked about as sick as any man could, stood by the door with a pad and pencil in his hand. Doc Randolph was dictating his observations.

"Both bowel and bladder voided at death," he said calmly. "Which means the hanging was not post mortem – this is further confirmed by the discoloration of the victim's face and the swelling of his tongue. No secondary abrasions about the throat in partner with no signs of restraint at the wrists seem to indicate the victim did not struggle. This could be attributed to a broken neck, or to other factors that may have left the victim incapacitated. Further, this could indicate the victim had no will to struggle." The doctor turned toward Tom and said, "This may be nothing more than a suicide."

The possibility had not occurred to Tom. He took the news as encouraging and then struggled with his sense of relief.

"He came in through the back," Tom said, checking on Gil to make sure the deputy wrote that bit down. "The door is jimmied."

"Why did you think this was connected to the Ashton boy?" Doc Randolph asked, still circling the body, peering upward at the boy's head.

"Two young men dead," Tom said reluctantly. "I didn't know the circumstances when I sent Gil after you."

Doc Randolph nodded and stepped away from the corpse. "I've seen all I can see for now. We best cut him down so I can take a closer look."

Tom looked around the lodge and found what he needed on a tabletop across the room. He went to the table and yanked the cloth from it, then returned to the center of the room. "Gil, bring your knife."

Standing on a chair, with the cloth wrapped around the boy's torso and hips, Tom held tight while Gil, standing on a table, worked his blade through the rope. David Williams crashed down, sending Tom and the chair toppling. He struck his head on the polished planks and the dead boy's weight pinned him until his momentary daze passed. Then he rolled the corpse off, sending it face down on the floor. Doc Randolph didn't pay any mind to Tom, who climbed to his feet, holding the back of his head and gasping for breath. Instead, the doctor focused his attention on the cloth-wrapped body.

Doc Randolph made some humming sounds and grunted twice. He knelt down and, using a slender metal rod like an empty pen, poked and prodded the back of the Williams boy's head. He hummed again, and then looked at Tom.

"So much for suicide," the doctor said.

"I don't follow."

"The victim took multiple blows to the back of the cranium. I noticed the blood on the rope, but assumed it was from abrasion. It's not. Someone knocked the boy out with a blunt instrument, likely before bringing him here. The damage might have been severe enough to explain why the victim didn't struggle."

"You've mentioned that before. What struggle are you talking about?" Tom asked.

"Yes," the doctor said heavily as if disappointed. "What would your natural reaction be should someone decide to hang you? Would you just dangle there and think what a shame it was you wouldn't get to finish that Hemingway novel you were reading, or would you do everything in your power to save yourself?" The doctor cocked his head to the side and twisted his face as if strangling. "If you chose the latter, as most rational folks would, you'd attack that thing responsible for your impending death, which is to say, the rope, and the only part of the rope you'd have access to is that bit around your throat." He made scratching motions at his neck, to illustrate his point. "I'll look closer, but I saw no marks to indicate he struggled, and since his hands weren't bound and he had every opportunity to do so, I'm forced to believe he was otherwise incapable, which a severe trauma to the head might explain."

"Okay," Tom said. A blush of embarrassment rose on his cheeks, and he checked on Gil to see if the young deputy had noticed. Gil seemed too involved with what he was writing on his notepad. "So, we are dealing with a murder, but it doesn't look like the same situation we had with the Ashton boy."

"Not exactly true," Doc Randolph said.

"Because the killer didn't murder his victim outright," Tom said quickly.

This seemed to impress the doctor who nodded his head. "In both cases, the killer made a definite effort to *place* the bodies. He didn't hide his victims or let them fall where he found them."

"He put them where he knew they would be found," Tom said, his heart sinking at what he knew would come next.

"I suggest we check the boy's mouth."

And there, they found another lacquered snuffbox. And inside that, they found another note.

⫴

Tom helped load the body into Doc Randolph's car, and Gil rode with the doctor the six blocks to his office. After helping get the body inside, Gil was to proceed out to Brett Fletcher's place with the latest note to have it translated. Meanwhile, Tom went to the apartment in back of the lodge and had a long talk with Mort Grant. Rex stood in the corner of the room silently as Tom questioned the lodge manager, and Mrs. Grant hovered around the edges of the conversation, a perpetual sheen of tears covering her red eyes. At times she would interject, but it was only to repeat something her husband had said, and then she'd cry and flit from the living area to the kitchen and back again. The interview was productive only in establishing a window of opportunity for the killer. Mort assured Tom that he checked the locks on the doors and the shutters every night, because the lodge had expensive whiskeys and vintage wines. Further, he had closed the lodge at the stroke of eleven as demanded in the bylaws – except in the event of a special occasion – and he and his wife had set about the business of sweeping and mopping and polishing. Mort restocked the liquor and reset the room. This took the couple until just after midnight. Maggie exited through the back, but Mort followed his father's ritual, which meant walking around the property. He did this to be sure none of the lodge's members had over imbibed, putting themselves in a less than honorable condition near the lodge. Because of the Fourth of July Celebration, Mort and Maggie had not opened the lodge at four in the afternoon as was customary, but rather waited until just before six – at the request of the city's mayor

– to assure "men spent an appropriate amount of time with their families before seeking the intellectual stimulation of the lodge" (the mayor's words as reported by Mort). Upon entering the lodge, Mort discovered the hanged body of David Williams. Unfortunately, his wife also witnessed the dreadful thing. He'd called the sheriff's office, and Tom knew the rest.

The sheriff asked Mort to repeat his story twice, and then he asked the manager to accompany him and Rex back to the office to repeat it a third time for an official report. Mort insisted his wife come along, afraid to leave her alone.

Gil called the station from the Fletcher house and read the translation of the note:

One less gun against the Reich.
Four executed for crimes against the Fatherland.
I will have them all in time.
Happy Independence Day, you stupid fucks.

The young deputy had found himself unable to say the last word until Tom had threatened him with disciplinary action. Then he'd stuttered it out as quickly as his naïve tongue would allow him.

Tom ordered Gil back to the station. He slammed down the phone and fell back in his chair. Across the desk from him, Rex – looking simultaneously sad and furious – pounded a fist into his palm as if eager to hurt someone.

The ledger on the desk between them only served to remind Tom that time was wasting as they waited for their only witness. Lily Reeves had reported a prowler outside of the Williams house late the previous night, and Tom had been trying to track her down since returning to the station.

"Where is she?" Tom asked.

"I sent Dick and Walter out to the lake to see if she's there. I'm calling her house every ten minutes, and I've tried reaching her daughters but so far no luck. My guess is she went to the celebration with her family and then out to the lake for the nighttime festivities. It is tradition."

"What about Deke Williams?"

"His boss at the paper mill said he was in Monroe, Louisiana on a buying trip. He's been gone since day before yesterday. He's not scheduled to be back for a few days yet, but I'll put Gil on tracking down hotels in the area when he gets back from Brett's place."

"So what does that leave us?" Tom asked.

"A pile of horseshit," Rex replied. "We'll get the patrol out in the morning to question all the businesses in the area. Maybe one of the shop owners was out late and saw something we can use."

"The city was all but closed down today," Tom reminded. "The murderer could have just as easily gone into the Ranger Lodge at noon to finish up his work."

"Well then, maybe someone saw that," Rex said. "I don't know."

"That makes two of us," Tom said.

His sour stomach rolled, sending acid to the back of his throat, and he swallowed hard against it. He thought about the description Lilly Reeves had given – a man in a Stetson and a duster – and he tried to picture the man, wondering why a German would adopt such a uniquely American costume. He certainly couldn't think it would help him blend in, not in a city like Barnard.

So what was he after, this cowboy? What was he trying to say?

Eleven: Tim Randall

After word got out about the second boy's killing, the city coiled in shock. I say coiled because even in those first few days you could feel something building – a tension woven into the hot, dry air – and it was only a matter of time before the dumb-founded citizens lashed out. A second note had been found, also written in German, and the paper had run a drawing of the killer, but it only showed a faceless man dressed in a Stetson and duster. The *Register* had taken to referring to the murderer as the "Gray Cowboy" or "Cowboy" for short. I felt particularly bad. David Williams wasn't a close friend of mine, but he was closer to my age than Harold Ashton had been, and I'd seen him in school for a number of years. All I knew of Harold Ashton's persona had been second hand information. David I'd known, and I'd liked him, so his death cut deeper. We hadn't gone to Harold Ashton's funeral, but Ma insisted I put on my suit and together we walked to the Baptist Church on Bennington for David's services. I heard a lot of angry talk in the vestibule. Even the women spoke of finding the killer and stringing him up. Some even used profanity, which surprised me, particularly there in the church's lobby. Carl Baker and his family appeared in the doorway of the church, all properly dressed for the ser-vices and coming to pay their respects for Mr. Williams' loss, but a crowd of men gathered, blocking the family's entrance and ushering them onto the front lawn. Ma held onto my shoulder, keeping me from racing outside to see what was being said. In the end, the Bakers walked away and the men, all old and weathered and fearsome looking, stomped back to the church. The services seemed to go on for a very long time, and I became drowsy in the over-hot room. Ma cried and held my hand tightly, and I tried to sit up straight as I'd been taught, but it became harder and harder to keep my eyes open. After the service, we returned home so Ma could pick up the pie she'd baked for Mr. Williams. I stood at the window and looked across the street at Ernst Lang's house and squinted against the shadows on his porch to see if there was any movement, but it was midday and the German was probably working on a chair. When we arrived at the Williams house, Polly Davenport, Mr. Williams' sister, took the pie from my mother and gave her a light hug, before leading us both back to the kitchen. The counters were covered in Dutch ovens and skillets and ceramic bowls. Silver spoon handles jutted from many of the containers and the smells went straight to my belly. I felt suddenly ravenous as if I could eat every bit of food Mr. Williams' friends had brought for him, but before Ma fixed us plates we walked through the house, which brimmed with solemn people, all dressed so nicely but appearing hunched as if broken by David Williams' death, until we found Mr. Williams in the backyard, sitting on a wooden bench, surrounded by a dozen people I didn't recognize. Ma told Mr. Williams how sorry she was for his loss, and I said, "David was a good guy," which brought a hard smile from Mr. Williams. Back inside, Ma put little portions of food on a plate for me, and I wolfed them down. That night, Ma stayed home from work for the third night in a row. I sat at the window, staring at the house across the street, hoping to catch a glimpse of my neighbor.

The next day, the sheriff announced an eight o'clock curfew for women and children under the age of eighteen to be in effect until he rescinded it.

The windows at the front of Weigle's Butcher Shop were smashed out. Two German men were beaten outside of the Mueller Beer Hall by a group of men who'd been waiting on the street. Sheriff Rabbit hadn't found a villain to blame, so folks were finding villains of their own.

Ma took the threat seriously. She had to return to her job, but she refused to leave me alone at night, and though I complained, she asked my grandmother to stay with me while she worked her shifts at the factory. Grandma didn't approve of the radio dramas I liked best – the mysteries and crime shows and creepy thrillers – so in the evenings my house was filled with the sounds of the Lennon Sisters, Kay Kyser and his orchestra, and other bouncy musical programs that I found dreadful. On the nights Bum couldn't sleep over, I stayed in my room, reading old comic books – because Ma wouldn't spend the little money she made on new ones – and tried to tune out the happy-as-you-please crooners pounding on my walls like party guests. Every night around ten, Grandma fell asleep on the sofa, the radio still blaring, and I would climb out of my window and creep to the front porch (believing my proximity to the house was enough to ensure my safety, wholly disregarding the fact that David Williams had been snatched from his own bed in the middle of the night). Hidden in the shadows, I'd sit on the bench my daddy had built and observe the German's house.

One night Mr. Lang startled me, though he likely didn't know he'd done it. I'd made my way to the bench and had just gotten my butt settled on the wooden slats when the lamp in the German's living room came on. A moment later the front door opened, and Mr. Lang, wearing nothing but swimming trunks stood in the doorway. I froze where I sat, uncertain if he could see me. It was a moonless night, and the lake to my right showed as nothing but a black void, but a line of light cut through the living room curtains on the far side of my porch, and perhaps some of its glow touched me. As for the German, he appeared simultaneously very small, because I viewed him from a distance, but also enormous as his broad chest seemed to span the door from frame to frame. I held my breath, waiting for some sign that he had seen me. He stepped forward, putting the light at his back. In silhouette he appeared smaller. The

German stood before the door for several minutes, and then he went back inside.

The next night a man visited Mr. Lang. I saw him walking quickly on the far sidewalk, tall yet otherwise indistinct. The German let this man into his house, and a dim light coming from a back room – his kitchen or bedroom – extinguished soon after. Not ten minutes later, I saw the man returning the way he'd come down Dodd Street. Only after he'd vanished in the shadows on the corner did the lights come back on in the German's house, and fearing Mr. Lang would again come outside, I slipped off the porch and returned to my room. That night in bed, terrible scenarios of spies and saboteurs and killers kept me awake until my mother returned from her shift.

Two weeks after David had been killed, Mr. Weigle moved to Fredericksburg to live with his daughter and her family. Also in those two weeks, a young man from a German family was run down by a car out on the farm road. No one knew who ran the boy down, and the papers called it an accident. The boy died the next morning. Fist fights became common occurrences at the Longhorn Tavern, Mitch's Roadhouse and the Mueller Beer Hall. No such disrespect was shown at the Ranger's Lodge, because it had not yet reopened for business since the afternoon Mort Grant had found David Williams hanging from a rafter.

On an overcast Saturday afternoon late in July, when the air felt like steam and the eclipsed sun still managed to cook the city, Bum and I walked into town. Ma had given me a quarter to see a movie at the Paramount, but Bum's daddy wouldn't give him a cent so we used the quarter to buy sodas at Delrubio's. Instead of taking stools at the counter, watching Clete Browning's tongue wag through his chipped and missing teeth, we sat at a table beneath a ceiling fan that whipped around like a propeller. Bum stabbed his soda with a straw while I set on mine as if I'd been wandering a desert for days.

After we'd finished our drinks we lingered at the shop, postponing the walk back home through the day's heat as long as we could. We browsed through the magazines and comic books for thirty minutes, and Bum picked up a copy of *Weird Tales*, the cover of which showed a cloaked figure at the mouth of a cave or a tunnel, pointing threateningly at a young couple huddled by candlelight. I read the names on the cover, Lovecraft, Bloch, and Bedford-Jones but they didn't mean a thing to me. My preference was for comics with bigger-than-life characters like Superman, The Human Torch, Captain Marvel and The Flash. Besides, comics only cost a dime, whereas the magazine Bum held cost fifteen cents.

"This looks good," he said, his nose about an inch from the page he was reading. "They don't have these at the library."

"Another fine reason to avoid the place," I said, reaching for a comic book to peruse while Bum scanned the magazine. I had fifteen cents left in my pocket, but couldn't commit the limited amount to any single issue.

Eventually, Mr. Browning chased us out, told us to go to the library if we wanted to read, and Bum thought that was a pretty good idea, but I nixed it quick. I wanted to go back home and maybe swim for a while to get the sweat off and see what Ma had left for supper. Soon the stores in town would be closing and the walk home would be fogged by clouds of dust kicked up by car tires. The drought had lasted all spring and summer and you couldn't walk three steps without a fog of grit rising from your heels.

We were well away from downtown, only a couple of blocks from my house when we noticed Hugo Jones and his buddies had taken some shade beneath an old oak sprouting from Mrs. Parmer's yard.

They stood halfway between Crosby and Dodd on Bennington, leaning against the Parmers' split-rail fence. Hugo smoked a cigarette. Ben Livingston and Austin Chitwood were at his sides, and the three seemed deep in conversation, until Hugo looked up and asked Bum and me to come over for a chat.

There didn't seem to be any reason not to do as he asked.

Hugo wasn't a typical bully, not like Bobby Lawrence or Tucker Manetti, who would target kids and chase them down, hurling insults before shoving their victims around a while. Hugo took a more sinister approach. He'd start a conversation – it could be as innocent as talking about the weather – and somewhere along the line, his eyes would go dark and a switch in his head would click and the punches would soon follow.

I knew this about Hugo, but Bum and I were much younger than his usual victims, and he'd never given us so much as a go to hell up to that point, so while we feared him the way we were meant to, we didn't actually figure him a threat.

"You're the Randall kid," he said, as if he'd heard about me before. He looked at Bum, whose older brother Mudbug had been friends with Hugo before getting sent off to fight. "Bum," Hugo said with a nod.

"Hey, Hugo."

"You headed to the lake?" Hugo asked.

"Yeah," I replied. "It's by my house."

"Good day for it. Just make sure you're out before sunset. Place is swarming with mosquitoes and moccasins once it starts to get dark."

"We will," Bum said nervously. "There's a curfew."

And Hugo asked us about where we'd been and how we'd spent the afternoon. He joked with us, and his buddies, Ben and Austin, laughed a lot, and it never occurred to me that the conversation was leading anywhere. In fact, it felt good to have a talk with an older boy, made me feel mature.

Then Hugo said, "You know we patrol out here at night, keeping an eye out for that Cowboy?"

And I made the mistake of admitting I'd seen them on the night the sheriff had found Harold Ashton's body. It had struck me as a way to confirm what Hugo had said, while making it sound like I was in the know. It was also a big mistake.

"You live on Dodd Street?" Hugo asked casually around the cigarette in his mouth.

"Yeah, like I said, by the lake."

"Well we have a problem, Tim Randall," Hugo said, and I saw the darkness like inky water running into his eyes. "We don't patrol Dodd Street."

I explained that I hadn't seen them from my living-room window or front porch. I told them I saw them at the corner of Worth. Bum confirmed my claim by explaining that I'd gone out on my own that night.

This intrigued Hugo, who nodded his head. He dropped his cigarette on the sidewalk and stepped on it, raising a small disturbance in the dust. Ben rapped Austin's shoulder with the back of his hand as if saying, *Get a load of this.*

Then Hugo lunged at me. He grabbed me by the front of the shirt and hauled me forward. Bum yelped and immediately started begging Hugo to let me go, but both Ben and Austin were moving forward, intercepting Bum, who wouldn't have presented much of a threat anyway.

Hugo's dark eyes were only inches from mine. I could feel the heat coming off of his acne-ruined face, and when he spoke again, his breath washed into my nostrils like sewer water passing downstream from a fire.

"You spied on us?" Hugo asked. "You following us around?"

"No," I told him. "I was just playing a game, hiding by a house."

"But you listened in on what we were saying?"

He didn't know that for sure, but it dawned on me that he was genuinely concerned I'd heard something I shouldn't have. I said no about fifty times. I told him I didn't hear a thing, I just saw them, but he had already reached a violent place.

The rest is a blur. He punched me in the gut, and then in the mouth, and I dropped to the sidewalk as more blows struck the side of my head and shoulder. I remember he dragged me along the sidewalk, shouting words my terrified mind overpowered with screams of its own. Tears scalded my eyes, though not from any specific pain. Fear made me cry, because I didn't know how to stop what was happening, or even understand why it had happened.

A crisp drone, like the beating of a hummingbird's wings, came up in my ears, and through it came a calm, deep voice that I didn't immediately recognize. Hugo Jones shouted, "Goddamn Kraut," and at first I was confused, because I wasn't German and neither was Bum, so his pejorative made no sense.

"If you three want a fight, you come see me," Mr. Lang said, his voice so even he might have been inviting the boys over for a snack or some sweet tea. "Go home, now. *Go.*" He barked the last word, and Hugo upped his insult to "Fucking Kraut," but I could hear his boots stomping the pavement as he said it.

The hum receded, making way for the pain. At first it was a general anguish that seemed to surround me as if I lay in a pool of it, but as my heartbeat slowed and my mind cleared, individual agonies presented themselves. My split lip burned. A knot on my forehead ached. A scrape on my knee stung. My stomach felt bruised and cramped. A stitch of embarrassment joined the physical pain; I hated that my best friend and neighbor were seeing me cry. I couldn't stop it, though. Sobs broke loose in my chest and fled through my mouth and nose, and more than anything I wanted the shameful display to end.

Mr. Lang helped me to my feet and looked me over with concern. His scarred face appeared particularly flat to me just then but his eyes were warm.

"Yes, good," he said. "If you can stand up, you'll live."

Bum rushed to us and grabbed my arm. He put it around his neck to help support my weight. "Thank you, Mr. Lang," he said, rapidly. "We'll be okay now."

"Nuh," said my neighbor. "Your friend should have his cuts cleaned. You bring him to my house."

"No, that's okay. I'll just take him home."

From the anxiety in my friend's voice, I knew he was thinking about his father's warning to keep well away from the Germans in town.

"But his mother is not there," Mr. Lang countered. "Do you know how to dress wounds? Nuh, I didn't think so. You boys come to my house, and Ernst will take care of your friend."

Bum made to protest again, but I interrupted with "Thanks, Mr. Lang, I'd appreciate that."

Leaning on Bum, we walked to the end of the block. Once inside my neighbor's house, he instructed Bum to help me onto the small green sofa and then walked into his kitchen. He returned a moment later with a bottle of Coca-Cola, which he gave to Bum.

"Th-thanks," Bum said, holding the bottle like a trophy.

"You are welcome," Mr. Lang replied. "Now, sit down next to your friend there while I mend him."

"I'm okay," I said, suddenly self-conscious of my beaten state.

"Nuh, you're still bleeding," he replied. "It was a bad fight."

"All fights are bad," Bum said.

"Maybe you are right," the German said, though Bum's claim clearly amused the man. He stood in front of the sofa, looking down at us. His gaze drifted from Bum to me, and he said, "The next time, you kick him here." Mr. Lang reached down and formed a cup with his fingers that covered his crotch.

"Pa said that's below the belt," Bum argued. "He says it's unfair."

"All fights are unfair," my neighbor said. "One man will always be bigger or faster or smarter. That boy was older and stronger and more experienced. Do you think he cared about fighting fair? Nuh, he cared about winning. That's why he won."

He left us on the sofa and walked into the hall. Wiping the tears from my eyes, I winced. The skin at my brow was tender, and I felt a knot pushing through. My lips were also swelling, puffing up like a bee had stung them. Ma was going to throw a fit when she saw me — face bruised, pants torn, shirt stained. I felt worse then, because the last thing I wanted was to give her something else to worry about. Mr. Lang returned to the room with a small tin box. He knelt on the floor before me, putting the container in the space between my feet.

"What did you do to this boy?" he asked as he withdrew a small amber bottle from the tin.

"Nothing." The word leapt from my throat like a denial of guilt. "I didn't do anything to him. He's just a bully. I don't know why he hit me."

My neighbor seemed to cough, but a moment later, I realized it was a blunt chuckle. "He hit you because he is human, yes?"

"He's just a creep," Bum said.

Mr. Lang shook his head. He retrieved a small cloth from the tin and upended the mouth of the bottle against it. "You call him a creep. Good. Yes. He is a creep, but that is in your mind. In his mind, he is a hero."

He pressed the dampened cloth to my split lip. Iodine. I should have seen it coming, but I was too distracted by the German's words. The fluid entered my wound and mixed with the blood, sending a hot sheet of pain across the lower half of my face. I tried to lean back on the sofa, but Mr. Lang shot out an arm, wrapping his hand around the back of my head, holding me in place.

"It hurts, yes? But it's helping you. Sometimes pain isn't the enemy."

His nose was close to mine then as he held my head between his palm and the cloth. I looked at his scarred face, the deep lines, nearly matching on each of his cheeks the shallow valley at the ridge of his nose. Despite the force he was employing and the agony his cloth delivered, his eyes were soft and kind.

"You think it is mean to hurt someone, yes? I hurt you now, but I am not being mean. Do you see? Nuh, you don't." He pulled away. Again he upended the bottle against the cloth. "Your father is far away from here, and he is hurting people, and he is right to do it because they will hurt him if he doesn't. He is hurting people, but he is not a bad man." Mr. Lang screwed the cap back on the bottle and replaced it in the tin. He straightened his back and puffed out his chest. "He is a soldier. A hero." He made a fist and thumped his chest. The performance made me smile, which ripped open the cut on my lip. In a flash, Mr. Lang had the cloth against my cheek and another blossom of pain erupted on my face. "The men he is fighting don't think him a hero. They think he is a monster. That's how they can fight him."

"They're just filthy Krauts," I said.

Mr. Lang produced another of those coughing laughs. "Yes," he said brightly, genuinely amused by the statement. "Filthy Japs and Krauts and Jerries and Nips." He seemed very pleased with the words. He pulled the cloth from my face and dropped it into the tin. Securing the lid, he grasped the box and stood.

He crossed the room and again entered the hall, leaving me to wonder if I had hurt his feelings or angered him, though he seemed nothing but happy. When he returned he stood on the far side of the living room, back straight, eyes sharp. He put his hands on his hips, appraising us like a sergeant inspecting his squad.

"You need ice for your head," he announced. He spun on his heels and marched into the hall again.

Bum nudged my shoulder and pointed rapidly at the front door. He clearly didn't want to spend another minute in Mr. Lang's house. I shook my head and put a finger to my swollen lips so he didn't say anything that might get us in trouble.

From the kitchen, I heard my neighbor hacking at a block of ice with a pick. Strange grunts accompanied the sounds of chopping and I realized Mr. Lang was laughing. Anxiety rolled through my veins, lighting up my nerves with tension. The laughter sounded harsh and crazy. Mr. Lang marched back into the living room, holding a rag that bulged around a hunk of ice the size of my fist. He put the cloth to my brow.

"You hold this," he said, "and I'll teach you about bullies and wars and men, yes?"

"Okay," I said.

"You are a man, yes?"

"I guess." I didn't feel much like a man with my wounds and the ice against my head, but I understood what he meant.

"And you?" he asked of Bum, who nodded cautiously. "I am a man, yes?"

"Yeah," Bum and I agreed in unison.

"So, we are all men. You agree?"

"Sure," I said.

"You see me and you say, 'Good morning, Ernst, isn't the weather nice?' because we are civilized human beings. You don't hate me, because we are, in this moment the same. You couldn't just pull out a gun and shoot old Ernst, because he is a man like you, yes?"

"I suppose."

"Now imagine we are at war. You and I wear different uniforms. We aim guns at each other. You are an American and I am a Kraut. You would shoot me then, yes?"

"You're not a Kraut."

"No? Why? I am German. I love my country. What makes me different?"

"You just are," I said. He was my neighbor. He'd helped me. He wasn't some lunatic butcher under Hitler's command.

"Nuh," he said, appearing frustrated. He looked around the room and scratched the back of his neck. "You do not want to understand," he muttered. Then his eyes lit up and he turned back to me. Absently, he kicked his shoes off, sliding them across the floor to thump against the wall. "Your name is Tim, yes?"

"Uh huh." He knew that so why was he asking?

"What if I called you something else? What if I decided to call you Tater, because you like your mother's potato salad so much?"

Bum laughed nervously and poked me with his elbow. "You're a Tater."

"Yes. It isn't a bad word is it? Maybe funny. Maybe a little odd. But it's not a bad word, nuh?"

"I suppose not."

"Good," Ernst said. He took three long strides across the floor and leapt onto the sofa next to Bum, who screeched and slid close to me. Mr. Lang stood at his full height and peered down. "I have just taken away your name and made you a thing. You are no longer a young boy called Tim who likes to swim and eat potato salad. You're now a Tater, yes? You are not an individual man, but a Tater like all of those other boys who like their mothers' potato salad."

"A lot of people like potato salad," Bum said.

"Yes," he agreed. "A lot of people and they are all Taters. Now, I look at you and I don't see Tim or his fat friend, I see a Tater, and I see that Taters wear torn pants and dirty shirts. You are sloppy like a pig. I think it must be true that you never bathe. Certainly you can't be smart. A person who is smart knows to keep his clothes clean and his face washed. How very terrible Taters are because they are filthy, wretched brutes that can't even keep their clothes clean."

He took a step back and climbed onto the arm of the sofa. He teetered for a moment. Then he raised his hands and put his palms against the ceiling to steady himself. "And I took care of you after you were hurt. You didn't thank me."

"I was…"

"You didn't thank me," Mr. Lang interrupted. "Therefore Taters are ungrateful and selfish. And you came into my house and sat on my sofa and got dirt on it. So Taters are also inconsiderate." He pretended to shiver. "What awful creatures these Taters are. They are nothing like me. I am clean and smart and grateful and considerate. I am a human being, with feelings. You are a thing, a nasty ungrateful thing."

What did this have to do with war or bullies or anything? Taters weren't real. They were just these fictional things he'd made up. I wasn't a Tater. I was still Tim.

My neighbor hopped off the arm of the sofa and landed on the floor with a *thunk*. He walked to the wall and grabbed his shoes, then sat in the rocking chair next to the couch.

"You call them Krauts," Ernst said, leaning forward to tie his shoes, "but they were just little boys who liked their mothers' cooking and liked to swim and hike and play games. If you knew that, it would be harder to kill them, yes? It is easier to kill a thing than a little boy."

"You can't be saying the Nazis are good?" Bum asked.

"No," Ernst replied quickly. "No, they aren't good. They are sick. *He* made them sick. *He* twisted them. I'm saying they're human. Like you and me and that boy who beat you up. That boy didn't see Tim. He saw something low and beneath himself, and that made it easy for him to hurt you. The Nazis have done the same to the Jew and the gypsy. I watched it happen. They need to find things to hate so that they won't hate themselves."

"Not all people are bullies," Bum said defiantly, standing from the sofa. "Good people don't go around trying to hurt each other."

"Then I am wrong," Mr. Lang said. A cloud of distraction ran over his face and then vanished. He forced a smile, though his eyes still seemed engaged by distant thoughts. "Yes. Good. No more talk of it." He helped me to my feet and patted me on the back. "You go home now. I hope you feel better soon."

And we were dismissed. Mr. Lang didn't even try to argue with Bum. He didn't need to. My neighbor had won the argument. We simply didn't understand what we were arguing about, and by the time I understood it many days later, the damage was irrevocably done.

𝔗𝔴𝔢𝔩𝔳𝔢: 𝔗𝔥𝔢 𝔊𝔢𝔯𝔪𝔞𝔫

July 27, 1944 – Translated from the German

I act foolishly with the boys. It is exciting to be addressing new minds not yet set in their beliefs, though my elation gets away from me and I climb on the sofa like a drunkard using a bar for a pulpit. At first I am a teacher instructing the boys, and then I am a child, performing buffoonery for his friends, and when this oddity of character dawns on me, the fear that my mind and actions are not my own takes hold. I end the conversation and send my neighbor Tim and his fat friend away.

Rarely have I ventured out since the second boy was found. I hear of the disharmony in town and see the anger in the eyes of the Americans, and though I am not afraid of these people, neither am I comfortable amid so much simmering emotion. They carry the fear and anger of revolutionaries but suppress the action, and for this I should be grateful as the hate they hold is for my countrymen. Still it reminds me of the worst days of the Weimar, when all was thought but nothing was done.

The excitement of my young guests has passed, leaving me saddened and convinced that my own company will not be good tonight. It is better to get out of this cell house and go. It is fortunate the sheriff's curfew applies only to women and children. I consider the Longhorn Tavern, but know my greeting there will be harsh, and the Mueller Beer Hall is out of the question, because for all of my dislike of the repressed revolutionary, I loathe to see it more on the faces of my countrymen, so I choose to walk out of town to Mitch's. On the walk, I think of what I told the boys and feel a compulsion to have them back in the house so that they might learn more of soldiers and human beings, but my neighbor's friend was afraid – perhaps thinking me the killer of young men – and I do not think they will return.

The walk is long. July is a hellish month in this place – always hot and dry. By the time I reach Mitch's my throat is parched, and I already wish to be back in my own house.

This place is dishonest. Not like the beer halls at home, where even the lies were infused with truth. These people know no better. It is their culture to be dishonest, to be masks and types rather than individual human beings. The building itself is a deceit. The walls are simple pine planks sealed with paste, more like fencing than the walls of a proper business. Tables made from old casks with wooden disk tops stand about the room. Light bulbs like hanged white kittens dangle from the rafters, emitting scant illumination, providing much darkness in the corners for those who drink alone. Smoke rests in a thick cloud over the bar as I enter, casting a dozen men and women in gray haze. All heads turn when I enter. They look. Some nod their heads. Others scowl. The rest realize I'm of no interest to them and turn back to the bar. They've seen me a hundred times over the years, and I am nothing but another German to them.

An old man in a tattered felt hat plays his guitar on a stage made of beer crates. A frown cuts a face that resembles a pale desiccated gourd. His gray suit is old. The knees mended with black patches a dozen times over. Clawed hands clamp filthy strings. The music shares a rhythm with the polka, but not the joy. The tempo is too slow. A minor key. The music reminds me of death.

At the bar, I order a beer, or rather what these people call beer. Even the drink is deceitful. It has no depth. It is a weak beverage made of grain, aspiring to be more. The man behind the bar is named Howard and he is attractive – broad shoulders and thick forearms. The arms of a man who appreciates labor. A soldier's arms. Howard reminds me of William Powell, only thicker in the neck and face with a full mustache rather than the pencil-thin whiskers the actor wears. Such painstaking vanity is beyond these people.

I pay for my drink and cross to a table. Standing behind it, I watch the man on the stage and the way his hand moves in gentle strokes over the front of his guitar as if he is comforting a dying dog in his lap.

The weathered guitar player ends his song and begins another that sounds like the last. There is no happiness here. The men at the bar laugh at crass jokes about Niggers and Bean-eaters and Japs and Krauts. They play patriot, condemning all that is not of their culture, but they share no military victory among them, so their boasts are meaningless, their pride empty. Pretenses to intellect are laughably brittle. One man suggests the Third Reich is nothing more than a madman's device. His companions agree and toast his idiocy, unaware of the Chicken Farmer and the Pilot and the others who feed the figurehead lies and repulsive strategies. They don't understand the core of this evil. Few do. I was there when it began, yet even I underestimated the brutal juggernaut that destroys my homeland.

The fool turns from his audience to glare at me. He is a foul-looking man with a pocked bulb nose and a prominent brow. I'm reminded of a Rottweiler. Such a dog and this man share the same eyes, always alert for weakness and meat.

I meet his gaze but offer no expression such a dolt is likely to interpret. Once I would have been bold. His stupidity would have put the blood in my cock and the argument in my throat, but no more. Ernst is gone and Ernst lives.

The king is dead, yes?

The man turns away from me, refocusing his attention on his friends. He makes a comment and they all laugh. Two of his drunken companions look in my direction, confirming that I have just been insulted. I drink my beer and look at the old man and his guitar.

From the corner of my eye, I notice a couple at the end of the bar. The woman is stout with waves of curly hair pushed back in barettes. The bands of her undergarments create trenches in her fat. Lumps and rolls strain against her snug dress. It has magnolia blossoms printed on cloth the color of midnight sky. The man next to her is smiling. He is masculine of feature and bearing, though wholly unremarkable. I would not notice this face in a crowd. He has worn a suit to this place, which strikes me as discordant with the atmosphere. Perhaps he is a salesman traveling through. He nods and leans close to the woman's ear, perhaps to tell her a secret but his eyes fall on me.

A group of three men enters. The door slams open amid guffaws of laughter. They lean on one another, already intoxicated though it is still very early. They are Germans and they speak boisterously. Memories of home cut my chest. Among this group, I recognize my friend Karl Baecker. He has changed the spelling of his name to Carl Baker. He called this assimilation. Karl is dead and Carl lives, yes?

For a moment I wonder why they are not at the beer garden in town, and it occurs to me, they are returning from Austin. Carl lifts a hand in greeting and calls my name. One member of his party is uncommonly tall. He is a thin-armed man with white hair and a mustache the color of carrot soup. His attention falls on me, and his words stutter mid-sentence, and he halts in the center of the room as Carl and the other man continue to the bar. This towering German makes no secret of his interest in my face. His attention is uncomfortable. I do not match his stare as I had with the Rottweiler-eyed fool at the bar. Instead, I pretend to find interest in the old guitarist's dreary music.

He taps a foot in time with his dirge. A hole at the toe of his brown shoe has been patched with cardboard.

The man finishes looking at me and joins Carl at the end of the bar. Next to them, the fat woman and the unremarkable man lean closer together, allowing Carl to speak his order to Howard. The tall man taps Carl's shoulder impatiently. His lips move frantically. He is suddenly flushed. The third man in the group, who is built short and round, peers around his back and his eyes narrow.

He shakes his head, which only infuriates the tall man.

It is time for me to leave. I finish my beer and set the bottle on the table. Before I reach the door a man shouts.

"Murderer," he calls. "Brute."

Turning slowly toward his voice, my pulse quickens. Now the blood is in my cock and my skin tingles. The men and women at the bar look on with confusion. The tall man is shouting in German, and though they do not understand the words, they recognize the prelude to violence. It is a tune these people enjoy.

"Eh?" I call.

"Stormtrooper scum," the tall man bellows, and he shakes his fist at me, and there is a folding knife in that fist, and Carl and the fat man hold my accuser back. Carl has his shoulders. The fat man his waist. "Thug. Brute. Murderer."

"Take this shit outside, you crazy Kraut fuck," Howard calls.

The old man stops playing his guitar. He stands from the wooden stool and backs off of the beer crates.

My accuser tears himself free of Carl, who is too drunk to recapture him. As the tall man moves forward, he drags his obese friend over the floor comically. Obscenities pour from his lips as he struggles to remove the fat anchor from his waist. He screams the name of a dead man – a name profoundly familiar to me – and I am lost.

With a twist of his hips, the corpulent friend is cast aside and the tall man charges forward. The knife comes down to his waist. His grip and the positioning of the weapon tell me he's been taught to fight – tells me he is willing to kill. The woman at the bar giggles loudly. The men begin shouting approval. Howard and Carl are the only ones to voice opposition to the impending conflict. The others are already drunk on blood. This is their coliseum.

The tall man bears down on me. As I expect, his knife arcs upward before he plants his feet. He is still moving, which makes him vulnerable. Yes, he was taught to fight, but he doesn't fight well. Stepping out of the blade's path is easy. I twist my body and let his momentum carry him into my range. A fist to his ear disorients him, sends him teetering to the side, and a second blow to his kidneys drops him to the floor, and he is easy to kill now. Exposed. Weak. I could apply my hands like a vice to either side of his head and snap his neck. I could punch his throat and crush his windpipe. I could break his arm and take his knife and sink the blade deep into his chest.

I realize I am cursing this man. Vulgar expressions rumble from my throat like the growls of a wounded cur. My palm slaps his head and my curling fingers ensnare his white hair. I am behind him now and I pull back so that he can see my face. He swings with the knife. Predictable and foolish. With a simple motion, I could drive it into his eye. But I turn aside as the blade slashes smoke-filled air. I snatch his wrist and turn it until the joint pops and the knife clatters to the floor. I yank the tall man's hair and feel strands come loose in my palm. He cries out. Again he calls me thug and brute and murderer.

His friends, Carl and the fat man, are near me now. I feel them at my back. Their voices are desperate, but they sound so far away and scratching as if shouting at me through a hailstorm. A hand falls on my shoulder and I coil my body, twisting to see what idiot has touched me. It is Carl, of course. His eyes are pools of worry, overflowing with tears, and he begs me to leave the tall man alone. He calls the man Udo, says they are cousins. The name means nothing to me. Names are for the corpse registry, for the carvers of stones. I am turning away when I notice the fat man's face. It is a childlike face, the face of a boy who is seeing violence for the first time. It frightens him, and his expression of fear pours through me like cold water.

I release Udo and brush strands of his hair from my palm.

"He thought you were someone else," Carl said frantically. "I'm sorry, Ernst. We've been drinking and it's muddled his thoughts. I'm so sorry. He thought you were someone else, someone who died many years ago."

I put up my hands and back toward the door. A smile moves my lips. Carl smiles in return. The fat man similarly grins with relief.

I embrace the residue of violence like a lost friend, holding it tightly to my chest, where its familiarity warms me.

Outside, the night air caresses my face. A band of plum lines the horizon to the west. I lean against the side of the building, smoking a cigarette. The violence is still with me, and I am made peaceful by its swaddling. Few would understand my admiration for conflict. I am no sadist, nor a masochist. If anything I am absolutely sensible about it. It is man's nature. Some, like the Indian Gandhi, will extol the virtues of peace and passivity. Ridiculous. If man were a soft creature, he would still crawl through the mud. No. Without struggle mankind would be no more interesting than the sunflower plant. Only through violence, rebellion, conflict was our history possible. Nietzsche wrote of this. He rightly points out that deviation fuels progress. Happy people, the truly content, have no cause for revolt, no motive for war, so we are created a dissatisfied and greedy species. Naturally we will also be a violent species, taking what we imagine should be ours, killing for gods we imagine will one day bring us peace. These justifications for conflict are lies – they are imaginings like fairies and witches – but the violence they fuel is true and honest. It is man's way. To refute this truth is to hate the self.

For many years I knew little but conflict, fighting for ideals that lifted the violence to acts of valor. No more a soldier, I now reject battle and will instigate no discord, though I will not deny it, as my actions in the bar clearly show. Conflict is an opiate but one I no longer crave.

I crush the remains of my cigarette under my shoe and work it into the dirt. I am surprised to find I'm not alone at the side of the bar.

Standing at the corner is the unremarkable-looking man in the dark suit. He looks at me as if concerned. I say hello to the man, but he doesn't immediately reply. He appears to be forming words in his mind, but they tangle and knot and he cannot speak.

"Will you try to kill me, too?" I ask. It is a joke, but the man's face blossoms in surprise. His head shakes quickly. "Good," I say.

"No, I...." His voice is deep but he is not a confident man. Words confound him.

What does he want?

"I was just going to ask you for a cigarette."

"Ah, good. Yes." I give him one and take another for myself.

He inhales smoke, again looking at me like I am an injured child. The expression insults me, but I feel I am not interpreting it properly.

"I thought that guy was going to kill you."

"He was going to kill me. I decided it better he didn't."

"Yeah," this man says with a chuckle. "You look like you can take care of yourself."

"I've seen a number of good fights. This one, tonight, was not so good."

"What was he calling you?"

"What do men always call each other? He believed I was a thing he hated and he labeled me such. It doesn't matter if I was this thing or not. He simply wanted an excuse to fight."

"Did you screw his wife or something?"

"I have no use for women."

Like many to whom I've said these words, his face darkens with confusion. He does not understand my meaning. In the beer halls and brothels and cabarets back home, such an admission surprised no one. It was understood without explanation, but those were places of honesty. Not like this place. These people and their masks, their roles. A man is this. A woman is that. In this place, there is John Wayne and there is Vivien Leigh. They are stories they've created for themselves. The truth of them lies buried deep: layered clothing against the cold.

"No use for them?" this man asks.

"Yes. I grew up among men. A soldier."

This seems to amuse him. He smiles around the cigarette. He pulls it from his mouth and says, "I can think of one use for a woman."

"And I cannot."

It is then that I recognize the question he was asking. I have already answered it.

"A lot of people would call that a sickness."

"What is the difference between a lot of people and a pack of dogs? People are led by ideas, and they believe that if they don't share the ideas they will be left behind to starve."

"I don't follow."

"People fear being alone."

"And you don't?"

"Alone is not so bad."

"You're a strange guy."

"Yes," I say. "You should be concerned about a man as strange as me."

"You're not so bad. Are you?"

"You should get back to your woman," I tell him.

"She's not mine. Just a whore looking for a tumble."

"That's an ugly word: whore."

"I thought you had no use for women?"

"I have no use for a lion, but I respect it."

"Yeah, well. I've already said my good nights to her. I was hoping I might find a bar in town, someplace that wasn't quite so depressing."

"You go to the Longhorn Tavern. They are happier there."

"Is that where you're headed?"

"No. Ernst is going home."

"Your name is Ernst?"

"Yes."

The man extends his arm to shake my hand but he does not offer his name. I understand him now. He tries to remain hidden, waiting to be drawn out. It is a tiresome flirtation, but common in this place. If I say nothing, he will go away. His desire means less to him than his role. But he will drive me home if I ask him, and he will come inside and have a beer if I ask him, and he will fuck if I ask him, so when it is finished he can tell himself he is without responsibility for the incident. He is a soldier waiting for orders, though he doesn't understand the cause for which he fights.

Once, I was a captain. I led men. They followed my orders and fought for my cause.

This man would be no different.

⁜

He lies on my bed. Naked. Face down. I was in the kitchen putting away the beer bottles when he walked into my room. He undressed and lay on the bed. His head is turned away from me, facing the wall. His arms embrace a pillow. The pose and what it suggests disgusts me. He behaves like an animal in the woods, indifferent to the beast that mounts him.

"Nuh," I tell him. "This is no good."

"Oh, Christ," he says. Fear edges his words.

Naturally he misunderstands me.

He hurries from the bed and reaches for his trousers. I circle the bed and stop him. Clasping his unremarkable face in my hands, I hold him tightly and force his face close to mine. The fright in his eyes is saddening. He thinks I mean him harm, and he tries to pull away.

My grasp is too strong. I give him a light shake.

"Look at me," I tell him. "Look at me."

"Christ," he repeats, now a prayer.

I kiss him then. My lips press against his but he does not reciprocate. He struggles even more as if I have tried to bite him. I pull away and shake his head again.

"Look at me," I say.

"What are you doing?" he asks as if I am a criminal holding a razor to his neck.

"You do what I say. In the end, it is all the same to you."

"What are you talking about?"

"You don't understand because you don't want to understand."

I kiss him again and this time I don't pull away. I keep my lips to his until he is certain I am not hurting him, and he responds slowly, but eventually his jaw loosens and his lips soften, and his hands slide over my shoulders and hold me tightly. I release his head and embrace him gently. Skin passes beneath my palms. Muscles not yet relaxed meet my touch. I move my mouth to his neck. His head falls back to allow me access to his throat. My tongue traces down his chest and my hand goes to his cock. This is better. This is good.

⑃

He wakes me from a dream of bullets and leaves of blood and tells me he must go. I tell him that is good and he says that he will stay in Barnard another night and will be back the next week and then again in a few week's time, and I am confused by the recitation of his schedule as I feel it has nothing to do with me, but he asks if he might call, perhaps tomorrow or during a future visit, and I tell him yes, he may call. I climb out of bed and walk to the kitchen, feeling his gaze on my skin like whispered breath. In the kitchen I write my phone number on a scrap of paper and hand it to him, feeling I have accomplished nothing but the waste of paper and ink. I escort him to the door and he walks into the darkness.

A boy in Munich once said he loved me, and I laughed, imagining he was playing some bedroom game, pretending we were husband and wife, but he played no game and his admission made me cruel. I wish I had understood what his words had meant. So long ago. His name escapes me now, but I wonder where that boy is. Did he find a companion who was not so ignorant as to misinterpret his declaration?

Is he happy? Is he even alive?

𝕿𝖍𝖎𝖗𝖙𝖊𝖊𝖓: 𝕾𝖍𝖊𝖗𝖎𝖋𝖋 𝕿𝖔𝖒 𝕽𝖆𝖇𝖇𝖎𝖙

Sunday morning, Tom Rabbit dressed for church in his best cotton suit. Downstairs, Estella prepared his breakfast. He knotted his tie three times before he finally got it right, and then he cinched it to his collar and smoothed it over the lapel of his shirt. Looking at himself in the mirror, he saw the toll the last five weeks had taken on his face. He looked drawn and dog tired, hardly a full night's sleep since he'd pulled Harold Ashton out of those woods, and his days had become exhausting rituals of listening to complaints about his competency, writing down inane tip-offs, and interrogating the local Germans in the hope that one of them knew something – or someone – that could bring peace back to Barnard.

He ate his breakfast slowly and drank only half of his normal cup of coffee. The aching knot in his gut hadn't let up. Most days it chose to be no more noticeable than a dull throb, but today it burned in his belly like a coal, and Tom felt his breakfast hitting that coal like kerosene.

The waiting ate at him. Sure as the sun rose, another boy was going to turn up. If Harold Ashton had been the only victim, Tom could have taken minor consolation in the idea that a drifter had murdered the boy, but after David Williams, Tom felt certain their killer was here to stay, and if Tom didn't do his job, the killer would find himself another young man to add to his list. Exactly how long this list was Tom didn't know. They had found two victims but the murderer's notes put the number at four. Doc Randolph had suggested these additional victims might not have come from Barnard, but could be remnants of an earlier spree carried out in another city or another country. Tom preferred that idea, though was hesitant to believe it.

He pushed a wedge of bread around on his plate, but instead of eating it he dropped the soggy bit on the remains of his eggs and pushed the plate away. Estella patted his shoulder and he turned to find her worried expression.

"Thank you," Tom said. "It was very good. S'pose I'm not hungry."

Estella smiled and retrieved the plate. She carried it to the sink and placed it in the basin. Then she turned to Tom and said, "Sheriff Rabbit?"

"Yes," he replied, not looking up from the table.

"I am going to my mother's today after church. May I stay there tonight?"

"Of course, Estella," he said. Only then did he realize that she was speaking, and the fact that her pronunciation was so good took another moment for Tom to process. When it did, he smiled broadly. "You said that very well."

"Thank you, Sheriff Rabbit," Estella said. "My aunt teaches me."

"It's nice to hear a woman's voice around here again," Tom said.

The phone on the wall above his right shoulder rang. The sound of phone bells had become repugnant to Tom since lately the device had brought him nothing but bad news. He closed his eyes at the second ring and took a deep breath, stomach churning like a volcanic pit.

The call came from Big Lenny Elliot, who lived a few blocks off Kramer Lake on San Jose Street. His eldest boy, Little Lenny, sixteen years old and nearly a twin for his daddy, was nowhere to be found.

||||

The Elliot household was in an uproar when Tom arrived. Big Lenny threw the door open and ushered Tom inside the untidy home. Clothes, papers, dishes, toys, and kids were everywhere. Big Lenny had married his wife, Kathy, young, and they hadn't wasted a moment before starting to bring babies into the world. Thirty-three-years old and the man already had eleven children to feed, and Kathy was good and plump with another one. Little Lenny had been the first, and worry boiled beneath his parents' skin.

Tom stood in the living room, feeling like he had been dropped in the middle of a particularly unkempt schoolhouse. Small faces surrounded him, looking up at him expectantly. Some smiled. Others looked at him like he was a two-headed calf.

"He went to bed at ten, like always," Big Lenny said. "Always at ten. I don't care what's on the radio."

"Is there any chance he left the house early for some reason?"

"Naw, sir," Big Lenny said. "I get up before anyone else. The one thing my boy and me don't share is rising with the sun. He'll sleep all day if we let him, but he's young yet."

"What about last night?" Tom asked. "Could he have slipped out of the house after you folks went to bed?"

"Why on earth would he have done that? And if he did, where is he now?"

A little girl waddled up to Tom and slapped his knee before the toddler giggled and scurried off to her mother's skirt. Two boys stopped playing with a toy wooden truck on the sofa and started jabbering questions at Tom nonstop, asking about trains and horses and bank robbers and radio programs. Big Lenny looked at Kathy and said, "Would you settle these children down?"

She gave her husband a wounded look and placed her hands on her belly as if protecting the child within from his voice.

"Why don't you show me the boy's room," Tom said. "Maybe we can have a private talk."

"You're the sheriff," Big Lenny said, turning on his heels and leading Tom to the back of the house. They passed through the kitchen and Big Lenny stopped at the threshold of the mudroom. Tom peered inside and saw a simple cot laid out with a pillow and rough woolen blanket. "Little Lenny couldn't sleep, sharing a room with his four brothers so he took this space here. Been just fine for him the last year."

"Did you make the bed this morning?"

"Naw, sir," Big Lenny said. "Everything's just the way we found it."

The pillow looked fluffed and the blanket lay neatly over the cot's shallow mattress. Things appeared neat, orderly. It didn't look like Little Lenny had been dragged from his bed. Maybe someone he'd known had come to the door and asked him outside, or the Cowboy might have coerced him at gunpoint, but would the killer have waited for Lenny to make his bed?

"Does Little Lenny have a girl in town?" Tom asked.

"Naw, sir," the man said. "None that I heard about, and he wouldn't keep something like that quiet."

"Has he stayed out all night before?" Tom asked. "Maybe stirring up trouble with friends?"

"Naw, sir, and I know what you're trying to do, Sheriff, and I already thought about this every which way. He's gone and I know someone took him, and I know you have to get out there and find him before he ends up like that Ashton boy or Deke's son. You got to find him, because it will kill Kathy if anything happens to that boy."

Tom noted the hitch in Big Lenny's voice and saw the moisture at the man's eyes. He nodded his head and crossed the mudroom. A row of dirty children's boots stood by the door, arranged smallest to largest.

"Are Lenny's boots gone?"

"I didn't think to check," Big Lenny said, leaning into the room. He eyed the row of boots and nodded his head. "They aren't there."

"Do you know if Lenny kept this back door locked while he was sleeping?"

"Since the Ashton boy and all."

"Have you called his friends? Just checked to see if he got restless last night."

"I'm not a complete fool, Sheriff. Of course I called around, but no one seen him, and you know why no one seen him, and you have to find him. I don't care if you and your men have to search every German house in the city. You best find my boy before he ends up like Harold Ashton and David Williams."

"Settle down, Lenny," Tom said. "It looks like his bed was made and he had time to put on his boots. Looks like he left of his own mind, and that's a good sign. I'll bet he comes home before the morning is done, but me and my men are going to follow up on this right away, so's you and Kathy can get back your piece of mind. Now, I want you to write down the names of Lenny's closest friends and whatever phone numbers you might have for them. He might have said something to them about where he was going."

"I already told you...."

"Yes, but folks are going to know this is serious business if they're talking to the sheriff and not the boy's daddy. Kids'll cover each other up, but only so much. You get me those names. And I'd appreciate it if you could keep your children out of the backyard until my men have had a chance to look it over."

Big Lenny nodded distractedly and then backed into the kitchen. There was a sheet of paper by the phone and a pencil lay across it. The man called for his wife and then set to writing. When Kathy appeared with a toddler in her arms, the little girl riding the hump of her mama's belly, Big Lenny told her to keep the kids corralled until the sheriff said otherwise.

"Please," Tom added.

"Yes, Sheriff," Kathy replied sibilantly. She covered her mouth after speaking and dropped her eyes, and then hurried from the kitchen.

"She'll keep them out of your way," Big Lenny said, scribbling on the pad. "If she's good at anything, she's good at herding this barnyard we got here."

"I'm sure she's a fine mother," Tom said. "My men should be along shortly. I'm going into the backyard. You send them on back when they get here."

"Yes, sir," Big Lenny said.

Tom reached for the doorknob, and then stopped himself, fearing his prints might smear those of the killer: if the Cowboy had left any. For all of his rationalization to Big Lenny, Tom didn't believe a single consoling word of it, though he was glad it sounded sensible in his ears. Another boy was gone. He'd not been able to stop it. Tom walked through the kitchen and back into the messy living room with all of the curious faces and by the time he reached the front door he all but ran, and when he hit the porch he veered left and hurried to the rail. He jumped it smoothly and ran between the houses. The first sob bucked in his chest as he reached the gate to the backyard. By the time he opened the gate and got it closed behind him, his jaws were clenched and his eyes squeezed tight as he fought to keep from bawling like a child.

Fourteen: Tim Randall

Ma's favorite record that summer, at least the one she played the most, was "I'll Walk Alone." Whenever she sat down to write a letter to my daddy Dinah Shore's voice filled the house with bittersweet emotion, crooning to some nameless beau who was presumably stationed overseas. The song always needled at me. Ma looked miserable whenever she played it.

She hadn't received a letter from Daddy in weeks, so she wrote him twice as many. Rita Marshall showed up just before noon to tell us that Little Lenny Elliot was missing, and my mother collapsed under the news, and I could tell she was considering calling her mother to come watch me again or maybe taking another night off of work, but she didn't. Instead, she sat me down and asked me to stay in the house and to promise I wouldn't break curfew, which I did. She looked so tired and scared I had to promise. When she left the house that evening, she carried a letter to my daddy against her purse, stamped and ready for the mailbox.

Bum and I went to the lake to cool off after supper, and we kept the water up to our chins. Late in the afternoon, I noticed a tall man walking up to Mr. Lang's door. He didn't look familiar, certainly no one from the neighborhood, and the sight of him reminded me of the other men who had visited my neighbor in the previous months – their arrival after sunset, their visits so brief.

In the twenty-four hours since I'd sat in his living room, with iodine drying in my wounds and Mr. Lang bouncing on his sofa to emphasize his point about Taters, I'd found myself inordinately interested in the man. I thought about him constantly, so bobbing in the lake and keeping up my end of the conversation with Bum, I watched his house, wondering about the stranger he'd just welcomed over his threshold.

When it got dark, Bum and I climbed out of the water and dried off. We dressed, but instead of heading back to the house and keeping my promise to Ma, I dropped down on the grass and just looked at the lake, which had deepened to the shade of a plum's skin.

"We should get inside," Bum said.

I knew he was worried about the Cowboy, and I had more than a little fear about the killer myself, but we were close to the house and our neighbors' houses and they'd hear us if we kicked up a fuss. Plus, we were in the middle of the grassy patch between the road and the lake. It wasn't like the Cowboy could sneak up on us, and we both knew better than to let a stranger get too close. I explained all of this to Bum, who reacted as I'd expected him to, with a shaking of his head and a soft-spoken line of reasoning, attempting to disassemble my argument point by point.

And then he added, "Plus, we're breaking curfew and that's against the law, and if we get caught our folks are going to beat us 'til next Wednesday."

He had a point, though Ma had only whipped me once since my father had gone to war. Still I wasn't ready to go back into the stifling, motionless air of the house just yet. A gentle breeze blew from the lake to take the edge off the heat, and the stars twinkled above our heads like an upended city hanging from the heavens. Bum threatened to go inside without me, but he didn't. After the night I'd called his bluff and gone wandering on my own, he knew better than to test my resolve.

"I'm getting eaten alive out here," he muttered, slapping a palm against his neck.

"You do anything but complain?" I asked.

"You give me any reason to do anything else?" he replied.

"Fine," I said. I climbed to my feet and turned back toward Dodd Street.

Except for a dim rectangle of light on the lake-facing side Mr. Lang's house was dark. A shadow played against the curtains – oddly rhythmic in its motion. Curiosity fell over me in a wave, as I stood transfixed by the window.

"Did you hear that?" Bum whispered, grabbing my arm.

"Hear what?"

"Someone in the bushes."

I hated taking my eyes away from Mr. Lang's window, but the fear in Bum's voice sounded authentic. I scanned the shrubs to our left and saw nothing but tufts of black against a blacker background. The shrubs on our right looked little different. Listening intently, I heard the common noises of crickets and somewhere across the lake an owl hooted in the night.

"You're nuts," I told him.

"Someone's here," he insisted. "Let's go back inside. Please, Tim."

My friend could have been pulling my leg and telling a tale to get his way. I knew full well no one could move around brush that thick without making a good amount of noise, and I hadn't heard a thing, which wasn't to say the prospect hadn't shaken me. A low blaze of fear began to burn in my stomach. The fates of Harold, David and most recently Little Lenny Elliot hadn't faded from my memory, so I had to agree that distancing ourselves from the field was a good idea.

That didn't mean I was ready to go inside just yet, though. I turned back to Mr. Lang's window, and without saying a word, I started walking toward it.

"Where are you going?" Bum asked.

"On our last mission of the summer," I replied.

"Mission? Tim, I'm not kidding. Someone is out here."

"And they'll think we're going to Mr. Lang's for help, if you keep your voice down."

"We should go inside."

"Look, Bum," I whispered, "we're just going up to the window. I know he's home because he let a friend in a while ago. If anyone tries to jump us, we'll make a racket and he'll come out and help."

"Why don't we just go up to the front door?"

But we were already in Mr. Lang's side yard. I put a finger to my lips and continued toward the window. From behind us, I heard a branch snap and my skin shriveled up. Then I looked through a part in Mr. Lang's curtains, and what I saw there drove away the momentary fear, bringing instead a physiological vibration, humming and buzzing through my veins.

Mr. Lang and another man were on the German's bed. Both were naked, their skin appearing slick and smooth in the dull light cast by a bedside lamp. The man was bent forward, clutching a pillow and facing away from the window, and Mr. Lang knelt behind him, hands resting on the man's buttocks as he moved his hips forward and back. My mind crackled as the details of this union scored my thoughts like memories delivered by a branding iron. Mr. Lang's sweat-slathered chest, bulging with strain. His guest's thick legs, covered in filaments of pale hair with rivulets of sweat drawing trails along the muscles. A muscular arm flexing against a pillow. The arc of the man's back. The force of the German's thrusts. The scene was confusing, exciting, and my breath stopped as the union of these men roared locomotive fast through the tunnels of my eyes. Only a second before I'd been ready to run at the sound of a twig snap, but in that instant, watching those two men, I didn't think anything could move me.

At my side, Bum mumbled desperately. "I don't want to see this."

I couldn't reply. The sight through the gap in the curtains emptied me of reason.

Then a hand wrapped around my mouth, and the coiling emotion in my belly hardened into absolute terror. I was lifted from my feet and yanked around. In that instant, I saw that someone else had Bum and was similarly spinning him. My heart climbed to the back of my throat and my heart raced as if I were falling from the edge of a cliff. Once the rotation was complete, I found myself in front of Hugo Jones, whose face was lit by the orange glow of a burning cigarette.

He withdrew the smoke and lifted a finger to his lips. *Shh.*

Then he walked past where I struggled against the hands holding me. I tried to spot Bum again, but couldn't turn my head. My fear receded by a fraction as I came to realize that Ben Livingston or Austin Chitwood held me and not the murderous Gray Cowboy, but I didn't feel safe. Hugo and his friends might not have been killers but they weren't kind, as Hugo had proven only the day before, and while I thought these things, I was again being hoisted in the air and turned, this time facing Mr. Lang's house again.

Hugo Jones stood at the window. His back as straight and rigid as a brick wall. He shook his head so slowly the motion was barely perceptible. He seemed to be as enrapt by the scene in the bedroom as I had been.

Finally he backed away from the glass.

When he turned to us, his eyes appeared as black pits in his face.

"Take those two back to the lawn and let 'em loose," he whispered. "We got bigger fish to fry."

The two boys did as they were instructed, waddling away from Mr. Lang's house with Bum and me in their grasp. In the middle of the grassy field, Austin Chitwood made us promise with nods of our heads that we'd keep quiet. We agreed eagerly. Then Ben Livingston released me, and Austin released Bum and the two of us tore off across the grass, making a straight line to my front door.

Bum, reeling from fear, muttered his anger distractedly. He stood frozen in the living room, incredulous that I should be so reckless and further, that I should involve him in my irresponsible behavior.

Electric currents of emotion bombarded me, distracting my thoughts and crackling in my ears so I could barely hear my friend's words. The sensual and the terrible battled. Scorched images of my neighbor and his guest smoldered in my mind. I knew what I had seen and could even name it, but the act struck me as wholly foreign, and for all of its erotic power, recalling the union of Mr. Lang and that stranger also left me feeling sickened and sad. I felt a profound disappointment in my neighbor, as though he'd lied, making me believe he was one thing, when in fact he was a different thing entirely. My heart continued to race like a hummingbird's from the encounter with Hugo that had followed. How could I defend myself to Bum? He was right about everything and I told him so.

"If it weren't after curfew, I'd go home right now," he said.

I was about to apologize again when Hugo knocked on the screen door and let himself and the other two boys into my house.

"You can't be here," Bum said as if he were talking to a leprechaun that had suddenly appeared through the living room carpet.

"We need to talk," Hugo said, strutting across the room to stand by the fireplace. Ben and Austin remained by the front door, arms crossed like guards at a bank vault. "Your ma's still at work?"

Though a lie might have served me better, I remained too shaken to form one. I nodded my head. After throwing a quick look at Bum, who had turned paler than a fish belly, I returned my attention to the older boy.

"I want you two to keep your mouths shut about what you saw," Hugo said. His tone was soft and familiar, like an older brother offering a sincere warning. He stood by the fireplace with authority. His cheeks burned red beneath the purple smudges of acne. "Kids like you shouldn't have to see a thing like that. If I thought you could forget it, I'd tell you to give it a try, but you can't unsee a thing."

"W-we didn't see a-anything," Bum spluttered.

"You saw," Hugo said. "And that's about the worst thing a man can see. A man treating another man like a woman isn't natural. In fact, it's flat-out evil. But it could be worse. Damnation, you two are lucky to be alive."

I didn't understand what he meant. Had he seen something different through the bedroom curtains than I had? Had he seen my neighbor kill that man? Hugo's voice was colored with concern, not threat, and I felt certain he was acting in a protective manner. He stood silently, nodding his head. Then he withdrew a cigarette from his pocket and lit it. He pinched the cigarette between his fingers and pulled it from his lips. He waved his hand back and forth, fingers directed at my front door and the two boys standing there, drawing gray-blue trails of smoke in the air.

"We'll take things from here," Hugo said. "You two just keep quiet until we figure out what to do about this, and you keep yourselves away from that pervert or he's likely to do you the way he did Harold and those other boys."

"Did he kill that man?" I asked.

"Maybe so," Hugo replied earnestly. "A man that can do what we saw is capable of doing anything. But he sure as shit isn't going to kill anyone else. You just stay away from him, and you lock that front door good and tight after we leave. If that Nazi bastard comes over here, you pick up your daddy's gun and protect your home."

Then the three boys left. Hurriedly I closed the front door and locked it tight the way Hugo had instructed. Bum remained stricken in the center of the room, white and motionless like a statue. I ran past him and through the kitchen and locked the back door, and then I checked the windows to make sure they were latched. The heat would build oven hot, but Hugo's conviction had become my own. Though he hadn't divulged what he'd seen in that room – beyond the same scene I'd witnessed – it must have been serious.

"It's all locked up," I told Bum after I was finished.

"I think I want to go to sleep," he replied distantly. Then he turned around and walked into the hall, disappearing around the corner.

As for me, I couldn't sleep. I paced the living room thinking about the atrocities occurring so close to my home, perpetrated by a trusted neighbor, a man I'd thought of as my friend until

I'd seen him for what he was. The pleasant sentiments I'd harbored for the man evaporated as I marched to and fro across the carpet, because of what this German was and the crimes I was coming to believe he'd committed. Rape and murder? Hugo hadn't revealed what he'd seen but it was clear the older boy believed the German was the Cowboy the papers had been writing about – a brutal killer of boys –and I wished Ben hadn't dragged me away from that window, so I could have seen the damning evidence. Amid my agitation a quiet voice in a distant chamber of my mind insisted that Hugo and I were wrong. The voice spoke to the German's generosity and kindness. It reminded me that the man had tended my cuts after his accuser had beaten me. Except the voice was so calm, serene like the rustle of wind across the tops of trees – all but drowned by the torrent of indictments leveled at the German that bellowed through my thoughts.

When I finally went into my room I stepped over Bum, who lay on the floor, wrapped in a blanket and facing the space beneath my bed. I went to the window. If I leaned close to the glass, I could see through the gap between my house and the Reddings' house next door, giving me an unobstructed view of Mr. Lang's porch across the street, and I sat there on the windowsill, eyes fixed, until Ma got back from her shift at the factory. Then I climbed into bed and pretended to be asleep when she opened the bedroom door to check on me. Once the door closed, I remained in bed. Then the soft strains of "I'll Walk Alone" drifted through the walls. I must have fallen asleep soon after, but in the middle of the night I woke and returned to my position at the glass.

The twin states of somnolent and agitated played against one another. My eyes badly wanted to close, but there was a strong possibility that my neighbor Mr. Lang was a murderer – he certainly wasn't normal – and my curiosity evolved into a kind of resolve; it was my responsibility to watch his house, my duty. What if he decided to cross the street in the middle of the night and snatch Bum or me? What if he hurt Ma? As I sat there I remembered what he'd done to that man in his room, could still picture Mr. Lang's chest, swollen with strain and covered in a shimmering layer of sweat. And though I could not recall the expression the German had worn, I imagined it would be cruel and twisted like the grinning façade of a torturer who enjoyed his craft.

The lights went on in the German's living room after I'd been at the window for what seemed like hours. The sudden burst of illumination startled me, and I leapt off the sill and went to Bum to shake him awake.

Then I returned to my post, peering through darkness to the rectangle of light open at the front of the German's house. Two men stood on the threshold. They shook hands and the other man left, walking casually to the street and passing from my line of sight.

"What's going on?" Bum asked dreamily.

"The other man just left."

"So Mr. Lang didn't kill him."

"That doesn't mean anything."

"Hugo's full of hot air," Bum said. Then he drifted back to sleep.

Fifteen: The German

July 24, 1944 – Translated from the German

Last night the man with the unremarkable face returned. He did not wait for cover of darkness, but rather arrived near seven as I was preparing a late supper of eggs and bacon, and he joined me for the meal and for a drink after and we sat on the sofa and spoke like friends, and I thought on how long it had been since I'd shared such a conversation, and it seemed like a very long time. When living in New Orleans, I'd met a man named Richert who was handsome and intelligent and showed great strength, and he asked me to visit him in Barnard, Texas, and I agreed because I loathed New Orleans, despite its indulgences. There was much laughter in New Orleans, much frivolity, and much celebration, but it all seemed to mask something foul beneath, like a lace handkerchief draped over the face of a leper. And I took the train to Austin, Texas, and Richert met me at the station and drove me to Barnard, and a sense of calm settled on me in this place. A time away from big cities enticed me. *Peace* enticed me. Richert and I became frequent companions and we spoke as friends. At times I grew restless because conflict was as ingrained in me as the color of my eyes, but after so many years of struggle, I believed I could let it go – wanted to let it go. Richert gave me a car, because he had three, and he paid for much of my house beside the lake because he had a family estate and could buy what he pleased, and though we rarely walked in public together, we spent much time in each other's company. When he died from a weakness of the heart of which he'd never spoken, his will spoke of me as his "faithful servant" and I was to retain the car and the house and even a small sum of money. At the time the generosity of his request was overshadowed by the humiliation and insult of it. I was no man's servant. I had led armies and held onto the pride of having done so. I loathed his memory, and then I destroyed it for myself, finding flaw with his every physical and mental attribute. I thought to sell his tarnished gifts and find some new home, but the comfort of this place, the heated days and serene nights kept me. Was he the last man with whom I'd shared both cock and mind, and if so how had I not noticed until now, and why did it suddenly strike me as a loss?

The unremarkable man reveals bits of his life as we chat. He is a machine-parts salesman from Houston, who is negotiating deals with the factory. He remains unmarried though his sisters and mother continue a search for his bride. Speaking of this amuses him, but there is fear in his eyes. I think to comment on his inexperience with women as it seems to mirror his inexperience with men, which he displayed so clearly the night before, but I keep my thoughts to myself, fearing the insult will end this talk among friends. He remembers fishing when he was a boy and an uncle who sucked his cock when they were alone in the woods, and he blames this uncle for etching confusion into his mind. Speaking of this visibly hurts him, so I pat him on the leg and tell him we should go outside for a time to catch the evening air, and he agrees.

In the backyard, he grins when he sees my chickens, and I tell him that I hate the birds, but I appreciate their eggs, and he thanks me again for the dinner.

"What are their names?" he asks, pointing at a lazy hen who sits in the port of her coup.

"Names?" I ask.

"Yes, what do you call them?"

"I call them chickens."

"But they don't have names?"

"Names are for the corpse registry and the carvers of stones," I say.

This comment – though meant as nothing more than flippancy – unsettles the unremarkable man and the fear is back in his eyes. I smile and clap him on the back and try to soothe his disquiet, but this man is not comfortable with thoughts of death, so I wait for the power of the comment to fade, and I ask if he would like another drink, and he tells me there is something else he would prefer. I still do not know this unremarkable man's name.

◧

The sun has set, and sweat cools on my belly and chest. A dim light from a single lamp sends shadows over the bed. Next to me the unremarkable man rests with his eyes closed and a vague smile pulling his lips. I smell dirt and rot, and think of a concrete cell and of being cold, colder than I've ever been before. I think of a blood-filled hole and flakes of scab dropping from my chest, and I wonder on how it is that I'm alive?

Was it the Bolivian? Did he impart this magic to me? Is it a flaw in my own design? Or am I like Caligari's narrator, perfectly mortal but deluded into believing the macabre in an attempt to camouflage my own infirmity?

In thinking of the Bolivian, his gaunt feminine face returns to me and once recognized he remains behind my eyes. Have I ever spoken of this man? Have I ever written down our meeting and the token of loathing he pressed into my palm?

I cannot remember...but I do remember.

Nearly twenty years ago I lost my post at the Reichstag and left my country for Bolivia and the City in the Pit.

I do not enjoy this assignment. As a military advisor, I witness the sloppiness of the troops and the indifference of the officers. Many times I attempt to show them the proper German way to train and deploy an army, but my efforts are rewarded with shrugs and laughter. More discouraging is the attitude of the Bolivians toward my disinterest in women. The Catholic

Church has already commandeered this place, and sins of flesh – particularly those they find unspeakable – are mocked and cause for much outrage. I grow frustrated with the culture, and though La Paz is a beautiful city, I enjoy it little. I come to call it the City in the Pit, because of the towering canyon of stone in which it sits, demeaning it the way its populace demeans me.

This night, as is often the case, I dine with officers in the hotel restaurant, eating bland pieces of fish and overcooked vegetables. I choose to excuse myself after the meal, but my hosts will not hear of it. Instead, they escort me upstairs. Whores wait for us in a vast suite. They lounge on sofas, drinking wine from the bottle, their breasts exposed shamelessly as if they have already performed their services. The assortment of breasts is surprising to me; some small as to be hardly noticeable, some great melon-sized; some still firm with youth, and others hanging like drained leather flasks. The men walk into the room smiling and laughing, reaching for selections from this unappetizing menu, whereas I remain frozen by the door. A tall captain named Zamora tells me to take my pick of the women, and I understand that he is testing my manhood, using a worthless scale for its measurement, and I take great offense from this insulting challenge, but I smile and bow politely. Then I wish him a good night and depart.

Downstairs I take a bottle of whiskey from the bar and carry it with me into the streets, cursing my hosts and drinking deeply. After an hour I am very drunk, and find myself wandering in a strange part of the city. All around me are low dark shops and the impression of larger buildings behind them. I turn about to get my bearings, but the darkness cloaks the hillsides, erasing topographical landmarks that might have guided me in the right direction. Drinking more and missing my homeland, where I might find myself in a steam bath with any number of attractive opportunities, I lean against a shop that reeks of rotted flowers and hear a clatter coming from down the street.

Men shout and stomp the road. To my drunken mind, it sounds like the approach of a full unit, but it is merely a handful of men – four, maybe five – chasing after another man with

sticks and harsh words. Though I have no interest in the squabbles of these Bolivians, a good fight strikes me as a wonderful
thing, and I push away from the wall.

The chased man wears white pants and a loose tunic, only
a shade darker than the trousers; his skin is so dark I make out
no features of his face. He is willowy thin and when he runs he
looks like a great marionette being jerked about by unskilled
hands. Mid-block he changes his course and dashes across the
street, away from where I stand and vanishes into a pitch-black
alley. Those behind him run with greater determination and far
more grace, but somehow, less speed. Though they gain on this
raggedy doll, it seems they should have had their prey in much
shorter order.

I leave the corner and cross the road, changing my grip
on the whiskey bottle as I approach the black corridor ahead,
where I see a number of shirted backs milling in the gloom. Still
they shout and a shrill cry comes from within, and I reach the
alley with a cock full of blood. Indifferent to the cause of the
chase – What care have I for the squabbles of these undisci-
plined people? – I believe the greater fight will come from the
pursuers, so it is they I attack. I shatter the whiskey bottle over a
black-haired head, dropping one of the men outright. His com-
rades turn to see what has caused the commotion, and I swing
the bottle again, slicing into the arm of a burly Bolivian with a
thick and scruffy beard. He clutches at his arm and looks at me
confused, and I bring my knee up to his balls and when he drops
and gapes up at me, I smash my forehead into the bridge of his
nose, and he falls unconscious on the paving stones. Hands are
on me now, holding my shoulders, seeking purchase on my
arms, but the fight is still building, and I will not be denied this
conflict. I dig in my feet and push back, shoving whichever man
has gotten behind me into a wall. His grip on my shoulders loosens and I step away in time to avoid a kick meant for my own
balls, but landing instead against this other man's thigh. I take
three punches to the face and one very painful blow to the ear.
Caramel-colored hands and faces surround me, but I continue
to struggle, striking out at every shape in the gloom. In time

two men run off and two lie on the stones at my feet. The last man tries to reason with me. He shouts and points deep into the alley, likely at the man he has been chasing, but he speaks the native gibberish these people called *Quechua* and I do not understand a word of it. I shout back in German, calling him weak and foolish and any number of obscenities. And if I were carrying my sidearm, I would shoot him then, so infuriating do I find the meaningless babble he launches at me. But I have no gun, and the bottle lies in useless shards around me. I charge the man, who continues to point, shaking his finger into the darkness at something I cannot see. My attack on this last man is brutal and were I not drunk I would end it much sooner, except I am very drunk and my body is charged as if imbued with the power of Thor himself. I punch teeth from the man's mouth; dislocate his right eye so that it bulges against his swelling lids; one hand is crushed into the stones by my polished boot; and he vomits blood until he finally lies quietly.

Now I am eager to see what manner of prey these men have cornered, because in their defeat I have made it mine.

I march down the alley, which smells of cat piss and rotten fruit. I withdraw a box of matches from my jacket pocket and strike one. In its flash – for it goes out almost immediately – I see the pale-clothed man crouching against a wall many meters away. Another match flares and I see that this beleaguered man is holding up a palm, though whether this is for assistance or to ward me off, I neither know nor care. When I reach him, I light another match and it keeps its flame. Up, I tell him. You stand up, now. Ernst has protected you.

In the firelight I gather some impression of his face. He has high cheekbones and large eyes, and at first I think that perhaps I have just saved a woman, but there is a masculinity to the man's jaw, and when he rises to his full height, six inches taller than myself, the question of his gender vanishes. The match burns down and I discard it – light another.

After such a fight, my body sings of muscle and confidence, and I have saved this wretch's life, for which he merely stares at me. I reach out a hand and touch his cheek and then caress his exotic skin. His eyes grow wide and he slaps my hand away and begins to babble at me in his native language, and hearing it again hits my temples like lightning, and I punch his full lips with every gram of force I can muster. In the dark I grope for him and he slaps at me, and I laugh at this game, until his long nails scratch my cheek.

I strike out with fists and knees and curses. Punching into shadows, hitting his chest and face and the stone wall. When he collapses, my boot suffices to continue the assault. It is easy to blame the whiskey, easier still to blame the ungrateful peasant at my feet, who has insulted my protection of him with repugnant dismissal.

As I straighten my clothing, the wretch begins a fresh chorus of incomprehensible chatter. With my energies spent I find the sing-song of his voice amusing; he is like a punished child making himself feel better with a lullaby. I take a step away and a hot palm wrap around my wrist, so I spin back to this broken peasant whom I cannot see, and feel something damp and writhing slapped into my palm and all the while, he continues the nonsensical chanting. So disturbing is the sensation on my hand, I do not even think to retaliate with violence but rather seek only to flee. I jerk my arm out of his grasp and back down the darkened alley, palm before my face trying to see what this man has placed there. It moves on my palm like a damp poultice or secreting insect, oozing toward gravity but I feel it stinging through my skin as well. I slap my hands together, which only sends spikes of pain into my palm and I scrub it against my trouser leg, which offers the same result. Keeping pace with me in the darkness is the wretched, beaten man. His voice rolls through the alley, taunting and brutal. Finally I reach a point where the light is sufficient to see what he has forced upon me, but there is nothing there. I search my hand front and back. The knuckles are split and ooze blood. The hand has swollen from so much violence, but whatever manner of creature had been put upon me is gone.

A week later I receive word that I am to return to Germany to take on a position of great authority, and the countdown to my execution begins.

※

I climb from the bed with stealth, so as not to disturb my guest and I walk into the living room for a cigarette. It is still early, I note – just after eleven o'clock. The cigarette tastes good to me. I turn on the lamp beside the sofa and look at the palm of my right hand; it is smooth and shows only the natural lines all men possess.

In this moment, I decide that I carry neither a Bolivian's curse nor a hereditary predisposition to endure. I am a man who is misremembering his past, nothing more, and though this speaks to insanity, it is far more rational than the mystical alternatives. Otherwise, what am I to call myself? Undead? Ghost?

The man with the unremarkable face speaks my name from the room. I crush the cigarette in the tray and return to him. He greets me from where he stands at the foot of the bed. His body is tall and firm and looks golden in the weak light of the lamp. We embrace and kiss and he turns in my arms, facing away so that my hands caress his stomach, and I place my ear against his cool back and listen for his heart, and when I hear the beating, I kiss him between the shoulder blades. Then I again listen for the rhythm.

"I like you, Ernst," he tells me.

"Yes. I like you, also."

This is good. To hold a body not eager to flee my touch, to be with a man that is not fire and then smoke – consuming then insubstantial – confirms I am no ghost merely inhabiting a place with no influence on it. In this moment, I am alive, and I hold him tightly to me, feeling the curve of his backside against my waist and the beat of his heart against my ear.

※

I remember the name of the boy whose declaration of love I met with laughter, and the boy's face returns to me, and I'm startled to remember that like me, his name was Ernst, and his face was very much like my own.

Sixteen: Sheriff Tom Rabbit

Monday morning, Tom sat in his office, facing Doc Randolph. The doctor puffed on his pipe and wore his customary expression of superiority, though he had added very little to the conversation since having arrived.

"It's like waiting to be executed," Tom said. "Two days and no body, but it's only a matter of time before Little Lenny's found, and I think things are going to blow up."

"Someone hit Mrs. Schultz with a rock this morning," the doctor said. "Gave her a good lump on the back of the head."

"Did she say who did it?" Tom asked, noting that the woman hadn't come into the station to report the attack.

"No. She said it was thrown and it knocked her down. By the time she got up and took a look around, there was no one to see."

"I guess I can add that to the Henckel boy who was run down and about fifty fights in the last few weeks. Lord, we're going to have Germans hanging from the trees in the park if we don't find this son of a bitch."

"You only need one to hang," Doc Randolph said. He took a deep puff on his pipe.

"Excuse me?"

"To defuse the situation," the doctor said. "This is purely hypothetical, of course, but let's say you brought in one of the less desirable German citizens on suspicion of these crimes. You don't actually charge him. There's no need to add busywork for yourself. More than likely you're going to have a mob of some kind form, which is perfectly natural. Even if they don't actually intend to murder this man, they will want to see him, so as to have a face for their hatred. You give them that. Let them see him, but make a stand against the vigilantes and warn them of severe repercussions should they attempt any action against him. Then, in the middle of the night, your suspect tries to escape and is subdued and killed in the process."

"Are you off your rocker?" Tom asked, appalled at the doctor's suggestion.

"Merely speculating," Doc Randolph said as if he were predicting the winner of a horse race and not plotting the murder of an innocent man. "Though it will be assumed by the mob, you've made no claim as to this man's guilt, so when the Cowboy again strikes, you cannot be held accountable. But you have brought a period of peace to the city, and you have kept additional attacks against your German constituency to a minimum, which at this point is likely to save a number of lives."

"That doesn't make it right."

"Indeed not," Doc Randolph agreed. "But again, this is all hypothetical. I am in no way suggesting what should be done, merely examining what could be done. After all, how much of your time is currently wasted on false or petty information? Half of your day is spent on the phone or reading ledger sheets. It's ridiculous. How can they expect you to focus on the important elements of these murders when they have you chasing all of their private geese for them?"

"What you're forgetting is that people are on guard right now. They're keeping their eyes open. We give them a dead guy, and they go back to their normal routine and suddenly the Cowboy has an easier time of it. At least people are scared enough now to protect themselves."

"For all of the good it did the Elliot boy."

Tom ground his teeth together and turned his attention toward the window. The urge to punch the smug doctor in the mouth flared, but Tom bit down on it. Half the time the son of a bitch infuriated him and the other half he intimidated him, so why Tom constantly allowed the man in his presence was a mystery.

"Okay, you've speculated," Tom said. He didn't want to talk about it anymore. The doctor's idea was far too simple and too tempting, and Tom wanted it out of his head. "We're not going to haul in a scapegoat."

"Sacrificial lamb is a more appropriate description."

"Call it what you like," Tom told the doctor. "If you don't have anything practical for me, I imagine you can head on back to your office."

Doc Randolph didn't move. In fact he smiled and relit his pipe as if Tom were being ridiculous. Tom was about to reiterate his desire for the old sawbones to hit the road when Rex poked his head into the office.

"Someone wants to talk to you," Rex said.

"Who's that?" Tom asked.

In reply Burl Jones pushed his way past the deputy and stomped up to Tom's desk where he glared down on the sheriff with a look of arrogance so sharp he might have learned the expression from Doc Randolph.

"I done what you couldn't do," Jones said.

"Yeah, and what's that, Burl?"

"I found the man that's been killing those boys."

After so many bad tip-offs Tom took the statement with a good amount of salt.

"Yeah, who's that?"

"A German faggot lives over on Dodd Street, not three blocks from the Elliot house.

"What's this man's name?"

"Lang. Ernst Lang."

"First I've heard of him. You see him with the Elliot boy?" Tom asked.

"No sir, but I didn't need to see him. My boy saw him clear enough."

"So where's your boy now? Don't you think he should talk to me if he witnessed a crime?"

"I don't want him hearing any more about this. It's unnatural, and he's a normal boy."

"Unnatural," Tom said, amused. "That's a kind word for murder."

"It's not just murder. The man's a sodomite."

"A what?" Tom asked. He knew the term from church, but only in a particular context, and he didn't understand what ancient cities had to do with the German.

"I believe Burl is saying that this Lang is a homosexual," Doc Randolph interjected.

"I'm going to need me a dictionary," Tom said.

"It's a pathology," Doc Randolph explained, "a sickness that makes a man sexually obsessed with other men. I've read a number of interesting studies on the condition."

"Sexually obsessed? You're talking about queers?" Tom asked.

"Yes, Tom," Doc Randolph said tersely, "we're talking about queers."

Burl Jones nodded emphatically with the doc's definition.

"So Hugo saw this Lang man with Little Lenny. When was this?"

"He didn't see nothing of the Elliot boy," Jones said. "But he saw Lang and another man doing their evil last night."

"Wait," Tom said. "Exactly what did Hugo see?"

"I just told you, he saw Lang having relations with another man. He's a sodomite. A goddamned faggot."

"But he didn't see Lang with Little Lenny Elliot?"

"He didn't have to see *that*," Burl roared. "He saw the scarred bastard mounting another man as clear as day. You need me to draw a picture for you?"

"Scarred bastard?" Tom said. He traced a line beneath his eyes with a finger, remembering the man he had seen at the city's Fourth of July celebration.

"That's the one, and I'm warning you, Tom Rabbit, if you don't do the job you get paid good money to do, I'll do it myself."

"You'll do no such thing, Jones. And I don't want you shooting your mouth off about this. Unless your boy saw Lang with Elliot, you've got nothing but manure to spread."

"Hold on, Tom," Doc Randolph said. "I wouldn't be so quick to dismiss this. He may have actually stumbled on the best lead you've yet had."

"That's right," Burl said triumphantly.

Doc Randolph sneered at Jones and shook his head. "It might be best if we spoke alone. I'm sure Mr. Jones wouldn't mind waiting with your men until we've gone over a few things."

"I got rights," Jones said.

"Of course you do," Doc Randolph said, placing his hand on Jones's shoulder. Gently he turned the man to the door and walked him toward it. "You go on out and talk to Rex and Don and Gil about them." Once he had Jones out of the office, the doctor closed the door and then spun on Tom, and said, "I hate that man."

"So why are you throwing logs on his fire?"

"Because my distaste for Burl Jones shouldn't supersede the value of his information."

"What value? He says he saw Lang with another man, doing.... Hell, I'm still not clear what."

"Don't be naïve. You know very well what we're talking about here."

But the truth was Tom didn't, not exactly. He knew about pansies and queers from schoolyard talk – kids who spoke funny or acted a bit sissy – and the other kids had made quite a bit of sport with them, sometimes going so far as to target them for fist fights after school, but every one of the kids Tom could remember who had gotten saddled with the name had grown up to lead perfectly normal lives – lives not so different from his own. Besides, the German he'd seen looked anything but sissy, so while Tom understood the unpleasant implications of Burl's accusation, he couldn't for the life of him fathom the connection Doc Randolph was making, and he said so.

"What does that have to do with Little Lenny Elliot, or David Williams, or Harold Ashton?"

"Quite simply, the man in question exhibits a debased morality, and this known deviance may be a single facet in a far more complex disturbance in his psyche."

"English, Doc."

"If he's capable of one crime, then he is capable of others. His sense of right and wrong is obviously distorted."

"Plenty of people will steal a nickel; it doesn't make them murderers."

"When all of this began, I told you about that killer, Albert Fish, and we discussed Jack the Ripper as well. In those cases, there was a sexual component to the crimes. Fish was a pedophile, a deviant against children, and his crimes included sexual molestation of the children he killed. One can extrapolate from the nature of Jack the Ripper's crimes, the violence against the female reproductive system, all the victims in the profession of sexual gratification, that he too was fulfilling an unwholesome sexual need. So if we use these as models, we might project that our murderer is likewise destroying that of which he is desirous. Homosexuality is not a common affliction, and though I did not discover any sexual interference of the victims that does not mean it didn't occur."

"You seem awfully confident," Tom said.

"You should talk to this man," Doc Randolph said.

〰

Tom didn't consider himself a worldly man, and generally he didn't lament his ignorance of the more cosmopolitan notions Doc Randolph threw around, but when it came to Ernst Lang – the man he drove across town to question – and the man's alleged sexual tastes, unusual as they were, Tom wished he had more information. He could rationalize Burl Jones's accusation against the German, but he felt nothing about it. Beyond schoolyard name calling and bullying, which all seemed to be based on some pale derivation of the actual sickness that had supposedly stricken Lang, Tom had no experience with the idea of homosexuality. Such things had never been discussed in his family's home or at the sheriff's office, and they didn't run stories about it in the *Barnard Register* or discuss it on the radio. So how was he supposed to feel about a subject that intellectually perplexed him and emotionally left him absolutely indifferent?

Parking the car across the street from Lang's house, Tom was reminded of a brief scene from Hemingway's *To Have and Have Not*, which he'd read a number of times in the last few years. Titles by Hemingway and Zane Grey made up the bulk of his home library, which consisted of less than twenty books occupying two whitewashed planks suspended by brackets on his living room wall. In the Hemingway novel two men had sat on a yacht, listening to Bach on a phonograph and bickering, and Tom had found their squabbling familiar, because he and Glynis had engaged in plenty of rows over the years. Further, he'd been amused by the way the author had written those two men the way he might write about a married couple, albeit a genuinely unhappy one, and he remembered finding the scene depressing because one of the men had seemed so trapped and forlorn and was contemplating suicide by scene's end.

He crossed the street thinking about this passage and wondered if Hemingway had been describing diseased men like the one he was about to meet. Then Tom wondered what possible difference it could make unless he decided to start a conversation about the book, which he didn't.

Tom knocked on the door and stepped away. He stood with his back straight and hands at his sides.

Remembering his first impression of Lang – the day he'd seen the man at the Fourth of July celebration – Tom recalled a powerful and cold thug who might very easily take the life of a boy. He'd felt intimidated by the blunt, scarred face and the German's unwavering stare, and standing on the man's porch, Tom felt a flutter of butterflies in anticipation of facing him again.

Lang opened the door, wearing a pair of gray slacks and no shirt. He was a short man, maybe five foot seven, if that. He carried an extra bit of weight on his frame, but the soft layer of flesh fell over the kind of muscle it took a lifetime of exertion to build. The man was badly scarred, and though Tom had seen worse in his day, these instances had been few. The scars on Lang's chest were small and round, and the sheriff suspected they were the souvenirs of bullet wounds. He counted three in all, then doubted his certainty of their cause when he noted their placement. No man could survive that kind of wounding he reasoned, not even this man with his bull build. Lang looked at Tom suspiciously and checked the street to the sheriff's back, as if expecting to see a posse on his heels.

"Yes?" he said curtly.

Tom introduced himself as the sheriff of Barnard, and asked if they could have a word or two.

"Yes," Lang said. "You come in. I will finish dressing."

"Were you going out?"

"Nuh," Lang called with no further explanation as he turned from the open door and walked to the hall on the far side of the living room.

The German had furnished his house sparsely with a small sofa covered in a rough green cotton fabric. A simple wooden rocking chair sat beside it and a lamp stood in the corner. There was a Montgomery Ward radio, but the walls were bare. No photographs. No pictures at all. The house was uncluttered and spotless, but the room's absolute lack of personal affects, of additional comforts beyond those of the barest minimum struck him as unnatural.

Lang reappeared wearing a short-sleeved white shirt that stretched tightly over his barreled chest. Shadows accentuated the deep scars on his cheeks and nose. He stood perfectly straight with his arms behind his back, looking like he was facing a firing squad, proud to give his life for a cause.

Tom walked closer to him and picked up the scent of rose water, the kind his wife had used on her neck when they were courting. The scent distracted him, reminding him of Glynis, whose memories engulfed and teased and added yet another layer to Tom's confusion.

"How can I help?" Lang asked.

"I have a few questions. You can sit if you like?"

"Nuh. Questions?"

"Just checking a few things. You're name is Ernst Lang?"

"Yes."

"And where do you work, Mr. Lang?"

"I am retired."

"Kind of young for that, aren't you?"

"I worked at the factory for a time, but the supervisor was inept. I make chairs now, but it is not a true vocation, merely a hobby."

Watching the German, Tom quickly got the impression the man had been questioned before. Lang did not seem the least bit shaken. His responses were direct, courteous and thorough.

"And how long have you lived in Barnard?"

"Seven years."

"But you were born in Germany?"

"Munich, yes."

"What brought you here?"

"I had reason to believe my homeland was no longer safe."

"The Nazis, huh?"

"Yes," Ernst replied. "Some of them."

Tom noted the oddity of this statement. *Some of them?*

"Can you tell me where you were last Saturday night?"

Lang's eyes changed then – little but a momentary flicker. If Tom hadn't been observing him so closely he would have missed it completely.

"Mitch's. It is out on the farm road."

"I'm familiar with it. Did you speak to anyone there? Anyone who could confirm what you're telling me?"

"I was only defending myself," Lang said dryly. "I did not start the fight, if that's what you think."

"You were in a fight?"

"I believed that was the reason for your interrogation."

"Didn't know a thing about it. When did you arrive at Mitch's?"

"Eight p.m."

"Did you drive there?"

"I walked. I always walk to conserve petrol for the war effort."

"And you walked home?"

"Nuh," he said. Again, uncertainty flashed in his eyes. "A friend drove me home."

"And what was this friend's name?"

"I'd rather not say."

"Excuse me?"

"I would prefer to keep that information to myself."

"It would be in your best interest to tell me."

"Yes? Would it? You still haven't told me why you are here."

"You know about those boys that were killed?"

"Sad business," Ernst said. "Is that why you are here? Because of those two boys?"

Tom noticed the man had said *two* boys, not three. The papers had been filled with stories about Little Lenny's disappearance, yet Lang only accounted for the Ashton and Williams boys in his question. Did that mean he was ignorant of the recent events, or had he just slipped and revealed that his latest victim was still alive?

"The boys are part of it."

"I know nothing of their deaths."

"We have some folks who aren't so sure. There's talk."

"People always talk. It's what makes them people."

"About you, I mean."

"And what do they say about Ernst?"

"Have you ever been married?"

"I prefer the company of men."

"That doesn't answer my question."

"But it should, yes? I have no use for women."

He made no attempt to refute the accusations of moral deviation Burl Jones had leveled against him, and an inexplicable discomfort settled over the sheriff. Lang struck Tom as masculine enough, certainly more masculine than many of the men in Barnard, yet what he confessed spoke against that and left Tom's mind in a knot.

"We had laws against such behavior in Germany, but it was ignored until the Nazis gained control. Do you have such laws here? Have I broken them?"

"I'm here because of those boys," he said, keeping the focus on matters he understood.

"And you believe that I am involved."

"Didn't you just admit to being a queer?"

"And you equate my deviation with that of a murderer of young men? I have hurt no one that did not try to hurt me first."

"You said you were in a fight."

"I have protected myself. Is that also a crime?"

"You don't look beat up."

"I know how to fight, Sheriff. It is one thing I am very good at."

"Is that how you got those?" Tom asked, indicating the German's face with a wave of his finger.

"I was injured in battle."

"You were in the war?"

"I was in *a* war. We did not win that war."

Was he talking about the Great War? He didn't look old enough, not that Tom knew the man's age.

"I am not the one who hurt those boys," Lang said. "You ask at Mitch's. They will tell you about Ernst."

"I intend to."

"Yes. Good. No more talk of it then." He broke his stiff-backed pose and walked up to the sheriff as if to show him out.

"We aren't finished here."

Lang's face clouded and when he replied his voice rumbled with anger.

"Then you take me to your jail until the next dead boy is found so that you are certain Ernst is not your criminal. I have been falsely accused before and I will not have it again. You arrest me and see. You will see I am no killer of children."

"Settle down, Mr. Lang. I just have a few more questions for you."

"Then ask them."

"Do you support the Nazi party?"

"Nuh," Lang said. "I was a socialist, many years ago, affiliated with a group that rose in power along with Hitler, though we viewed very different futures. I believed the government should serve its people; he believed the people should carry him to godhood. Ten years ago, he took action against us. Many men died in a few short days, and he was allowed to become the thing he is now."

"Were you attacked as well?"

"Yes. I was arrested and charged with treason, made a conspirator in a conspiracy that did not exist, all to gather the sheep around their shepherd. I should be dead, now. That is why I fled my country. My face is too well known for me to ever walk a German street in safety. I went to London and then to New York, and from there I traveled to New Orleans, and then here."

"Why here?" Tom asked.

"Another friend invited me."

"And what's his name?"

"I would prefer not to say, and it makes no difference. He is dead."

"Names would help your defense."

"I have nothing to defend myself against."

Tom continued his questions, asking the German where he was on the nights Harold Ashton and David Williams were abducted, and both times the German responded that he was at home alone. No one could confirm the information, but Tom's suspicions were already fading. Something about the man intimidated Tom, and the sheriff had no doubt that the German was capable of violence, but he did not think Ernst Lang had killed either of the boys or snatched Little Lenny Elliot. It might have been the man's composure or his honesty in answering the questions about his homosexual illness – Tom didn't know. The German had integrity, or perhaps a good façade of it.

Still Tom knew better than to trust a suspect at his word. He asked Ernst Lang to sit on the porch while Tom searched the house. The Elliot boy was still missing, and Tom checked every closet, every nook and the attic, but found no sign of a young man or the belongings of a young man. Nor did he find a Stetson or duster of any color, let alone of the gray Mrs. Reeves had described. He found a large ledger, bound in brown leather, and Tom leafed through it, noting the shape of Lang's penmanship, though unable to read any of the entries as they were written in German. He thought about the notes the killer had left and from memory compared them to the scrawl filling page after page of the journal, but the lettering seemed wholly different from the precise craftsmanship in the killer's notes. Noticing the chicken coop through the kitchen window, Tom let himself out into the backyard. Inside the wired fence, he kicked aside two hens as he made his way to the long narrow box. Lifting the lid, he felt a moment of dread, certain Little Lenny Elliot's dead eyes would greet him. Instead Tom saw four neat nests and boards covered in bird shit.

Upon finishing his search of Ernst Lang's home, he could not say the man was guilty, though he certainly wasn't ready to absolve him. Instead he called the sheriff's office from the phone in the German's kitchen, and asked Muriel to send Rex Burns out to Dodd Street. Tom wanted his deputy to park on the north side of the street near the middle of the block, and he wanted Rex to keep an eye on Lang's house. If the guy had snatched and hidden Little Lenny away, he could still lead them to the boy.

Then Tom asked the German back inside. He requested that Lang write "One less gun against the Reich," on a scrap of paper. The suspect did so without hesitation, but Tom had been unclear and Lang wrote the phrase in English. The second draft, this time in German, went into Tom's pocket. Though he wanted to give Rex ample time to drive across town to Dodd Street, Tom could think of no additional questions to ask of Lang. So he thanked the German and shook the man's hand, noting the strong dry grip, and said his good evening.

"You come back if you have more questions. I will be glad to help."

Tom pushed open the screen door and stepped onto the porch. A fly buzzed at his ear and Tom slapped it away. He looked across the field at the lake but it appeared as a pale blue smear, oddly unattractive beneath the scorching sun.

Noticing that the sheriff was not leaving, the German poked his head through the door. "Something else?" he asked.

"Are you really a queer?" Tom asked.

"Yes," Lang said without hesitation, "I am."

Western Union
A. N. Williams
President

1944 Aug 9   2 PM

THE SECRETARY OF WAR DESIRES ME TO EXPRESS HIS DEEP REGRET THAT YOUR HUSBAND PRIVATE FIRST CLASS FREDERICK RANDALL HAS BEEN REPORTED MISSING IN ACTION SINCE TWENTY THIRD JULY IN FRANCE IF FURTHER DETAILS OR OTHER INFORMATION ARE RECEIVED YOU WILL BE PROMPTLY NOTIFIED =

R A ULIO THE ADJUNCT GENERAL.

Seventeen: Tim Randall

The telegram arrived on Wednesday afternoon. I didn't hear the uniformed men knock on the door or my mother's attempt to greet them pleasantly. I'm sure she eyed the envelope the way she might an attacker's knife. Bum was helping his mother with chores around the Craddick house, so I was alone in my room, reading an old *Captain Marvel* comic when these sad events transpired. The first I knew of the note came when I got thirsty and went to the kitchen for a glass of water. Ma stood with her back to me and the phone against her ear. When she heard me walking behind her, she turned and tried to smile but it just made her look sick, and she let the smile fade, revealing a mask painted the grim shades of misery and loss. She told the caller that she'd call back and hung up the phone.

Though it was clear something terrible had happened, it did not occur to me that this dreadful news would concern my father. Another dead boy? was my first thought.

She asked me to sit at the kitchen table, and I saw the envelope lying beside an empty water glass. Sitting next to me, she turned her chair and put her hands on my shoulders and she ran a palm over my hair. Again, she tried to form that grotesque smile.

"We received a telegram today," she said.

I knew what that meant – everyone knew what it meant. The Washingtons had received a telegram to inform them of the heroic death of their son Chip. Mavis Clooney, who I'd seen through a cheap tin spyglass crying and laughing at the news from her radio, had received a telegram from the government about her husband. Despite the miserable expression on Ma's face, I quickly rationalized the news. The arrival of a telegram didn't mean my father was dead. Telegrams had been around long before the war. They'd been used to announce weddings and the births of children. I didn't want to know what our telegram said. If she never told me, I could go on believing that some distant cousin had just married a successful rancher in Seguin or Luling. My thoughts tumbled down this hill of optimism, scrabbling for purchase but finding little to hang on to.

"Your father is missing," Ma said with a cracking voice.

Then the tears came, and she pulled me into her arms, whispering about hope and prayers and telling me to be brave. From her hair and neck came the substantial fragrance of factory oil, and I remembered that before the war, she'd always smelled of flour and cinnamon. "Missing" became an enigma. It carried too many meanings in those moments, effectively making it meaningless. My father wasn't dead; he was "missing," and I no longer knew what the word meant, but every time the word appeared in my mind, a shock of sickness hit me in the stomach, an ice-cold spear driven through my navel, revolving and jabbing the tender tissues.

The word filled me, as unrelenting as the reek of factory oil wafting from my mother's flesh. There was no Cowboy. Harold Ashton and David Williams had never existed. I couldn't even picture my disturbed neighbor's face. There was only the feel of my mother's arms around me, the oil offending my nose, and the cryptic word.

The house soon filled with familiar faces. Rita Sherman was the first to arrive. She stormed into the house and immediately commandeered the place, setting on a pot of coffee and ushering me into my room to "clean up for company." My mother's parents arrived soon after, and my grandmother went to the table to join the other women while my grandfather stood in the corner of the kitchen – his pants hiked high on his great belly and arms crossed – with a hard frown cutting across his face as he gazed down on the women. Neighbors began arriving. I walked from the living room to the kitchen and back again, sorrowful faces hovering over me like ugly blossoms on tall plants, and they all said the same things: "We'll pray for Fred," "He's a strong man," "You be brave for your daddy."

Soon the odors from cooking food filled the house. The women who had gathered in the kitchen had begun the process of preparing a feast, and the men sat on the sofa and in the chairs in the living room, speaking quietly and I didn't know what I was supposed to do. I couldn't sit down. I couldn't distract myself with frying catfish or making biscuits. The freezing spear in my belly kept twisting, and I thought to dislodge the point with movement not understanding that it was the thing dragging me.

Unable to grasp what was expected of me, I disappeared into my bedroom and went to the window and pressed my cheek against the cool glass. A row of cars had formed in the dirt track next to the road. Across the street, Mr. Lang stood in his front yard staring at my father's house, and the sight of him incensed me.

This was his fault. Men like him had captured my father and thrown him in a cell, and they would cut him and beat him, and they'd laugh as they tortured him because that's the way Germans were. I thought about what I'd seen through Mr. Lang's window, the thing he'd done to that man – the worst thing one man can do to another – and the icy blade in my belly changed. It burned hot, searing the tissues so recently chilled.

I looked at his scarred face bathed in sunlight and found it monstrous. My fists tightened at my sides, mentally daring the German to come across the street and try to walk into my father's house. Right then, I believed I'd kill him if he tried it.

The Kraut son of a bitch.

The disgusting queer.

⁋

I was still sitting on the windowsill when my grandfather walked into my room. The German had disappeared into the shadows of his porch some time ago, but I kept my eyes on his house the way you keep an eye on a rabid dog in a distant field. My grandfather closed the bedroom door and crossed his arms over his enormous belly. The frown remained carved deep. Swollen pockets of wrinkled skin surrounded his eyes like small wasp nests, and his fleshy cheeks were red as if sunburned.

"Come away from the window, son," he told me.

I cast a final look at the yellow house across the street, and then did as I was asked, except I didn't know where else in the room to go. I settled for the bed and dropped onto it.

"You got a lot of people out there come to pay respects for your daddy," he said, his voice thick and warbling as if his vocal cords were as laden with fat as his belly. "It's not right you leaving your Ma alone with all of them folks, but I suspect you need some time to grieve on your own, and it's good not to make a show of it."

"Daddy's not dead," I muttered.

"Maybe he is and maybe he isn't," my grandfather said, "but one way or the other the man you knew won't be coming home. If he got himself hurt bad or if he got himself captured by the Krauts he's going to be changed. Even if those things didn't happen, he'll be changed because war does that to a man. Sometimes it's for the worse and sometimes it's for the better. You just don't know, and you have to be ready for that, because he may not be able to tell you it himself, and I know your ma isn't good at explaining things like this – complicated and all. So the sooner you get it in your head as a fact, the easier it's gonna be. We're praying your daddy is alive, but sometimes just being alive isn't the best thing for a man."

My grandfather had never said so many words to me before, and I wanted more than anything for the fat old man to shut up. His advice smacked of cruelty and inevitability, and maybe he didn't want Daddy to be dead like he said, but it sure sounded like he'd already buried the man.

"You think over what I said, and then you come on back out to be with your ma."

"Yes, sir."

Except I had no intention of thinking over what he'd said. My mind already raced with terrible thoughts of my own and there was no room for the callus old man's theories. After rising from the bed, I returned to the window and glared at the yellow house across the street.

The German was probably inside soiling some strange man, treating him like an animal. The memory of what I'd witnessed returned virulently, making my face hot and my stomach knot with sickness. He might have been killing another boy in there as friends and neighbors gathered in my daddy's house to pay their respects.

Eventually I left my room and found that the number of people in the house had tripled and swarms of concerned men and women huddled in the kitchen and living room, reminding me of the repast following David Williams' funeral, only no one had put on their Sunday clothes, and amid all of the quietly chatting neighbors and family, I wanted to scream, "He's not dead. He's just missing. Don't you stupid hayseeds know the difference?" but I kept the fury contained and wandered through the crowd, accepting premature condolences and falsely optimistic words of faith, prayer, and hope. Every palm that fell on my shoulder or patted my back took a little of me away on it. My grandfather stood against the back door, arms still crossed, watching over the room like a clean-shaved Santa Claus supervising a crew of inept elves. Women fussed and bickered at the stove as if they could create an adequate cure for grief by adding the right amount of salt or butter to a recipe. Ma sat at the kitchen table, flanked by her mother and Rita Sherman, and I pushed my way through to them. My grandfather approved of my actions with a shallow nod of his round head.

My presence was wholly unnecessary and I saw that right from the start. Ma cried and the women at her sides held and consoled her as best they could, and I thought to leave her to them, worried that the women would turn their comfort on me.

Imagining their soft perfumed bodies crushing in from both sides struck me as no different from drowning, and my nerves were too agitated to endure such a suffocating prospect. It was better to move and keep moving. I stopped long enough to put my arm around my mother to let her know I was there, and she stroked my cheek and asked if I wanted something to eat, and I told her I didn't, and I stayed for a minute – though it felt more like an hour – and excused myself, making my way back to the living room, not checking with my grandfather for his approval.

Then I was back in the theater of the absurd, its performers sending me conflicting messages. "You be strong. You're the man of the house now." "He'll be home before Christmas, just you wait and see." "He was a fine man. You should be very proud." "He just got separated from his men. I bet he's already back at camp and the telegram hasn't gotten here yet." And they insisted on patting me and squeezing my arm and shaking my hand, and bits of me clung to their hands like mud, and before I'd made it to the front door, I felt empty. Even my anger had receded to a ticking rhythm at my temples, hardly distinguishable from the hum of desolation in my chest.

More people had gathered on the porch, but there was nothing left of me for them to take, so I let them bestow their hope and grief and I let them pat my back, and I stared at the German's house across the street. Dust and pollen – or maybe it was just my agitation – cast a scrim of grit across the scene. I imagined I could see every sun-bleached speck in the air, every piece of filth that separated me from the degenerate who'd chosen my street to live on.

I thought of Daddy trapped in that house, imagined his Nazi captors had shipped him home to be tortured by our neighbor. The German's disgusting grimace eclipsed my father's face, and his muscled body moved perversely against him, and then Hugo Jones was standing beside me, and he said, "Hey, kid."

The blemishes on his face looked particularly inflamed on that afternoon, and it occurred to me that perhaps Hugo wore his anger in his skin instead of in his chest the way I had before its retreat to tick away like a beetle in my head.

"Hey, Hugo," I replied.

"I'm sorry about your daddy," he said, awkwardly.

"Yeah," I said, unable to come up with yet another response to a phrase I'd heard a hundred times already.

It never occurred to me to ask why Hugo had come to my house. We weren't friends and our families weren't close, but the house had filled with a spectrum of well wishers – some familiar and others nameless, so his presence struck me as normal enough.

"He's a hero," Hugo continued, "an honest to God hero."

"I guess."

Then we fell silent and I turned my gaze to the yellow house across the street.

Finally, Hugo said, "I'm sorry about clobbering you the other day."

I'd forgotten about the incident, or had simply chosen not to think about it. I told him it was okay.

"It's just we can't take any chances these days," he said. "It's like we're at war here, too, and I know you're not a snitch or anything – you're a good guy – but when I heard you were following us...."

Though I hadn't been following him and his friends that night, I didn't bother correcting him. Instead I kept my eyes on the shadowed porch of the German's house.

"Sheriff didn't do a damn thing about that faggot," Hugo said as if we'd been talking about my neighbor all along. "My daddy told him what we saw, told him everything, and the fool sheriff went on over to have a nice chat with the guy, like they were buddies or something."

"That's not right," I replied.

"Damn straight it ain't right. He's over there killing our friends. Hell, he's probably got Little Lenny tied up in his attic right now, and what's the sheriff doing about it? Nothing, that's what. If Sheriff Tom Rabbit had an ounce of man about him, we'd already have that Nazi fucker strung up in the center of town."

"Somebody ought to do something," I said.

"You're right about that. Get some men and some guns and show that faggot what God thinks of his Nazi ass."

Then someone was calling my name, and I turned to the front walk and saw Bum hurrying over the grass. At first, he looked like a stranger or someone long removed from my acquaintance, as if he didn't belong in my life anymore. Sweat ran over his face and had painted dark ovals on his shirt beneath his armpits, and his black hair lay messily over his brow. Before he reached the porch, I threw another glance at the yellow house, and the last words I'd said to Hugo whispered through my thoughts: *Somebody ought to do something.*

Eighteen: The German

August 9, 1944 – translated from the German

I feel sad for my neighbor Tim today. I hear the cars pulling up to the house and the people in the street, and my first thought is that Tim and his mother are having an afternoon party. The drawn expressions of concern on the guests' faces quickly snuff such light-hearted thoughts. I walk up to a man and woman just stepping out of their car. Both appear to have been molded from bread dough, their faces lumpy and pale. When I inquire of this flabby couple what is happening, the woman scowls at the sound of my voice, but the man responds curtly as if speaking to a servant, telling me that Tim's father is missing in battle, and the man adds that I should think twice about visiting the house.

I take his meaning and retreat to my yard, where I stand for some time watching the grieving people arrive and those who have gathered on the porch, and I think that I should pay my respects, but understand I may not be welcome as I share the nationality of those who have hurt this family, and besides have nothing in the way of gift – food or flower – to offer with my sympathies, so I stand at the foot of my porch and observe until the ringing of the phone draws me inside.

It is the unremarkable man, and my sorrow for Tim and his family is distracted. A tingle rises on the back of my neck and trickles down my shoulder blades to gather and warm in my chest. My physical reaction to the sound of his voice startles me, and I soon feel the pull of a smile stretching my lips. He tells me that his mother and sister will be returning soon and he cannot stay on the telephone long, but he wanted to hear my voice, and I tell him that I am glad he has called.

"I may be in Barnard in a couple of days," he says. "The factory orders are still coming in, and I have a meeting with a manager at the paper mill to look at some of their equipment."

"Then you should come to dinner," I tell him.

"I was hoping you'd say that."

Then he makes a terrible joke about fat sausages and though the humor is low and predictable, I find myself laughing along and adding euphemisms of my own, and the conversation sparks many fond memories for me, memories of laughter and warmth, of time spent sharing opinions and bawdy insinuations with men who did not fear being overheard – men who claimed their identities and did not secrete them away behind rigid masks. For several minutes I lose myself to the heartening exchange and think how very much I want the unremarkable man in my home and my hands so that we can continue speaking as friends without the concern of his family's interruption, but too soon he announces the return of his sister and apologizes that he must hang up, and I tell him it was nice that he called and I hope to see him when he visits the city next.

He tells me, "You're a dream come true."

And I am without words, so I hang up the phone aware that I share his sentiment.

A moment of remorse comes and goes as I cross my kitchen to the back door and grab the pan of chicken feed from its shelf. I am very happy but across the street my neighbor Tim is terribly sad. He did not share bitterness with his father as I had mine, and my heart – a second before light with the unremarkable man's voice – clenches tightly in my chest and I grieve for the boy, and this reaction astounds me with its suddenness and its clarity because I've always found the tragedies of war unsurprising and I have seen intimates murdered in the streets and fallen in fields and have felt their blood run through my fingers, and my thoughts were never for the companion lost, but rather trained on the enemies that had taken them. Vows of retaliation blossomed on those occasions not grief, and now I remember so few of their names.

The fat hens greet me at the door to their pen and I shake the shallow tin above their heads, scattering feed over the dirt, and I smile at the birds as they turn from me and waddle and cluck and peck at the dry kernels and seeds.

"You eat good," I tell them. "Today I don't hate you so much."

Watching my birds, my mind wanders. The emotions that delight me are not new, but they are so poorly maintained I'm surprised they continue to function.

I remember affection so easily attained that it seemed perpetual, a constant in which only faces and bodies changed. I remember seeing a poor sketch of my face on a tattered newspaper beneath the words "The Traitor is Dead."

I remember a marble pool filled with steaming water and beautiful men, and the feeling of my heart racing as I decide on my next companion. Moisture beaded on flesh, captured on hair like smooth crystals. Steam making the chamber a hazy vision. My eyes fall on a sinewy youth with wisps of blond hair pasted to his chest. Others have noticed this boy, and an ugly old man with a mole on his neck has cornered him and chats heatedly even as the boy tries to escape his attentions, and it is my intention to swim across the pool and interrupt this old man's unwholesome seduction and claim the sinewy youth as my own, knowing none in this place would question or deny me, but before I push away from the pool's wall, another young man appears on the marble ledge above me, and he is very broad and smooth and muscular, and he has shaved his mustache very thin and cropped his hair in the manner of mine, and were it not for his brawn and the unmarred skin of his cheeks, I might have thought myself looking at a mirror image of myself at his age. He is bold and drops into the water next to me and apologizes for splashing my face. Close to me the resemblance to my younger self remains strong, and I look at this boy with a profound sense of desire, because he appears the way I wish I could appear. Unlike this boy, my face is scarred and my body is tremendously soft from years of opulent meals, and I know that my merit as an intimate is directly related to the position of authority I hold. He makes no pretense at seduction but flatly states he wants to share a room with me, and I cast a look at the blond boy and his ugly suitor and find they are embracing.

The owner of this bath is an old acquaintance and keeps his finest room available to me, and I lead this boy to it. Along the way, he tells me his name is Ernst and he knows my name is Ernst, as well, and he knows of my position and comments often on my accomplishments, going so far as to remark on my commission in Bolivia. Despite his admiration, I grow tired of his voice and once we are in the room, I push him to the bed and fall on top of him and silence his accolades with my lips, and we fuck violently and then tenderly and then violently again and then, exhausted, I order one of the servants of the bath to bring us champagne. I was drunk when I met this boy and feel the sharp edges of sobriety returning. The champagne arrives and I place a second order for whiskey, and this youthful Ernst and I drink and talk and smoke cigars and the champagne is gone and much of the whiskey, and we fuck again and agree to meet in the baths a week later.

That night is much like the first. The next the same, and I think to invite him on holiday with me to Bad Wiessee but before I suggest this rendezvous he tells me he loves me and adores me, and I tell him that is woman's talk – the talk of wives – and I need no wife. Further, I sense he has grown too near to me, reciting much of my history as if it were his own. I've endured obsession once before and found it to be less than congenial, so my resolution to silence its echo is adamant. I regret this decision only because the boy's company brings lightness to my heart, but the misery on his face when I speak of distance is a cold spike in my chest, freezing all that it pierces, and I leave, refusing to see him again.

A strange thought follows this memory, and it is of this other, younger Ernst taking a blade to his face so that it will more resemble mine. This fancy – so like a memory – disturbs me, and I wonder if a boy's life could ever be so sad that he would willingly trade it for another man's.

I chuckle at the pecking chickens and scatter more feed for them as I am feeling generous, and I put away these bizarre notions. The unremarkable man's voice returns to me, bringing happiness and a profound calm, and the past and my place in it are forgotten as I recall our conversation and our moments of intimacy. I tell myself he is not unremarkable at all.

He tells me I am a dream.

Nineteen: Tim Randall

The day after the telegram arrived the house was dreadfully quiet. Ma didn't listen to her records or the radio; she didn't do anything at all except sit in the kitchen, drinking coffee and smoking cigarettes until Rita arrived, and then the two whispered and sampled the leftover salads and hot dishes prepared by our neighbors. Anger remained ticking in my head and I felt hollowed out and simultaneously bloated as if my stomach had expanded and hardened to stone, crushing the other organs to make room for the vast nothing at my center. Rita barged into my bedroom and sat on the edge of the bed, fixing a motherly frown of concern on me. With her make-up applied so thickly, her lips like bloody open wounds, she resembled a particularly cruel clown, even though her eyes were soft and warm and veined from crying. She rattled off a list of chores – picking up the yard, straightening my room, sweeping the porch – like these things were gifts she was giving me. My only response was a shrug and she grew stern, telling me that my mother shouldn't be bothered with such petty tasks. I got angry with her but I said nothing.

I didn't want to pick up the yard or sweep the porch, because I didn't want to be out front in view of my neighbor, the German. He'd see the pain on my face – or maybe he'd see the depth of the emptiness inside of me – and he'd take pride in knowing I hurt. Instead I picked up my room, and though it was an effort of half measures, I'd done something. Rita returned and nodded at the progress and pointed at the tumbling stack of comic books by the bed.

"I don't understand why you read those awful things," she said.

"Then don't read them," I responded, taking great joy in the astonishment my comment had brought to Rita's face.

Her dismay quickly resolved into simmering anger and she put her hands on her hips and pursed her ugly wound-red lips. "You pick those up or I'll burn them."

"And I'll get my daddy's rifle."

Another flare of shock lit her face, making her eyes grow wide and her mouth open in an O of disbelief.

"Timothy Randall," she snapped. "I will not have you talk to me that way."

I shrugged.

"Do you know what your mother is going through right now?" Rita asked. "She is suffering the torture of a Christian martyr."

"She's suffering you," I said, glaring at the fat woman in the doorway.

My mother arrived just then and she told Rita to leave me be, and Rita was outraged, launching into her account of what had happened. Ma interrupted her.

"Just leave him be," she said, sounding exhausted. She grasped her friend's arm and led her into the hall.

Rita cast a final furious glance my way and then followed my mother back to the kitchen. Then the house was silent again.

I couldn't stand it. The quiet fell around me like a tomb and then like a coffin, pressing in on my back and chest and shoulders all at once until I couldn't breathe. I ran out of my room and through the house until I reached the porch, and after checking to make sure the German wasn't watching me, I raced to the street and sprinted away.

〰

I'd thought to distract myself with the shops downtown, but this turned out to be a mistake. It seemed everyone in town knew me and had heard the fate of my father, which was wholly impossible, yet every pair of eyes that fell on me seemed to hold pity, and these compassionate glances only fueled my anxiety. Why did people have to look at me? Why couldn't they mind their own business?

I walked to the Ranger's Lodge, where they'd found the body of David Williams, and from there I continued to Santa Anna Street and headed south to the small white clapboard bus station. A gray bus pulled away from the loading platform as I approached, leaving two women in long green dresses standing in a cloud of dust. The women put their hands on their wide-brimmed hats as if to hold them in place through a wind gust, and they bent low, using the hats as screens against the powdery haze. Once the dust had settled both women grasped the handles of their suitcases and carried them off the low wooden platform, heading across the street toward St. David's Church. I stepped onto the planks and walked to the far side to take a seat on a long and narrow wooden bench.

I'd sat on this bench while my mother said goodbye to Daddy, and I'd watched them kiss – quickly and discreetly at first, and then more passionately as Ma's tears drew shimmering lines down her cheeks – and this is where I'd waved goodbye to my father as he climbed into the bus. He never turned to see my farewell gesture, but his own hand was lifted high, the back of it presented as the shadows of the bus engulfed him, and he took a seat on the far row across the aisle so that I couldn't see him through the window, and the bus pulled away, raising one of a thousand clouds of dust that would dot Barnard in the course of that day. Looking around the station platform I thought how desolate this side of the city looked, barren like a ghost town. Even the church across the street looked solemn and vacant, sitting on a bed of cracked clay earth. This was where I'd seen my father for the last time. Our final moments had been spent in this bleak, dusty, and dismal spot, and his last words to me were "See you soon." I thought about the notes he'd sent me, scraps of paper included in the real letters he sent to Ma, and they struck me as inadequate and cheap, and he should have told me about himself – anything about himself and what he was going through – but his notes had almost nothing to do with him or with me: *We're giving them a good run, Timmy. Be sure to behave yourself and mind your mother. Your father, Fred Randall.* And it wasn't enough, because it wasn't anything at all. I let myself hate him then. The anger flared. Then it died, receding to the beetles-in-the-walls ticking sound I'd grown accustomed to.

The stationmaster, who might have looked like a movie star were it not for the kidney shaped birthmark covering his neck and jaw, came outside and removed his cap. He noticed me on the bench and asked if he could help me. I got up and walked in the direction of town without replying.

I came upon Hugo and Ben and Austin as I rounded the corner onto Main Street. The three stood outside of Delrubio's. Hugo and Austin, who fidgeted like he was attached to an electric wire, smoked cigarettes in the shade, and Ben leaned against the drugstore's brick wall, his Stetson pushed low to shade his eyes. Hugo noticed me and lifted his hand in a half-wave and called me over. This seemed to amuse Austin Chitwood, until Hugo slapped the laughter out of the guy by backhanding him in the chest. Austin coughed out a thick cloud of cigarette smoke and hacked around the question, "What in the hell, Hugo?"

"Hey, buddy," Hugo said to me. "You doing okay?"

"I suppose."

"Good," he said.

"Yeah, Tim," Ben said. "I'm real sorry to hear about your daddy."

"Fucking Krauts," Austin added. "Can't trust a one of them. Killing everybody, even women and children. It ain't right."

"Daddy's just missing," I said, but it sounded wrong in my ears; it sounded like a lie.

"That's right," Hugo said. "I just hope they didn't take him prisoner is all."

The way he said it was ominous. My throat clenched tight around my reply so I kept silent.

"Better to die in battle," Austin said, shaking his head, "while he's still a man."

"Sure," I managed to say, though I didn't understand.

"They're all queer like Lang," Hugo said. "They prefer to fuck children, but they do it to prisoners, too. Take away their manhood so they won't try to be heroes, because a real and true man would rather rot in a cell then have to admit having that happen to him."

"Rather die," Austin said.

"But you don't have to worry about that," Hugo quickly added. "I bet your daddy just got lost in some woods, separated from his squad. He's probably killing a dozen Nazis an hour, working his way back to camp."

"Sure," I said, not convinced.

"That's the way it is," Hugo said. "I'm sure that's right. Your daddy is fighting on God's side, so you don't have to worry about him."

"It's that German across the street you should be worried about," Austin said, scratching behind his ear like a dog with fleas.

Hugo dropped his cigarette and ground it into the sidewalk and then immediately lit another. He looked up and down the street. A group of five Mexican women walked toward us, wearing loose dresses in vibrant shades of yellow, blue, and red, and he stepped back next to Ben. I did the same, waiting for the women to pass.

When they did, he said, "Austin's right, you know. We can't trust that horseshit sheriff to do what's right. I guess we've already seen that."

"I guess so," I said.

"We were thinking about doing something about him."

"Somebody should do something," I agreed.

"We might just," Hugo said.

"Like what?"

"Can't say," Hugo told me. "He's a queer and a murderer. It's man's business and we can't take any chances. Now don't get me wrong, I'm not saying you're a baby or anything like that, but you might get scared, lose your spine and go yellow."

"I'm no coward," I said.

"Not saying you are," Hugo replied. "I'm just saying that we can't take any chances. That Cowboy is tricky. He fooled Sheriff Rabbit easy enough, fooled everybody, so we have to step lightly."

I protested and promised, but the older boy released only the tiniest bits of information, bread crumbs to follow into a forest. Whenever anyone approached we all fell silent, waiting for them to pass. Ben and Austin nodded and added their agreement to Hugo's line of thinking, and the thing that most stuck with me was that these older boys were treating me like an equal, like a friend. They didn't censor their language or talk down to me. Hugo even offered me a puff of his cigarette, which I took, choking terribly on the smoke as he patted my back and told me, "It happens to everyone the first time."

They had included me in their conversation, and as it progressed, I realized with great pleasure that I was also being included in their plan.

Everything Hugo said made sense. His words illuminated the crimson gem of my anger, refracting and reflecting as it hit the facets of my rage, and the splinters of light it cast off crystallized, creating dangerous edges. They never revealed the details of their plan – what they intended to do to the German – but nonetheless I felt certain it would be the right thing, and by the time our conversation wound down I was entrenched in the darkness and Hugo held the only light, and I couldn't have found my way out on my own if I'd wanted to.

"You just put all of this out of your head until tomorrow," Hugo instructed. "We have plans of our own tonight, and you can't get mixed up in it. If you see that German piece of shit, you act nice like everything is just peachy. Don't let him know you're on to him. Then tomorrow you come to my house after your Ma goes to the factory. You'll receive your orders then."

"And don't tell anyone," Austin put in. "You keep this quiet."

"I will," I promised, though they hadn't told me anything at all.

"Good," Ben muttered from his place against the wall.

"We're going to show that son of a bitch he can't get away with his shit here," Hugo said. "He's got himself a real lesson to learn about that."

I walked home, swollen with pride, knowing I would be helping to teach the German his lesson.

⁘

Bum waited on my porch. I walked down Dodd Street, still wrapped in a sense of purpose and maturity, and I even managed to smile. When I looked at the German's house my smile did not falter; I wouldn't let it. The honed edges of my anger shifted upon seeing the place, jabbing and cutting at my gut, but I wouldn't show it on my face.

The German had fooled me. Tricked me. He'd pretended we were friends, even helped me once, but it was all a lie. He only wanted me to think I could trust him so that when he came to take me, to rape me and kill me, I wouldn't struggle. He'd probably done the same thing to Harold and David and Little Lenny Elliot. He was tricky, just the way Hugo had said. Well, let him try to fool me again, I thought. Just let him try.

Bum greeted me with a solemn handshake, and looking at his round, boyish face, I again felt that he didn't belong in my life anymore. We were friends but friends separated by a widening gap. He didn't understand my tragedy, and nothing he could say would alleviate the pain or the anger.

We spent the evening mostly in my room, saying little. He tried to get me to talk, but my thoughts had drifted to the yellow house across the street, where my missing daddy and those dead boys and every other misery I'd ever encountered resided. He stayed over night, sleeping on my bedroom floor like a protective hound, but I couldn't sleep. I went to the window a few times, but mostly stayed in bed, staring at the ceiling and wondering what Hugo and Ben and Austin had planned for the German.

And the thought warmed me, bouncing off the ruby of hate behind my ribs, lighting it up and making it grow.

Twenty: The German

August 11, 1944 – Translated from the German
The chickens are dead.

Their necks are wrung and their white bodies lie in the dirt of the backyard. I should have heard this happening, but my sleep was deeper than it has been in ages, rustled only by pleasant dreams. The gate of the back fence stands open and someone has carved a swastika in the wood, and my birds are dead.

Who has done this thing?

Twenty-One: Sheriff Tom Rabbit

Tom was at home having supper when the call from Big Lenny Elliot came through. His stomach couldn't take any more of the greasy food at Bob's Stop so he'd driven home, and had just sat down to a plate of grilled chicken and bell peppers Estella had prepared for him when the phone rang. His gut curdled at the sound, and he leaned back in the chair for a deep breath before standing and lifting the phone from the wall.

"I don't know how to tell you this, Sheriff," Big Lenny's drawling voice said. "But Little Lenny just walked through the door."

"Excuse me?" Tom said.

"The damn fool ran off to enlist, the way everyone thought Harold Ashton did. Folks made such a fuss about how brave and noble Harold was, Little Lenny got in his head to follow through on what Harold, God rest his soul, couldn't. He left a note but one of the young 'uns dragged it off the counter and painted over it with molasses, and neither Kathy nor I ever saw the damn thing. Then the damn fool tells the army he's seventeen and they pack him on home. Didn't even have enough sense to get his lie right."

"He's home?" Tom said, feeling tendrils of relief easing into his veins. This was about the only good news he'd had in weeks.

"Sorry we put you through the ringer on this one, Sheriff. I've a good mind to tan him from here 'til Tuesday, but I'm so damn happy to see him."

"Then leave your belt on and shake his hand," Tom said. "I'm glad everything worked out this way."

"Amen," Big Lenny said. "Amen."

"Thanks for calling, Lenny. Have a good night."

Tom hung up the phone and leaned against the wall, feeling positively light in his skin. Estella looked at him and smiled.

"Good news?" she asked.

"Very good news," he said.

The girl stepped up to Tom and pressed her cheek to his chest and said, "I am happy about it."

Tom remained motionless against the wall as if pinned by a stone and not the slight body of a beautiful girl. Estella wrapped her arms around his waist and peered up at him with her soft, chocolate-colored eyes, a look she'd frequently offered before Tom had invited her across the threshold of his bedroom, but he felt no desire for Estella now. She appeared younger to him, perhaps too young, and he thought back on their nights of intimacy with more than a little shame, though he didn't understand what element in their relationship had changed.

She'd come to his room two nights ago and he'd sent her away claiming exhaustion, which, while not strictly a lie – as he hadn't enjoyed a full night's sleep in weeks – was also not completely true. She was still beautiful, but Tom no longer drew desire from that beauty, and when he tried to pinpoint the moment his feelings about the girl had changed, he found himself at a loss.

Tom gently grasped Estella's shoulders and pushed her away. The warm expression on her face changed to one of confusion and then embarrassment.

"I am sorry," she muttered, lowering her head.

"Don't be sorry," he said still holding her shoulders. "You haven't done anything to be sorry about. I just have to get to the station. These days even good news requires a lot of work."

He smiled at the girl, but she continued looking at the floor. A needle of inexplicable guilt pierced his chest as he stepped away. At the door, holding his hat in his hands, he looked back at the girl in the kitchen, head down, arms crossed over her stomach looking so terribly unhappy and he tried to conjure a phrase that might make her feel better, but his tongue and his mind were dry.

Tom put on his hat and left the house. In the Packard he lit up a cigarette and smoked, trying to file and understand his maddening emotions, all the while telling himself he should return to the kitchen and Estella and try to explain what was in his head, except he didn't know what was in his head. So he finished the smoke and drove away.

⫘

At the station he instructed Muriel to call Walter back from Dodd Street. The surveillance on Ernst Lang had produced nothing of value, and with Little Lenny Elliot safe at home, the reason for having the German watched had been eliminated. There were better uses for the manpower. Besides, Tom still had strong doubts about Lang as a suspect in the Cowboy murders, no matter what Burl Jones or Doc Randolph said. Then he told her to get on the phone with Marty over to the *Barnard Register* and let the reporter know, Little Lenny was safe and sound.

Back in his office, Tom tried reading. A pile of reports had grown from the top of his desk – mostly interviews his men had conducted with suspects – and he needed to make a dent in the stack before he called it a night.

His mind wasn't on the work though. For the first time since Harold Ashton's body had been found, the business of the Cowboy became a secondary consideration.

Estella was in his thoughts, and he found it impossible to reconcile his feelings for the girl, which more and more resembled shame. They'd shared a bed several times in the last seven months, and he'd never given it a second thought – outside of pleasant reminiscences when he was away from her. He had never once forced her either physically or by threat to be with him, and she had invariably been the one to initiate their love-making usually by waiting in the hall outside of his room, yet he still felt as if he'd taken advantage of the girl.

But why? he wondered. What had changed?

He still thought of Estella as a wonderful girl, more so now that she had picked up a bit of the language, and he enjoyed hearing her voice in the house, glad that she no longer remained a mute spirit, flitting through the rooms. It made no sense that he should find her age inappropriate now, yet he did.

The certainty that he had done something wrong gnawed at him, and he chewed back, grinding his thoughts to mush, hoping an answer would appear in the gruel. He eventually decided it had to be the business with the Cowboy. The crimes and his inability to protect those young boys must have been getting to him. He didn't know how that might be, but it was an explanation he could accept even in its imprecision.

Twenty-Two: Tim Randall

Anticipation built in me throughout the day. Bum left early so he could get home to his chores, and I promised to call him later, though I had no intention of doing so. When I said goodbye, it felt like a real goodbye – one that genuinely ended an association. The minutes dragged. I found myself in a constant state of motion, going to the living-room window to observe the German's house; going to my room to pick up a comic book only to drop it after the first page failed to tame my wild thoughts; going to the kitchen and finding nothing appealed to my appetite; flipping through the radio dial, finding nothing important enough, funny enough, or exciting enough to keep my attention; and then back to the window to keep an eye on my neighbor, hoping with all my heart he stayed home so our operation wouldn't be postponed. I didn't know Hugo's plan, and that made the waiting all the harder. Speculation created myriad possibilities, and my mind fired like a machine gun barrage. I pictured the filthy German sitting on his couch with his hands tied in his lap and a hangdog expression on his scarred face as we presented him with irrefutable evidence of his guilt; I saw the man sobbing and begging for understanding, trying to bribe us so we didn't turn him in; I imagined the sheriff shaking my hand and congratulating me for my part in the deviant killer's capture. Childish thoughts woven from a thousand threads of radio-drama plot, where the hero was never in any genuine danger and always saved the day.

After a morning and afternoon of agitation, I was grateful when my mother appeared in the living room, wearing her work clothes and carrying her handbag and a sack supper. Between the threat of the Cowboy and the telegram from the government, my mother had taken several days off work, and she apologized and told me she had to go or she might lose her job. Her supervisor was already grumbling about her absences, making threats, and she wished she could stay home with me but she couldn't, and I said it was okay because I wanted her to go. I had plans of my own.

I waited ten agonizing minutes after my mother left to make sure she was well on her way to the factory and wouldn't be returning because she'd forgotten her kerchief or compact, and then I hurried outside to my bike. I was so eager to learn my role in the night's events I wasn't paying attention to the road and nearly got run down at the intersection by a delivery truck.

Hugo met me outside of his house, a two-story farmhouse with peeling lime green paint and a tattered roof, and he told me we would talk outside because his daddy was home with his little brothers, and he didn't want anyone overhearing. There wasn't much to hear.

"I want you to get him out of his house," Hugo said.

"How am I supposed to do that?"

"He doesn't know you're on to him," Hugo said. "Ask him to help you with a favor. We just need him out of his house for ten or fifteen minutes."

"When?"

"Ben and Austin are meeting me after supper. We'll drive over to the lake, probably park a couple of blocks away and walk it so he doesn't see the car. Just keep an eye on your front window. When you see us walk past, you get him out of the house and you keep him busy."

"Then what?"

"Send him on home. Leave the rest to us."

I frowned at this, feeling that I was being left out.

"You've got the most important job," Hugo said immediately. "If you don't get him out of the house, the whole plan is shit. Now head on home and keep your eyes peeled. If he goes out on his own you call."

"Okay," I said, uncertainly. "But what are you going to do?"

"You'll know soon enough," Hugo said. "Now head on home."

He turned around and walked inside. Much of the excitement I'd brought with me remained there on the front lawn. My job seemed so small and hardly important, no matter what Hugo said, and I didn't have any idea what kind of excuse I'd use to get the German out of his house. I couldn't exactly invite him to go swimming or to have him over to supper.

I pushed my bike to the intersection, feeling dejected. These feelings rapidly changed when I took the corner and saw a familiar face.

"Are you crazy?" Bum asked.

"What are you doing here?"

"What are *you* doing here?" he replied. He fixed me with a frown, and I shook my head at his childish expression. "Since when did you and Hugo become best pals?"

"Go home," I said. "You wouldn't understand."

"What are you up to?"

"Nothing. It's no big deal. He was just apologizing for hitting me the other day."

"I thought he did that at your house?"

"Well, he wanted to apologize again. Why are you following me anyway?"

"Because you're my friend," he said.

"Friends don't spy on each other."

"They don't lie to each other either," he said, sounding wounded. "Is this about your father?"

"It's about a lot of stuff, and you should mind your business."

"You're acting like a damn fool," Bum said. "Now tell me what's what."

"No."

"You're up to something, and I'm not going anywhere until you tell me what it is."

I knew how stubborn Bum could be, and I knew he'd recognize a lie the moment it left my lips. My only chance to get rid of him was to tell him something he would believe. So I made him swear an oath on his Ma's life, and then I told him what was what.

⫙

Bum tried a dozen times to talk me out of helping Hugo as I sat at the window. His thin, insistent voice grated at my ears, and I wanted him to shut up, but he kept on. Then I saw Hugo and the others strutting down the street, talking and laughing, and Ben Livingston swung a stick through the air like a baseball bat, and Austin Chitwood covered his mouth, suppressing a laugh, and Hugo seemed to be ignoring them both, marching ahead like a general, leading unwieldy troops.

"Don't go over there," Bum said. "Please, Tim, just stay here and listen to the radio, and if they come to the house send them away."

"Somebody's got to stop him," I said.

"Mr. Jones already reported him to Sheriff Rabbit," Bum pointed out. "You think if there was a doubt in his mind the sheriff would let Mr. Lang loose?"

"Sheriff Rabbit is as dumb as a mule's ass."

"Now you just sound like Hugo."

"Well maybe Hugo is right. You saw what he was doing to that man. You saw it."

"But he didn't kill him," Bum said. "You watched that man walk right out of his house and drive away."

"Did you ever think they might be in it together?"

My nerves were on edge, and I wanted to get moving, get it over with, like jumping into a cold lake all at once so my body would adjust to the temperature. Bum could flap his jaw all night long and it wasn't going to change what we'd seen or what needed to be done. How could my best friend be so blind? It seemed he just didn't want to see the truth. I decided Bum was afraid, and I understood that, but my daddy wasn't a coward and he hadn't raised a coward.

"You should just go home," I said. "You'll just make a mess of things."

Bum was stricken by my words. His face fell and it looked childish to my eyes.

"I'm not going anyplace," Bum said. "Somebody's got to look after you."

"I can look after myself," I said. "But if you come along just stay out of the way, and you remember the oath you took. You don't tell anybody about what we're doing until Sheriff Rabbit arrests him. We'll be heroes and there'll be plenty of time to tell our story then."

"Heroes," Bum whispered, unconvinced.

"If you're staying help me get the leg off of that table."

⫲

Hugo's instructions looped in my mind like a scratched phonograph recording – *get him out of the house, ten or fifteen minutes, get him out....* My hands shook violently as I crossed the street and climbed the German's porch steps. Next to me, Bum looked around the neighborhood anxiously, probably worried that a neighbor would see us, but I wasn't concerned about that. Folks were eating dinner. They wouldn't come out to their stoops until sunset, once the hellacious heat of the day had subsided. I felt scared enough, but my fear was focused on what lay behind Ernst Lang's door, not the interference of nosy neighbors.

The German opened the door and seemed surprised to see Bum and me, and a bolt of dread ran through me. My thoughts scrambled and when the German said, "Hello, boys," neither Bum nor I replied. His brow clouded and he opened the door further. He stood on the threshold looking over our shoulders at the street. "Is something wrong?"

"No, sir," Bum muttered.

Hearing my friend's voice brought me back to myself. He sounded so guilty and scared, I had to cover for the both of us.

"You look upset," the German said.

"No," I said, finally able to unknot my tongue. "Well sort of. I just…we kind of goofed. We didn't mean any harm, but we sort of broke something."

"What did you break?"

"A table. We broke one of its legs and we don't know how to get it back on, and I know you make those great chairs, and…."

"How did you break this table?"

"Bum fell on it," I said.

I didn't turn to see how Bum took this excuse, but the German laughed. "Yes, your friend could break many tables I think."

"Yeah," I said, trying to sound as amused as the German. "We were just messing around and I kind of shoved him and he fell. It wasn't his fault or anything. And like I said, we tried to fix it, but I'm afraid we'll just ruin it."

"I could come over in the morning," he said.

Suddenly I was afraid that the German was on to us. He looked suspicious, uncertain as if being asked to jump into a hole the bottom of which he couldn't see. I spoke quickly.

"Oh, Jeez. If Ma found out we wrecked her table she'd kill us. It was a present from her daddy, and she'd probably tan me for a month if she knew I broke it."

The German nodded slowly as I spoke. He looked from me to Bum and then said, "Yes. Good. You come in. I have supper on the stove, and I do not want it to burn."

I stepped over the threshold, but Bum didn't move. He visibly trembled, and his face was drained of color. Why hadn't he gone home the way I'd told him to? He was going to ruin everything.

"Your friend is afraid of me," the German said, bemused. "Am I so very scary?"

"Bum, come on, we don't want to keep Mr. Lang all night."

"I'm sorry," Bum said, but he remained frozen on the porch.

"Are you sure everything's all right?"

"Yeah," I said, too quickly. "Everything is fine. He's just really worried about breaking Ma's table. Bum, come on. You're being rude."

"Boys," the German said, "My supper is burning, so you just come in when you're ready. Or, if Ernst is too scary for your friend, wait here and I'll be right back after I turn off the stove and gather some tools."

Then, the German turned away from the door and walked across the living room, leaving me on the threshold to convince Bum. He didn't want to be convinced.

"He's been nice to you," Bum whispered. "He's done a bunch of chores for your ma and your neighbors. He's the one who mended you up after Hugo gave you a licking. Why are you doing this?"

"I can't believe you're on his side."

"I'm not on his side. There is no side because this shouldn't be happening."

"He called you fat."

"Everyone calls me fat," Bum replied. "I am fat. So what?"

"I don't see what's got you so knotted up," I said.

"What does Hugo think he can do that the sheriff can't?"

The German returned from the kitchen and said, "Would one of you boys go in the backyard and pick up my hammer while I get a few things from my workshop? It should be beside the chicken coop."

"Sure," I said.

"Oh," he announced, startling me. "I am very sorry to hear the news of your father, Tim. We'll hope he is in good health."

"Thanks," I said, turning away. The angry ticking in my head exploded into absolute rage, and it burned a path down my neck.

We walked through the German's house and continued outside. I looked at the chicken coop and it had been demolished. Scraps of splintered wood littered the dirt. The entire roof had been torn away and lay in the middle of the yard; the rest had been reduced to useless jagged planks. I turned away in confusion and was surprised to see Hugo and the other two already pressed up against the back of the German's house. Thoughts collided in my head as I gaped at the boys. Ben and Austin crouched, each holding lengths of board, but Hugo stood tall with a Colt revolver trained on the kitchen door.

"Tim," Bum muttered at my side, seeing exactly what I saw.

The sight of the weapon sent icy rivulets down my back. Hugo had said nothing about guns. The possibility had never occurred to me, and it scared me as I came to realize this really was adult business, like war, and people died in wars. Quickly I turned back to the pile of broken lumber, searching the mess for the German's hammer, so my neighbor wouldn't come outside. I tossed boards stained with white bird shit aside but found no sign of the tool I'd been sent to fetch.

"What are you doing?" Bum asked. His voice trembled horribly. "We can't be here."

"Just help me find the hammer," I said.

The German came out and said, "No luck?" He laughed at this and shook his head, walking down the two steps toward us. He didn't think to look around his yard.

"What happened to your coop?" I asked, hoping to keep his attention on me.

"Happened?" the German replied as if he couldn't see the demolished shack with his own eyes.

"Mr. Lang?" Bum said, sounding frightened to the core.

"Bum, shh," I said.

Behind the German, Hugo crept forward, the gun trained on the back of the man's head.

"No, Tim," my friend argued.

"Boys, what is going on?" the German asked. Then he must have heard Hugo, because the German spun around to face him. Taken off guard, Hugo's step stuttered and he came to a stop, but he kept the revolver aimed at the German. "What is this?"

"It's what you deserve," Hugo said.

My neighbor turned back to me with a question on his brow, and Hugo skipped forward to place the muzzle of his pistol against the man's head. The German spun quickly, slapping

Hugo's gun hand to the side and planting a fist in the boy's chest. Hugo tripped backward, landing hard on the ground. His gun had found its way into the German's hand, and dread filled me. The brawny man looked at the weapon and tossed it high, sending it soaring over the fence. Through all of this Ben and Austin remained motionless at the back of the house.

The German whipped back around, shot out his hand, and grabbed Bum by the collar.

"So you come for a fight?" he asked. "Little boys playing soldier?"

"Leave him alone," I shouted. "You get your hands off of him."

"You come into my home and attack me?" he bellowed in Bum's face. "Kill my birds? Ruin my fence?"

I didn't know what he meant about the birds or his fence, but Bum squealed, trying to get out of the man's grip, and seeing my friend so helpless affected me in an unexpected way. It felt as if a cascade of ice water fell over my head, leaving my skin and muscle numb in its wake. I walked to the German, and when he spun on me, I kicked him in the balls, the way he'd shown me. His eyes lit with surprise and the man dropped to his knees, his hand releasing Bum as it joined its match to cover his crotch. Then Ben Livingston strolled casually across the lawn and stepped in front of the German, cocking the board back like a baseball star. He swung and connected with the German's forehead, splitting the board in the process. The tremendous concussion sounded like a gunshot to my ears. The German rocked back on his knees, and for a second he seemed to struggle to right himself, and then blood poured from the new wound on his brow, his eyes rolled up and he dropped face first onto the grass.

I stared at him, suddenly aware that the radio-drama scenarios I'd imagine were nothing more substantial than the signals they'd been delivered on. A man lay unconscious at my feet, bleeding from his head, and the night was only getting started.

"Get him inside," Hugo called, climbing to his feet.

"Lord, you killed him," Bum said.

"He's not dead, yet," Hugo said. "Now you just keep your mouth shut."

"You killed him," Bum repeated, backing up the stairs.

"Don't be a baby," I scolded. "This is man's work, Bum. You keep your crying to yourself."

"I don't want any part of this," Bum mumbled.

"Look," Hugo said, "I don't know what you're doing here." He shot me a glare. "But you're part of this whether you like it or not, and if we don't tie him up he's going to kill you and the rest of us, so give us a hand."

Bum muttered incoherently next to me, blubbering.

"Stop it," I told him. "Just settle down."

"I want to go home."

"You're not leaving," Hugo said. "You're not taking one fucking step out of this house. You think I'm going to have you shooting off your mouth about this? No, sir. You're either with us or you're against us and if you're against us, I'll have Ben find another fucking board."

"But you killed him."

"We saved your life. You saw the look in his eyes, like a wild animal. That's how they are. So shut up and give us a hand."

"This shouldn't be happening," Bum said.

"We'll put him in the bedroom," Hugo said.

"What if he wakes up before we tie him down?" Ben asked.

"We beat him til he's sleeping again," Austin said.

But the German didn't wake up. We hauled him into the bedroom and dropped him on the bed. Then Ben left the bedroom, returning a minute later with a long coil of rope that they must have had hidden in the backyard. Hugo took it from his hands and immediately began cutting it into serviceable lengths. Ben took the strands and went to work, tying the unconscious German to the posts of his bed. It was done in no time, and Hugo walked around the bed, checking on the binds, nodding in approval at each station. He told us we had to get the German's clothes off and Austin burst out laughing. Ben asked why, and Hugo told him that it was necessary without further explanation. Since none of us understood or made a move to follow Hugo's order, he withdrew a buck knife from his belt and opened it and started cutting away the German's shirt, tearing along the seams from the sleeve to the waist. When he finished he tried to pull the garment away, but the German's weight secured the back of the shirt to the bed, so Hugo sliced it at the shoulders and tossed the rags into a corner. The pants took longer, but they came away clean. Bum stood just behind me crying, and I was too nervous myself to calm him down. Hugo insisted we should cover the German's face with something in case he woke up and started screaming. Austin found an old brown blanket in the closet and he draped it over the German's face, tucking corners in behind his head, giving the rough woolen fabric the shape of a hood, draping down about the German's shoulders and chest.

"Now what?" Ben asked.

And Hugo told him we waited for the German queer to wake up. He lit a cigarette and stared frowning at the naked man on the bed.

It was quiet for a time. The German lay sprawled, tied spread eagled with the brown blanket covering his face, and if it weren't for the gentle rise of the fabric when he took a breath, I'd have thought he was dead.

"He's going to scream," Austin said. "When he wakes up, he'll scream and the neighbors will hear."

"The blanket will muffle the worst of it," Hugo said. "Besides the next house isn't that close, but we'll probably need something for a gag when we take it off. Find some socks," he said to no one in particular.

Ben responded quickly and attacked the chest of drawers by the door. He handed a rolled-up pair to Hugo, who dropped them on the bed beside the unconscious man.

"We need to keep the front of the house dark," he said next. "We don't want people to think he's home, and someone has to stand guard up there in case his queer buddy comes back tonight."

"We gonna question him, too?" Austin asked.

"No. We have enough on our hands with this one. He'll go away if this one doesn't answer. Ben, you go close all the curtains and turn all the lights off. Blackout conditions in every room but this one. We got a moon tonight so we'll be able to see our way around once it gets dark."

"Consider it done," Ben said, scurrying out of the room.

"When you're done with that, you go out back and find my daddy's gun."

"What are we going to do to him?" Austin asked.

"Whatever we have to," Hugo replied. He took a drag off of his cigarette and glared at the bed. "Whatever it takes to get justice done."

⁕

Dark settled hard outside. Ben had found the Colt, and Hugo shoved it into his waistband. Austin Chitwood discovered a bottle of whiskey in the kitchen and brought it into the bedroom. The older boys passed the bottle around and when Hugo offered it to me, I took a small sip of the burning liquid and held back a cough. Bum just shook his head. Then Austin disappeared again and returned with the German's supper, eating the ham steak with the long fork my neighbor had used to push the meat around the skillet. The older boys kept passing the bottle between them, and I took a second and final sip. The whiskey was nearly gone when my neighbor began to stir.

The German muttered, his voice scarcely audible through the layers of wool covering his face. Then his body started to tremble. He shook so badly the bed clacked against the wall, and his attempts to move his arms became frantic. The ropes held. He shouted, but I didn't understand his words as he was speaking German. Next to me, Austin Chitwood laughed as if he were watching the Marx Brothers from the balcony of the Palace Theatre, and Hugo remained calm, standing sentinel over the bed, watching his captive struggle. The shouts became dreadful, and at one point, the German said in English, "Where is this place?" His voice cracked, and he pissed himself, sending a stream down his thigh to pool on the mattress between his legs. Hugo took a step away from the bed, shaking his head slowly, and Austin guffawed, pointing at the stain, and Ben said, "Would you look at that?"

For a flicker of time, my chest tightened. I felt as if I was on the verge of tears, pitying my neighbor, except I didn't want to pity him and I thought of those boys he'd killed – thought about my daddy – and my mercy evaporated. I checked on Bum in the corner and he looked ridiculous. Mouth open. Hands clapped over his ears. Eyes wide. He was near panic, and I knew he should have gone home and left this to us.

"Ben, take that blanket off his head. I'm going to start asking him questions." Hugo delivered the order around the cigarette in his mouth. He once again pulled the knife from his pocket and opened it. Casually he walked to the head of the bed and drove the knife point into the post there.

Ben did as he was told and removed the old brown blanket. He dropped it on the floor, and the German quickly looked around the room. Blood from his brow had smeared over his scarred face, making his eyes seem impossibly white. Whatever the cause of his fear and desperation, though, it was not us. In fact, his face relaxed and I noted a twitch at the corners of his mouth as if he were trying not to smile.

"Shouldn't you boys have given me kisses first?" he asked.

"Fuck you, queer," Hugo said.

"And you, neighbor Tim?" the German asked, "What did Ernst ever do to you?"

"Let him go," Bum said at my back. "Please, he didn't do anything."

"Shut your goddamned mouth, Craddick. You think this queer gives a shit about you? If the rest of us weren't here, he'd already have you bent over this bed, and then he'd slit your throat."

"No, he is too smooth and soft," the German said. "Like a woman. Like all of you."

Hugo leaned forward and punched the man in the mouth – three quick blows that sounded like a blade chopping ice.

"Think a woman could do that?"

The German spat a wad of blood on the mattress. "Nuh, a woman's fist might hurt," he taunted, though he was obviously dazed.

Hugo yanked the knife out of the bedpost and placed it against the meat high on the German's arm. Then he pressed, slicing into the skin. Next to me Bum gasped. The German just gritted his teeth and breathed deeply through his nose fighting back a scream. After Hugo finished the cut, the German spat out another wad of bloody phlegm that hit the edge of the mattress.

"You see your leader?" the German said. "He is a coward. He is no man."

Hugo made a second cut in the arm, this time applying more force and digging deep into the flesh. I turned away when I saw the blood welling up around the blade.

"They're going to kill him," Bum whispered.

"If I have to," Hugo said. "This is war. Do you understand? War? You just going to let these fuckers come to our country and murder us in our sleep?"

"We don't know if he did anything," Bum protested.

"You saw him," Hugo shouted. "You saw it as clear as day."

"We didn't see him kill anyone. He was just...."

"Bum, stop it," I said.

"Don't matter. He's a fucking pervert. Who else is going to cut up a kid but a pervert? He's a freak and he's going to confess or I'm going to bleed him out like a pig."

"I did not kill those children," the German said. "The sheriff knows this."

"Yeah, well, he's a shitheel," Hugo says. "He wouldn't know his dick from a rattler. You killed Harold and David and Lenny, and you're going to tell us you did it. You're going to tell us how you snatched them and fucked them and hollowed 'em out like deer. Then we're gonna get the sheriff and you're going to fry for it."

"You have made a mistake," the German said.

"No, Kraut, you're the one that made a mistake. You come here and think we're just going to let you kill us? Let you fuck us and then kill us?"

"Is that what you want?" he shouted at Hugo. The outburst took all of us off guard, and I recoiled, startled. "You want Ernst to fuck you? Is that why you have me tied up so you can sit on my cock when your friends aren't looking?"

Hugo brought the knife high, positioning it over the German's chest. Bum stumbled back into the door, causing a racket. He shrieked and fled the room. Looking at Hugo again, I saw that his position hadn't changed; he remained frozen with the knife poised for a killing blow.

"Go get him," Hugo growled, without turning away from his victim. "You want him to tell everyone in the city?"

Austin headed for the door, but I beat him to it, running as fast as I could down the hall, afraid he might hurt the boy I'd dragged into this business. Bum shouldn't have been there in the first place, and I wasn't going to let him get hurt just because he'd been worried about me. I burst into the living room but Bum was gone. The front door had been thrown open. I hurried to the threshold and the porch beyond, and saw my friend running to the end of the block as if monsters nipped at his heels. Austin grabbed me by the collar and dragged me off the porch, through the living room, and into the hall.

"The fat boy got away," Austin said, shoving me back into the room.

"Then we'd better make this quick," Hugo replied.

He drew deeply on his cigarette, making the end glow orange in the gloom. Then he pressed the hot end of the smoke into the German's leg. Tears streamed down the sides of my neighbor's face. His body quaked and sent the bed against the wall again, wood rapping wood in a horrible syncopation, but he refused to give Hugo any greater satisfaction, refused to scream.

Hugo finished with his cigarette. He ground the butt into the German's bedroom rug and took up his knife. Then he grabbed the German's left hand and wrapped his hand around one of the fingers.

"In those chink Fu-Manchu movies, they use bamboo," he mused. "You got any bamboo around here?"

Head turned, eyes wide, the German looked at the position of Hugo's blade at his fingertip and realizing his captor's intent began shouting in German. His voice was an incomprehensible storm of growls and grinding syllables, spoken at machine-gun speed and rising and falling from a terse tenor register to the deepest baritone. His muscles tensed violently as if in spasm, but he could not free himself from the ropes.

"Where's Little Lenny Elliot?" Hugo asked.

The German continued his harsh barrage, shouting like a madman at Hugo Jones. Spit flew from his lips in rabid flecks, splattering his shoulder and arms with froth. No one seemed concerned with neighbors hearing the man's shouts now. Hugo had been right: the next house on the road wasn't that close.

"Where is he?" Hugo demanded.

When the German responded with nothing more than his continued rage, Hugo drove the knife downward between the German's fingernail and the soft flesh beneath. The nail peeled back with a wet ripping sound, and Hugo finally received the scream he'd been waiting for.

This wounding was more awful than the cuts Hugo had made in the German's arm, because I could feel the knife at my own fingertip, and it was too much to bear. My stomach recoiled and I covered my mouth, trying to keep from vomiting on the German's floor. The hand at my collar loosened, and I heard Austin Chitwood say, "Gross," before I fled the room. I made it to the bathroom and retched, head spinning as if being filled with roiling swamp water. Oily and acidic, the vomit burned my throat. It coated my tongue, and my stomach convulsed again, and the murky and fluid thoughts in my head boiled faster. I shouldn't have been there. Bum had said this shouldn't be happening, and I suddenly knew he'd been right.

Once my belly was empty and my nerves recovered, I looked up to see Hugo Jones standing in the bathroom doorway. He gazed down on me with a sympathetic expression, as though he were genuinely concerned.

"This is what they're doing to your daddy right now," Hugo said. "That queer fucker's friends are peeling back his nails and cutting him, trying to get your daddy to rat out his command."

Sickness and confusion worked to make me mute.

"This is the only way we're going to find out what happened to those boys, and since Bum high-tailed it, and he's probably shooting his mouth off right now, we have to get the information fast. Now, you're just a kid so I don't expect you to watch any more."

I nodded my head and felt the tide of foul swamp water slosh against my skull.

"You go up front with Ben and keep an eye on the street. Austin and I are going to continue questioning the prisoner."

By now, Bum would have found help. He'd probably run to a neighbor's house and told them what was happening on Dodd Street, and they would call Sheriff Rabbit, and he would be on his way across town. All I knew was that I wanted the night to end. I prayed for it to be over, but this turned out to be a night of unanswered prayers.

Twenty-Three: Sheriff Tom Rabbit

"Sheriff, we have to go," Rex Burns called.

The tone in his deputy's voice made it clear that Tom should get to his feet and start moving before he began to question why he was moving. He rose from the chair and made his way into the front office of the sheriff's station. Rex was already at the door, holding it open.

"The Cowboy just snatched a kid off Bennington," Rex said. "We've got a witness that saw a black Ford drive right up to the kid. The driver got out and lifted the boy off the sidewalk and all but threw him in the car. Then he turned the Ford around and headed north."

"When did this happen?" Tom asked, following Rex out to the Packard.

"Now," Rex said. "It's happening now. I was talking to Regina, she lives at Bennington and Crosby, and she saw this kid running like the devil down the sidewalk when the Ford comes swooping across the street at him. The kid froze in the headlights and the guy just snatched him."

"Any chance this is a parent retrieving their kid after curfew?"

"He was wearing a gray Stetson and duster, Tom."

"Shit," Tom said. "You better drive. You got better night eyes than I do."

He tossed the deputy his keys and ran to the passenger side. Once the Packard was moving west, Tom picked up the microphone of the two-way radio and began instructing his men to proceed to Bennington.

"Walter already got the word out," Rex said. "With any luck this fucker is already face down in the dirt."

Tom doubted it. They only kept two patrol cars running at night, and Bennington was a long street, spanning the city from the southern border to the farm road cutting the upper edge of the city. Tom pictured the corner of Crosby Street and knew the Ford would already be north of Main by now. Then he considered the neighborhood, realizing Ernst Lang lived two blocks from the intersection where the crime had occurred. But Lang's car was a 1937 Buick 8, cream-colored and rusting around the fender, and according to Regina the vehicle had been traveling south, toward Dodd Street, and then had turned in the other direction.

"Did Regina say anything else about what she saw?"

"Honestly, I didn't give her much time," Rex said. "I figured we needed to move."

"Sure," Tom said. "There's Bennington."

"Yes, sir," Rex said.

He took the corner tight and the wheels cried against the pavement. Then Rex gunned the engine and sped down the nighttime road, headlights revealing gray pavement framed by brown grass. In the distance, Tom saw the twin red eyes of running lights.

"Any chance that's our guy?" Rex asked.

"Only one way to find out," Tom said. He lifted the microphone again and relayed their position. One of the patrol cars had been on the Farm Road when Walt called in the abduction, and they were approaching from the north. The other was still working its way back from Mitch's Roadhouse where another brawl had broken out. Tom told them to keep their eyes open for a black Ford, even though that was about the most common car in the country. "Walter," he said into the mouthpiece, "I want you to go pick up Regina Mason and show her the make and model catalogues to see if we can't narrow down the model and year of the Ford, and get as much information about the suspect as you can. Height. Weight. Anything. Radio back when you have information."

"Regina knows men better than cars," Rex said.

"Let's hope she was paying some attention to both. Any idea about the victim?"

"She didn't say."

"Hold on, the guy's turning."

Rex had done a good job of catching up to the car in front of them, and had narrowed the distance between them to three blocks. The car completed the turn and for a split second Tom saw it in profile. "Black Ford," he shouted, his heart tripping in his chest. "Son of a bitch. Stay on him."

Tom got back on the radio and redirected his men, and then leaned back and braced himself as Rex whipped around the corner, sending Tom halfway across the seat in the process.

"It's a Tudor sedan," Tom said. "Looks to be a thirty-nine or forty."

"Yes, sir," Rex said, "And he's seen us coming."

The Ford made a hard left ahead, and Tom caught the sound of its squealing tires. Rex kept on the gas pedal.

"Where's the plate?" Tom asked.

"Doesn't have one. Son of a bitch took it off."

They followed the car on a circuitous route through the neighborhoods north of downtown, Tom sliding across the street or slamming into the passenger door, depending on which direction his deputy turned the Packard. On a particularly tight right turn, Rex jumped the curb and Tom flew into the air. Dropping back to the seat in a moment of disorientation, he checked the road ahead and saw the driver's door of the Ford opening.

"What's he doing?" Rex asked.

Tom didn't know. The driver's door remained open, though how it stayed open with the Ford moving at such a speed he didn't know. A pale form emerged and seemed to hover above the running board, and then it dropped to the road like a bag of feed, rolling and bouncing before coming to a stop in the road to be captured in the headlights of the Packard.

"Shit," Rex spat.

The view in the windshield blurred before Tom realized Rex had cranked the wheel to the left. He cracked his shoulder against the door, and the Packard flew across the street and hopped the curb, punching through a white picket fence at the front of a yard before rocking to a halt.

"You all right?" Rex asked.

"What the hell are you thinking?" Tom asked.

Rex was already opening the door when he replied, "He threw the kid out, Tom. He tossed the kid into the street."

Tom turned in his seat and cast frantic looks through the windows, searching for proof of what Rex had told him. And there not far from the curb he saw a lump in a pale blue shirt and dungarees, and his heart tripped double-time in his chest as he reached for the door handle.

They ran to the boy, who lay curled like a caterpillar in the road. Neighbors began to emerge from their houses, and a woman screamed, and Tom called for everyone to stay back. Then he told Rex to get on the radio to phone for an ambulance. After that he instructed his deputy to let the other patrols know which direction the Ford was headed but they should focus the search on the areas northwest of town. That's where the driver had been heading before noticing Tom and Rex on his tail. Logic dictated that was the direction the driver had wanted to go. Then Tom turned his attention to the boy.

He was young, years younger than either Harold Ashton or David Williams. Blood covered what little of the front of the boy's shirt Tom could see. Carefully he rolled the kid onto his back, and saw the neat cut, angling down from the left ear. He didn't recognize the boy, but he was in bad shape. The driver had opened his throat. Blood pulsed from the gash, and Tom took the handkerchief from his pocket, pressed it to the wound, and prayed it wasn't too late. The plump boy's chest showed no sign of respiration, but when Tom leaned in, he felt the gentlest of breaths on his cheek.

"He's alive," Tom shouted. "Get the ambulance here fast."

Holding the cloth to the wound, Tom looked at the crowd gathering in the street. Something fouled his vision. Men and women hugged one another against the terrible sight in the road, but the faces appeared blurred as if he looked through a faulty lens, only the very center of which showed true.

Tom stood back when the ambulance arrived and let the medics do their job, and then he rode with the boy to the county hospital, frequently questioning the medic about the boy's condition. In addition to the cut at his throat, he'd sustained a broken arm, and a severe blow to the head, plus a number of abrasions from rolling across the pavement. The only question the medic couldn't answer was the most important question in Tom's mind. "Is he going to make it?"

At the hospital, they took the wounded boy down a hallway, leaving Tom alone. He asked the nurse if he could use her phone for police business, and she lifted it onto the counter for him. He radioed the station to see if there had been an arrest.

"They lost him," Walter said. "They're driving around north of town, but the guy is probably laying low someplace."

"Wake everyone up," Tom said. "I want every deputy and patrolman on the streets. One man to a car so we can cover more ground. You get Muriel out of bed and have her cover the office so you can join them. In the meantime, put together a list of everyone you know in town that owns a black Ford Tudor – thirty-nine or forty – and have it waiting for me. Did you get any more information from Regina?"

"She's just gotten here, Sheriff," Walter said.

Frustration came upon him in a wave and then quickly receded. "You find out everything she saw, right down to the kinds of shoes this bastard was wearing. And once Muriel comes in, get out on the street."

"Yes, sir."

His thoughts turned back to the victim. He didn't know the boy, but somewhere his parents had to be worried sick.

"Has anyone called in to report a missing boy?" Tom asked into the phone.

"That's the thing, Sheriff," Walter replied.

"What do you mean?"

"We have two reports."

"Two?"

"Ben Livingston and Austin Chitwood."

Tom rolled the names over in his head. He knew Livingston and Chitwood well enough. They wasted their time with Hugo Jones, and both were too old to be the injured boy. They were probably drinking beer with Hugo out to the flats or by the lake, ignoring the curfew as always.

He waited at the hospital for Don Niall to relieve him, and then he took his deputy's car to search the streets. Before Tom left the hospital he spoke with a doctor about the injured boy, and the news wasn't good. The boy was unconscious and based on the severity of the head trauma, not to mention the amount of blood he'd lost, there was no guarantee he would ever wake up. If he did, his brain might be so scrambled he wouldn't remember his own name, let alone the name of the man who had abducted him. Even with such a somber prognosis, Tom instructed Don to stay for updates on his condition and to be on hand if the boy managed to wake and was able to speak.

⁜

Tom drove a circuitous route north of town, occasionally stopping in the middle of the road to chat with one of his deputies who was heading the opposite direction. No news came over the radio, at least none that gave him much hope. Don reported from the hospital and the injured boy's condition hadn't changed. The doctors wanted to move him to one of the larger facilities in Austin but feared what such a trip might do to the boy. So far they had no identification for the kid.

It was half past midnight when Muriel called with a report about another missing boy, and Tom shook his head with frustration and gripped his angry stomach, listening to the dispatcher give him the boy's name and the situation.

Tim Randall's mother had returned from a swing shift at the factory to find her son missing and the living room in disarray. The woman was panicked, and when Muriel read off the address, Tom's gut twisted into a burning knot. The Randall house sat less than two blocks from where their John Doe had been snatched by the Cowboy. It didn't take a lot of detective work to figure Tim Randall was the boy Tom had seen tossed out of the speeding Ford like a sack of garbage.

He drove the Packard across town, his mind wandering and his gaze sweeping, still on guard for the black Ford. He didn't expect to see the car. They'd had about as close to luck as they were going to get he figured, but it didn't stop him from braking frequently when the back end of a black car caught his eye.

At Dodd Street he parked at the curb in front of the address Muriel had read to him. All of the lights in the house were on, and he could see a slender woman with long brunette hair pacing frantically in front of the window with a cigarette to her lips. Climbing out of the car, he threw a glance at Ernst Lang's house on the lot by the lakefront. Like the other houses, all except the Randall home, the lights were out. He took a few steps down the street to see that the man's Buick remained parked in the carport, and there it was. Of course that didn't mean the man was home. In fact, Tom didn't understand exactly what he was trying to put together. Did he still believe Lang was involved?

Mrs. Randall met him at the door, frantic with wide green eyes covered in a pool of tears. She drew heavily on the cigarette pinched between her fingers, drawing the smoke into her lungs and holding it there. Tom observed an overturned table with one of the legs lying askew on the carpet and he winced at the sight, hoping Mrs. Randall hadn't noticed his reaction.

The first thing he asked was to see a picture of Tim. Their conversation would be sorrowfully brief if it were the boy he'd left at the hospital. Mrs. Randall led him across the room to the fireplace mantel and lifted a wooden framed photograph. Handed it to him.

The boy in the picture wasn't the boy in the hospital, Tom realized. He didn't remotely resemble the kid Tom had tended on the street and in the ambulance. This discovery brought him no relief, however. It only added a new layer to his anxiety. If the boy in the hospital wasn't Tim Randall, then who was he, and where was this woman's son?

"When did you see your son last, Mrs. Randall?"

"Before I left for work. He was waiting for his friend Bum to come over, and I told him to mind the curfew. I had his grand-mother staying here for a few weeks to keep an eye on him, but she couldn't keep doing it, because Daddy needed her at home."

Mrs. Randall began sobbing. She stubbed her cigarette out in a tray and wiped at her eyes and nose with a handkerchief, and then she grabbed the pack of cigarettes off the mantel to light another one.

"Who's Bum?" Tom asked.

"His friend," Mrs. Randall replied. "Bum Craddick. I don't know what his parents were thinking when they named him. Such a shame to go through life with a name like that. He and his family live a few blocks over on Worth Street. The boys are joined at the hip like Mutt and Jeff."

"Can you describe the Craddick boy?"

"He's a pudgy boy," Mrs. Randall said. "He's got black hair and he wears it too long."

Tom nodded, feeling the description sink in like a virus. "And you said that his parents live on Worth Street?"

"Yes."

Tom questioned Mrs. Randall, asking for details about her son's other friends and where he was most likely to have been playing earlier in the evening, and he asked what Tim had been wearing the last time she'd seen him and if Tim could have run away for any reason. It was all very familiar to him after investi-gating the thankfully false abduction of Little Lenny Elliot. But as he spoke and Mrs. Randall answered, he felt the pull of his car and the two-way radio. He had to get someone from the station to speak with Bum Craddick's parents, or he had to do it himself. The various threads of his thoughts kept winding and unwinding and he missed much of Mrs. Randall's information.

Finally, with his notepad filled with his scrawled writing, Tom suggested that Mrs. Randall have her parents or a friend come stay with her while he began the investigation.

He excused himself to return to his car to radio in the information. Muriel Iverson interrupted him.

"A nurse at the hospital recognized Bum," she said. "She called his parents straight away, so they're already driving to the hospital. Don called in and said there had been no change. He hasn't woken up yet."

"Any word from the patrols?"

"No, sir. They haven't found anything yet."

"Well, you tell them that we're looking for a second boy now. His name is Tim Randall." Tom read off the description and explained the situation to Muriel who gasped at the news.

"He took both of them?" she said.

"We don't know that, yet. Just get the description out and radio me with any news."

"Yes, sir," Muriel said.

Tom turned the radio volume up so he would hear it from the street and then he walked to the end of the block, where Dodd intersected with Bennington. At the intersection he headed north and followed Bennington three blocks where it intersected with Cactus and he looked around.

If he had Regina's story straight, the Craddick boy would have been running up the other side of the street, because she'd said that the driver had crossed the lane, aiming the nose of the car at the boy before getting out to grab him. He checked over his shoulder at the distant street sign for Dodd, then looked ahead. Worth Street was three blocks up. Tom crossed the street. The boy seemed to have been running home, which wasn't a strange thing to do, except in this scenario it felt wrong. If he and Tim Randall were playing and Tim got snatched, wouldn't Bum have run to the nearest lit-up house instead of tearing down the street?

And if this had happened in the Randall's front yard or on the street, surely a neighbor would have heard the commotion out front and called it in. The Randall kid and his friend wouldn't both go quietly. So that left the possibility that the Cowboy had parked to the north and walked down to Dodd Street, entered the home and snatched Tim Randall, breaking the table in the process and sending Bum Craddick fleeing, but then how had the Cowboy managed to get back to his car with the Randall kid, fire up the engine, and still intercept Bum?

It didn't work in Tom's mind. He returned to Dodd Street and his Packard and he lit a cigarette and thought the facts over, and the series of events made no sense, no matter how he put them together.

He looked up and down the street, his gaze touching each darkened house. His attention fell on the last house – Lang's house – and he decided that if he needed a place to start questioning folks that was as good a place as any.

Twenty-Four: Tim Randall

I think I could have left anytime I'd wanted to, and many times I felt I should get out of the German's house and away from the terrible groans and muffled screams coming from my neighbor's bedroom, except I stayed. Ben Livingston didn't seem to care what I did. He probably wouldn't have said "Boo" if I'd stood from the sofa and walked to the front door and told him good night before crossing the street to my house. But I didn't leave. Why didn't I leave? What I'd seen was awful, and what I imagined Hugo doing to the German was even more so. Why did I stay?

My willingness to believe the German's guilt outweighed my unease with what was being done to him. I had fitted myself into a terrible situation, and the only way to account for that decision was to wholeheartedly believe that the German's punishment was deserved, his crimes unforgivable. He suffered because he deserved to suffer. If he wasn't wrong, inexplicably wrong, then what we inflicted on him could never have been right.

The German's tirades had stopped, leaving only the dreadful, animal grunts. Maybe they'd put the rolled-up socks in his mouth after all. I could hear Hugo and Austin, particularly when they were laughing, which was happening more and more frequently, though the walls muddled and made their talk incomprehensible. I kept wondering why Bum hadn't sent help, and I figured it was because of the oath I'd made him take, and half the time I spent in the living room, I wished I'd run off with him. Except I hadn't. I sat there on the sofa where the German had made a show for me only days before and cursed the man for being monstrous – so monstrous I was forced into the ugly business of capturing him. Ben remained in the room with me, often appearing bored and anxious. Sometimes he chuckled when he heard his friends laughing. Sometimes he muttered, "Fucking queer."

It felt as if I'd been on the sofa all night but it couldn't have been more than two or three hours. Austin emerged from the bedroom and said, "Get in here."

"My turn?" Ben asked eagerly.

"Both of you," Austin said, sounding good and puffed up with his accomplishment. "The prisoner's got something to say to you."

I looked nervously from Ben to Austin and realized that my chance to leave had passed. The fear that engulfed me in that moment was sick inducing, and I worried that I might vomit again. I didn't want to see what had been done to the German. I had to believe it was justified, but I didn't want to see it.

"I'll drag your ass in there again," Austin warned.

Standing from the sofa, I took a step forward and my stomach rolled and clenched. I swallowed hard against the gagging at the back of my throat and followed the boys to the room.

At first, I thought the German had been skinned alive. His head lolled, rolling lazily from side to side, but the mask of blood that had smeared his face seemed to have become a glistening crimson shawl, covering him from his chest to his scalp. Sweat covered his legs and forearms. Black burns – round like pernicious freckles – dotted his thigh. His cheek and brow were swollen badly as was his left hand, where Hugo had taken a second fingernail. A thick pool of blood had gathered under his arm where I could make out the lines of four deep gashes.

Hugo stood by the bed, holding a sock in his hand that appeared to be weighted down with a potato or a rock. He looked up at me, and then back to the German.

"Say it," Hugo ordered.

"*Nein*," the German muttered. His voice rumbled low, weak, and coarse. "Not him. Not with a child in the room."

"He was old enough to stomp your ass."

"*Nein*," the German repeated.

Hugo swung the sock with a vicious windmill motion and slammed it across the German's chest. It sounded like a steak hitting dirt. The German grunted in pain and launched into another bout of angry, incomprehensible dialogue, though he couldn't muster the strength to shout.

"Say it," Hugo said. "Confess to them."

The German looked in my direction, but I didn't believe he was seeing me. What little expression I could discern on his face, seemed too soft and kind for the situation – for me. It made his words all the harder to understand.

"I killed those three boys," the German whispered. "I raped them and killed them and left notes for the sheriff."

Hugo swung again.

"Tell it right," Hugo said. "Tell it all."

The German made a low growling sound like he was clearing his throat, and he shook his head slowly as if to get an annoying drop of water out of his ear. His eyes, so white against the crimson mask, found mine and the expression he offered was one of absolute pity. Hugo wound up and swung the sock with all of his might, whipping it hard against the German's side. I heard something crack like a twig beneath the dull slap. The German gritted his teeth against a shrill squeal, which managed to escape through his nose with a spray of snot. He squeezed his eyes closed, sending tears to carve pale streams through the blood on his face.

"Tell it right," Hugo whispered. "Then we'll call the sheriff and he'll take your ass to jail and maybe a doctor will fix you up before they send you to the chair."

"I took Harold Ashton and kept him tied up in my attic so I could fuck him whenever I wanted to. He was a very pretty boy and I fucked him often, but he kept crying so I cut him open and scraped everything out so the sheriff wouldn't know what

I'd done. I kidnapped David Williams from his home but I only fucked him once because he was fat and ugly, and he smelled like old onions, so I hung him in the Ranger's Lodge so all of you would see him and know that no place in your city was safe." The German breathed raggedly. His eyes remained on me, but there was no pity left to color them. Instead, his fury burned as if I alone bore the weight of his loathing, and again I wondered if he was seeing me at all. "The last boy I stole from his bed, out from under the noses of his parents, and I fucked him in his backyard, on the grass after I put a rock in his mouth so he couldn't scream, and I dragged him to the lake and fucked him again and then I cut his throat and threw his body into the water."

A hard breath rattled from the German's lips and he closed his eyes. Tried to swallow. Choked and took another rasping breath.

"Finish it," Hugo said. "Finish your confession."

Eyes closed, the German whispered. "I am a Nazi and a faggot and I killed those three boys after I fucked them because that's what faggots do."

"Who was next?" Hugo asked. "Who were you going to fuck and murder next?"

The German's eyes fluttered open and he again fixed me with a dreadful, hate-filled glare. I trembled violently under it.

"You," he said, eyes never wavering from mine.

His confession came together in my head like electric wires completing a circuit. It was true. All of it. Hugo had gotten the man to confess, and the German's sick past and his grotesque plan for me erased what little sense I had retained.

I walked forward and took the sock from Hugo's hand, felt the weight of it hanging like an extension of my arm. The monster on the bed continued to watch me, and I thought I saw that twitch at the corners of his mouth, that near-smile that he'd fought when we'd first removed the blanket from the queer's face.

The weight of the sock felt good and I swung it, hitting the German's chest feebly, and he did smile then, and he began muttering in German, and I knew he was calling me a baby and weak. Ben moved in on the other side of the bed, holding a knife of his own and Austin lit a fresh cigarette for the burning. The German's disdain only emboldened me and my next blow was solid, and the next and the next, and I kept hitting him and Ben scored his arm and Austin burned him until the German again cried out, and Hugo shoved the roll of socks back into his mouth, and on and on it went until he fell silent and stared like a corpse at the ceiling, no longer able to voice or respond to the trauma in any physical way, but we didn't stop. Not even then. Not even when I felt certain he was dead.

Twenty-Five: Sheriff Tom Rabbit

When Uncle Stan Moffat blew his head off with a shotgun, his mama was the one that called Sheriff Tom Rabbit. Tom walked into that bedroom and saw Uncle Stan's remains draped across that bed with the top of his head opened like the mouth of a volcano – a volcano that had just erupted all over the walls and bed clothes. It was a damned sight. A mother shouldn't have to see that, and Tom didn't want to see it, but he'd admit he'd seen worse. Harold Ashton and David Williams were bad in a wholly different way, because Tom could still sense their fear – boys shouldn't know such fear. But seeing Ernst Lang trussed up on his bed naked and cut with those boys looking down at him their eyes fired up with an ugly, ugly passion like they were looking at their first woman…was about the worst thing he'd ever seen. His gut tumbled and tried to climb on up the back of his throat.

A lot of blood covered the German. His face wore a mask of it, making his eyes look bigger and whiter like a couple of eggs floating in a tomato soup. Ernst's body quaked uncontrollably.

Those four boys. What in the name of God had they been thinking?

"We got him, Sheriff," Hugo Jones said proudly. "We got the queer bastard."

"Let him up," Tom said. None of the boys moved. They looked at him like he was dancing around the room in a dress, and Tom honestly couldn't remember if he'd actually spoken the words that first time, so he repeated the order. "Let him up!"

"But he's the Cowboy. He confessed," Hugo protested.

"Yeah," Austin Chitwood added. "He confessed to being a spy and a Nazi and a pervert. He killed Harold and David and Little Lenny."

"No, he didn't," the sheriff said. "Jesus Christ, he didn't touch them."

"But he confessed," Hugo insisted. "He's a damned pervert."

"Let him up!" Tom yelled, and this time, the Randall boy moved.

He didn't do as Tom said, though. Tim Randall fled the room and a second later Tom heard the porch door swing out with a squeal, then slam. The sheriff looked back at the German, and those big white eyes were burning, and he understood the Randall boy's fear. Once Lang was loose, that bull-built bastard would rip those kids' heads off. How they'd gotten the best of him in the first place, Tom didn't know, but he'd seen enough violence for one night.

"You boys get out of here," he said.

"Are you gonna arrest him?" Hugo asked, crossing his arms over his chest defiantly.

"I'm going to arrest *you*, Hugo Jones," Tom said. "What you've done here breaks too many laws for me to list, but you are going to answer for each and every one of them. Now you get out of this house. I'm letting this man loose, and if he has a mind to break your stupid necks, I'm inclined to turn the other way and let him."

"My pa won't stand for this."

"Then you send him to me. Now, get the fuck out of this house."

The curse seemed to do the trick. Boys were used to throwing those words around easy enough amongst themselves, but hearing an adult invoke such an obscenity got their attention. And it was a good thing too, because the German's condition so disturbed Tom he had a strong urge to break some necks himself.

The boys fled, all but Hugo, who strutted across the floor like he'd gotten the best of the sheriff. Infuriated by his manner, Tom hauled off and slapped the boy upside his head. Hugo yelped, and Tom was glad to hear it. "This is on your head, Hugo Jones."

"I ain't...."

Tom didn't let the puffed up little bastard say another word. Instead, his palm made a second visit to the boy's head. This time, Hugo cried out and then he stumbled out of the room, leaving the sheriff alone with Ernst Lang.

At the bedside, the man's wounds were clear enough. The boys had burned him and cut him. His skin was bruised and swollen in so many places Tom figured the man was lucky to be conscious. Using his knife, the sheriff freed Ernst's ankles. Then he pulled a pair of rolled up socks out of his mouth. The German didn't make a sound. Not a thank you or a damn you; not a whimper or a sigh, so Tom went to work on the rope at his wrist, freeing his left arm first. Then the sheriff circled the bed and sliced through the hemp securing Ernst's right arm to the wooden bed frame.

"*Scheisse!*" the German said. It was meant to be a shout, but it snapped in his throat, dry and brittle like the crushing of dead leaves. "*Scheisse! Verdammete Scheisse!*" Ernst bolted upright. He lunged in Tom's direction, throwing himself from the mattress. But his legs must have been starved for circulation, and he crumbled to his knees.

He startled Tom so badly the sheriff spun away, holding his knife out in a defensive stance. Kneeling on the floor and looking up as if in furious prayer, Ernst stared at the blade in the sheriff's hand. The German wanted the knife. Tom didn't know if the man thought he might use it on him or those boys or everyone in Barnard, but the blade rapt his attention.

"Settle down, now. You're hurt bad and a bit muddled." Truth was the German seemed out of his mind, but it looked to Tom like he had sufficient reason for it. "We have to take care of you."

"Out," Ernst said. "Just...out...my house."

"I can't leave you in this condition, Ernst. You're not thinking clearly."

A low growl rumbled in the German's throat.

"How long were they here?" the sheriff asked. "How long they have you tied up?"

"Don't know," Lang said. His eyes lost that hungry cast and they clouded over. The lids drooped, and he leaned forward on his hands. "Last night. At sunset."

"Let me call an ambulance. You're hurt real bad."

"No. *Nein*. No."

"You need help."

He slapped the air with one of his large hands, sweeping the thought away like a mosquito. "You see the kind of help I get."

"At least get back into the bed. I'll find some things to patch you up. Just get back in...."

"The bed...." Ernst interrupted, but the sentence ended. He grunted heavily as if releasing a great burden from his shoulders. The sound came again, only harsher, rasping – a dull file on a length of mesquite. The noise grew more frequent, almost panting like a dog about to retch. His head lowered and his muscled back expanded and contracted furiously.

Tom had never seen anything like it and didn't know what it meant. He only knew he needed to get the man to a hospital.

"The bed," Ernst repeated quickly between raking breaths, "shit and piss and blood." He inhaled deeply. The air fled him in those short sawing grunts. He gasped again. "You sleep in it." He tried to get to his feet and failed. His second attempt was no more successful. He crawled forward and spread out on the floor, lying on his back. "Water, yes? A glass of water, yes?"

"Sure."

Tom returned his knife to its sheath and walked to the kitchen. He poured a glass of water, then carried it back to the room, where he knelt by the wounded man's side, holding his head and helping his drink. After the glass was drained, Tom set it aside and began checking Ernst's wounds. One of his thighs had a long gash that drew a line from his knee nearly to his privates. The boys had removed two of his fingernails and ragged flesh framed the purple wounds beneath. Black circles on his outer thighs looked to be the work of cigarettes; they oozed clear fluid. The German's belly was one purple smear of bruise. Similar marks covered both of his arms. These didn't worry Tom as much as the cuts, though. The boys had carved his arm like notching a gun butt. Four on the left and three on the right. They still oozed blood.

"Nice boys, nuh?" Ernst said.

"They'll pay accounts for this."

"And how much is a German deviant worth?"

"As much as anyone else, I suppose."

"You're too old to be so stupid."

The sheriff ignored the comment and told him he had to get an ambulance. Ernst was bleeding all over the floor, and there might have been more damage inside. Tom didn't know. The sheriff could manage snakebite and maybe a broken arm. The German's wounds were well beyond his medical abilities.

"No," Ernst said, staring up at Tom from the floor.

"You could bleed to death."

"I stink."

"They'll clean you up."

"The bath, yes? You run the bath."

"No, I'm not running the bath, you goddamn fool. You could bleed out. Jesus, Ernst, the last thing you should be thinking about is the way you smell."

"So I deserve no dignity?"

Tom didn't know what to make of that. Dignity? Was the German so damn proud he was willing to die rather than be seen with a smear of shit on him?

The situation had Tom perplexed. He couldn't carry the man out of the house. Lang was too heavy for that, though Tom could have dragged him, he figured it would do more harm than good. Finally, he decided to grant Lang's request for a bath. If nothing else, it would give Tom time to get Doc Randolph down to Dodd Street.

He left Ernst on the floor and walked into the bathroom. The stopper went into the drain and he turned on the faucet.

Then Tom slipped back into the hall and made his way to the phone in Ernst's kitchen. The Doc's wife, Myrna, told him the doctor would be on down to Dodd Street as soon as he could. A few minutes later, the sheriff helped Ernst to the tub. The man moaned in pain when they reached the bedroom threshold and Tom stopped uncertain.

"The bath," Lang insisted, his voice pinched.

The water turned pink as his bulk slid into the tub. The wounds on his arms opened like tiny mouths drooling blood into the water. Ernst lifted a small towel from the edge of the tub, using the right hand, which still had all of its fingernails intact; he struggled with the cloth's weight as if it were lead rather than cotton. Dipping the towel into the foul water, he brought it to his face and dabbed gently across his forehead, cleaning away the sweat and blood accumulated there. With the skin clean, Tom saw a purple welt the size of an acorn on the man's right brow. Rivulets of crimson rose through the water like smoke from the wounds on his arms. Once his face was clean, Lang dragged the towel over his chin and down his throat. He winced but did not stop the motion. The towel slid lower and he passed it over his privates. Then the cloth grazed the cuts and burns on his legs. Lang cried out. It was a terrible sound, a squeal of animal agony. He gritted his teeth, biting off its tail, then he squeezed his eyes shut, continuing to clean himself.

"Is there anything you need?" Tom asked. It was a jackass thing to say, but he didn't know what else to do. Watching the German bathe himself was like watching a gutshot man crawling around a field picking flowers.

"Those boys," Ernst said. His voice was stronger, though still drained. He draped the cloth over the side of the tub. What he did next shocked the sheriff. The German grasped his privates in one of his hands, not covering them, but circling them and squeezing. "Those boys were afraid of my cock, yes? That's why I still have it. They talked about cutting it off, but none of them would touch it. I'm lucky, yes?"

Tom looked away toward the sink and nodded. "Sure," he said.

"They tried to act so brave, so cruel, but they were afraid. They hold their own cocks every day, but mine terrified them."

"Ernst, you shouldn't talk just now."

"Ah, it scares you, too. Good. Enough. No more talk of it."

"Thank you."

Tom was grateful when Doc Randolph finally arrived, though the doctor cursed him out something fierce for having put the German in the tub, but once he set to mending Lang's wounds Tom was forgotten. They helped the German to the sofa, and the Doc got to work and Tom went back into the bedroom where he collected the ropes and set them in a pile by the door. Then he stripped off the dirty sheets and took them to the back porch to air out. The mattress beneath was also stained, but there wasn't anything to be done about that just then.

Once the doc had Ernst patched up, he gave the man a shot of something and together they helped Lang outside and into Doc Randolph's car.

"He'll stay in the hospital for a day or so. Keep an eye out for infection. You mind telling me who did this to that man?"

Tom did mind, and he didn't say. The doctor would know soon enough anyway. Doc Randolph shook his head, disappointed, then he climbed in his car and drove off.

Tom closed up the German's house and drove back to the station. He'd have a deputy round up the three older boys, wake their folks, and give them all something to chew over while he worked on his report. In the morning – at least later in the morning – he'd call Estella and ask her to run by Lang's house to clean up those sheets and do what she could with his mattress.

The German might as well have a clean bed when he got home.

Twenty-Six: Tim Randall

I didn't sleep.

My mind overflowed with sound and motion – a big band dance filled with trampled and bloody dancers, twirling to a blaring, discordant dirge. Even my mother's demands for answers couldn't break through the cacophony. Once home, I flew past her and ran into my bedroom and collapsed on the bed, curling into a ball, and she instantly followed to ask where I had been and what I had been doing and was I okay, and I said nothing. She sobbed and held me, convinced I was the victim.

Amid screams pouring from the German's bloody face, I remembered the sheriff's words: *Jesus Christ, he didn't touch them.* At the time, his certainty had been like a splash of cold water delivered in unison with an electric shock. I felt my own certainty then: Hugo had manipulated me – had manipulated *everything*. My mind was too shattered to identify the specific deceits, but one moment I firmly believed my neighbor was a monster, and in the next I saw him as the casualty of monsters – beaten, cut, bloody. Innocent.

Later in the morning my mother returned to my room. Her demeanor had changed, but she continued to cry. In a terse voice, she told me to get up and straighten my clothes. Comb my hair. Deputy Gilbert Perry was waiting in the living room to take us into town. He greeted me with a sour expression and a stern, "Morning," and then he led us outside.

Ma sat next to me in the police car, silent and wiping the tears from her eyes. At the police station, Gilbert limped around the car and opened the door and when I stepped out, I felt his hand on my back, as if ready to grab me should I decide to run. Inside, Ma and I were led into a small, poorly lit room that smelled like cigarettes and sweat. A fan clacked noisily as it pushed warm air around the cinderblock cell. We were asked to sit at a table, and then Deputy Gil shambled out of the room, leaving me alone with my mother, who insisted on answers.

"Timothy George Randall, you tell me what this is all about."

"I don't know," I said, and it wasn't far from the truth. The dance continued in my head – one bloody face after another, though they were all the German's face contorted in different ways. I could no longer summon the rage that had so easily guided me into his house, that had made his wounding justified. So I didn't know what *this* was all about, because I couldn't understand how any of it had happened.

"He said you kidnapped a man," she pressed. "He said you hurt him very badly."

"Yes," I replied. That's exactly what had happened, but I didn't want to remember it that way. I wanted to remember how brave we'd been, how smart we'd been, how we'd made the German confess. We were heroes.

Laughable.

"How could you do this?" Ma asked. "Timmy, how? I don't understand."

"Yes," I said again.

The interrogation room door opened and Sheriff Rabbit walked in, followed by Deputy Burns. Both of them looked like they'd just come from the funeral of someone they loved. My belly twisted tight with sickness and the dance played on in my head, the music faster, the dancers all the more damaged.

Deputy Burns took the chair across from me. He dropped down in it and glared over the table. Sheriff Rabbit remained standing.

"Mrs. Randall," he said, "I want you to understand the seriousness of this business, and further, I want you to know that I witnessed the crime in question, so I would appreciate the cooperation of you and your son. It'll make life easier for all of us."

Ma nodded at this and threw a frightened look at me.

"Tim," Sheriff Rabbit said, "we know what happened, so there's no use in lying about it. We've already spoken to Hugo and Ben and Austin, and we have their statements on file. We know you entered the residence of Ernst Lang..." Ma gasped at the mention of our neighbor's name. "...and that you proceeded to subdue, restrain, and commit acts of violence on the man. Can you tell me why you did this?"

"He was a queer," I said. "He was a murderer. He was a German."

"And why did you think Lang was a murderer? Did you have any evidence?"

"Hugo saw something through his window," I said.

"And what did he see?"

"He wouldn't tell me."

"But Hugo convinced you that Ernst Lang had murdered Harold Ashton and David Williams."

"And Little Lenny."

"Little Lenny Elliot came home yesterday," Sheriff Rabbit said.

"But he confessed," I whispered, knowing how empty it sounded.

Deputy Burns spoke up then. His voice rolled over his tongue like a thresher chopping through a field of stone columns. "I'm thinking you'd confess to a whole lot of things yourself if you were tied to a bed and cut up and burned with cigarettes. Now, I don't have much use for Lang's sort, and I sure don't have much liking for them. I see a queer and I pop him in the jaw to let him know he best look the other way. I handle it like a man and I move on. But you could have killed that son of bitch, Tim. It's a goddamn miracle you didn't. Then it wouldn't matter a bit if he was queer or not; you'd be a murderer. That sound good to you?"

I couldn't respond. Fear and anger rolled off of Ma; I could feel it falling over me, clinging like the stink of cigarette smoke.

"His father is missing," she said. "We just got the telegram the other day. He's been out of his mind with worry. We both have."

"You have my deepest regrets," Sheriff Rabbit said dryly, "but that doesn't excuse the crimes in question."

"He's just a little boy," Ma continued. "He's confused. He's not a criminal."

"The law says different," Deputy Burns said. "You can't go around almost killing folks, even if they are queer."

"That's enough, Rex," Sheriff Rabbit said. "Tim, I want you to take a moment and think really clearly, and then I want you to start at the beginning. I want you to tell me when Hugo Jones first approached you about this business, and then I want to hear in your own words what happened last night. Deputy Burns is going to write it all down, and remember we already have your accomplices' testimony, so you'd best stick close to the truth."

I considered a number of lies but lacked the strength to build them, so the truth trickled out in a sluggish stream. I told them what I'd seen through the German's window and that Hugo had seen the same thing and said he'd seen more. I told them about kicking the man in the balls because he wouldn't let loose of Bum, and I told them I beat the German with a sock, weighted down with a rock Hugo had picked up in the backyard, and finally when I'd come to the end of the story, I told them I was sorry.

"I'm sure Lang will be happy to hear it," the sheriff scoffed.

"Are you sure there hasn't been a mistake?" Ma asked, reaching for her last shred of hope. "About Mr. Lang, I mean. You're sure he's not involved with those murders?"

"We were in pursuit of the real Cowboy last night," Deputy Burns said. "He snatched another boy right off the street, not far from your house."

"Another boy?" Ma asked.

"Bum Craddick," Sheriff Rabbit said.

The name hit me like a club, sending me back in my chair. The room canted to the side and smeared at the edges as if suddenly framed in grease. Details began to melt – a wax diorama suspended over flame. I fainted then, dropping a hundred feet through my own head, and Bum's name followed me all the way down.

Twenty-Seven: The German

In the hospital they look at me like I am a murderer. The injections of morphine are given clumsily, harshly; they rip the bandages from my wounds like wolves rending meat; they press salve into my burns as if in punishment for my taking up a bed. They know I prefer the company of men, and they think I am no better than the murderer of children.

I think about the blades and the cigarettes and the beating, and in my fevered opiate state there is the certainty that I could kill children – those children. When the nurses and doctors are around I speak only German, and I do not turn away from their expressions of repugnance but rather force them to avert their eyes, and when my friend Carl Baker arrives wearing concern like a virgin's veil, I tell him to go home, because his weakness reminds me of my own. The sheriff comes to take a statement and asks me about my confession to the boys, and I tell him to go away, because I know I am innocent and so does he. Weakness and pain birthed my confession. The confession was meant to end the boys' clumsy torture. I am shamed by it. I should have been a soldier. I should have said nothing, for that is the extent of my guilt. The confession they forced me to repeat was meant only to titillate their leader – that boy faggot Hugo – and I knew that every utterance of rape filled his cock with blood and painted salacious pictures in his mind.

He is unable to differentiate sex and cruelty. To him they are one roiling, ugly mass like the effluent beneath a slaughterhouse drain.

Then a doctor comes for one final, cruel examination before telling me I will be going home, and he tells me that the Bible will end my confusion and show me the way, and I tell him that the confusion is his, and he sneers at me and says he'll pray for my soul, and I ask that he not waste his breath. A nurse and two orderlies arrive with a wheelchair. The men in white grab my wounded arms roughly with the pretense of helping me to the chair, and I shake them off of me, spitting obscenities at the idiot men.

And for the first time in this new life I know hate, the genuine and honest hate that once drove me to command a legion while simultaneously following a lunatic. What fragile peace I had found will never be reclaimed, and I consider all that is not me to be loathsome, insignificant, and expendable.

Except that is a poor deceit. All that is me similarly suffers this hatred.

A taxi drives me home. My sheets have been cleaned and the bed is made and the floors have been scrubbed with a cleanser and lemon juice and I still smell the blood and the piss and the shit and the cigarette stink of that boy faggot's breath. I want to break everything I see. I want to burn it all down.

I don't want to feel this way again. The scalding rage in my chest, once familiar to the point of imperceptibility, has been absent these last years, blessedly snuffed and cooled and soothed. No more. Is this the nature of the Bolivian's curse? To never know peace, to approach the promise of it only to have it set afire and reduced to powder-soft ashes?

I sit on the porch drinking whiskey. It is cheap and harsh on my throat, but I guzzle the foul liquor because I don't know what else to do. New wounds and old scars ache. Every pain I've ever known is with me. The lines on my cheeks and chin scald like red-hot wires. Holes open in my chest. Bullets break skin and bone and organ. Knives cut into my arms and my legs. A child burns my thigh with a cigarette. And I drink this shitty whiskey hoping to numb the persistent misery.

It isn't right.

Cruelty is not taught. It is as certain as a compass point. One can be instructed in the specifics of cruelty, like one can be taught to use a spoon, a knife, a fork, but even without these skills a man will still eat. The need is with us. If man has any superiority to animals in this regard it is his ability to control the brutal impulses – should he choose to – but this is more than offset by the imagination he has been given, an imagination that allows perversions of creativity such as those employed by the Spanish Inquisition, and the prison camps built for wars. Torture is particular to man. He is very good at it.

Tim Randall walks out of his house. The little fucker keeps his head down. He doesn't look at me. Good. Very good. If he looks at me, I will kill him. I will break this bottle over his head and open his neck with a shard. I'll watch him gasp and convulse, trying to draw breath through the hole in his throat. I'll spit on him and grind his pained face beneath the heel of my boot.

I was a captain. I was respected. I commanded a force of four million men. My name brought fear. Esteem. There was only one equal to my power – my very good friend – and he had me murdered. Unable to face the task himself, he ordered some milk-fed bitch with aspirations of greatness to put the bullets in me. I was a captain. Men dropped to their knees before me, in admiration and supplication. The aphrodisiac of supremacy wafted from my pores like the goddamn rose water I use to mask the scent of dirt. I took what I wanted. Before the betrayal and the passing, I was Thor walking the streets of man.

But children never brought Thor to his knees.

I take another drink and feel the whiskey erode the tissues. My eyes never leave the boy. He hurries down the road looking only at the sidewalk beneath his feet, racing away from the source of his shame. Would he walk with less haste, would he strut with pride if he knew he had conquered Thor?

I came to this place to find serenity. In the cities there is nothing but struggle. I thought to remove myself, first to New Orleans, and finally to this place. But a trivial population doesn't guarantee peace.

Over the years I had convinced myself that brutality required motive, but this is a fool's deceit. Cruelty *is* the motive; religion and politics and resources are simply the cloth man weaves to curtain his desires for violence. All ideologies are inherently wrong. None have worked. None have emerged as dominant to the point of suppressing all others, and if this is true – if time has not proven a thing irrefutable – then a thing is a lie. Religion and politics encourage violence so that the meek will proudly throw away breath and flesh because their rot fertilizes fat succulent flora. Men thrive in these gardens of atrocity, proudly tending the blossoms, convinced that the clusters of lovely, vibrant petals – their gods, their governments, their belief in an unquestionable right to destroy all that does not resemble them – are worth the blood and the meat that feed the stalks.

A car stops before my house. It is a familiar car. The car belongs to a man whose face is unremarkable. I would not notice this face in a crowd.

"Ernst," the man says, and I realize I still don't know his name.

"Have a drink," I say, handing the bottle to him. "Drink. Have a cigarette."

"What happened to you?" he asks.

"Happened?" I ask. "Nothing happened. Everything is normal. Everything is as it will always be."

"You've been in another fight," he says.

The unremarkable face wears a frown. He pities me, and it makes me sick. My fist clenches. Pain from my mutilated fingers stabs, but I keep it at my side. He is weak, so fucking weak. He's not worth my hate but like all others it is bestowed upon him. The pain from my wounds turns liquid, spreading over my skin like acid. Every nerve erupts with agony and I close my eyes against it. When I open them, the man kneels at my side.

"Did you come to fuck?" I ask.

His face burns red and he jerks his head around to see if there is anyone in the street to hear.

"I...just.... I wanted to see you."

"Ah, good, yes. You wanted to see me."

"Can we go inside?" he asks.

"It stinks inside," I tell him. "We'll talk here. You can see me here."

"Yeah," he says, but he is not certain. His eyes widen with fright and he quickly stands moving to my left side. "Jesus, Ernst, you're bleeding."

I look at my shirt and blood stains the cloth at my shoulder. My wounds are seeping. The unremarkable man is concerned, but I am not. Much more blood than this has escaped me in the past. I take another drink from the bottle and offer it to him.

"Did you hear me?" he says. "You're bleeding. What happened to you?"

"Like you said, I was in another fight."

"Was it the same man?"

I do not know what he means. What man?

"Did he come after you again?"

Then it occurs to me he means Carl Baker's cousin: the coward Udo – the man who did not fight well.

I put the bottle on the table, ignoring the unremarkable man. I take a cigarette and light it and lean back in my chair.

"Do you want me to leave?" he asks.

"Yes, I want you to leave," I tell him.

"Can I come see you again?"

"Yes, you can come see me again."

"You really are a strange man, Ernst."

"Yes, I am a strange man," I say, blowing a cloud of smoke into the air. Through the smoke I see Tim Randall's house. The sight of it infuriates me. I am drunk, I realize, but that simply frees my tongue. "And who are you?"

"Excuse me?"

"Who the fuck are you?" I say harshly. "Another coward in a nation of cowards? A terrified child afraid to offend his parents? A cocksucking piece of filth who wants his pleasures kept in secrecy because he cannot say I am a man, and I am this kind of man, and to hell with the masks you want me to wear? What kind of man is that? What does he call himself?"

The children's torture is on my skin; their despicable words ring in my ears. I feel their breath and their spit and their hands and their blades and the tiny fires they use to sear my skin.

All moments are this moment because nothing has changed. Everything that has happened or will happen occurs in this time. Past and future are the same variegated smear of fluids leaking from an infected wound. At the center of this wound is this moment, this oozing agonizing second, and when it passes, another moment, equally as impure and painful occurs.

The unremarkable man is angry now. He rights himself and straightens his back as if with pride. What does he know of pride?

I was a fucking captain.

I was....

It doesn't matter. Ernst is dead.

"You really are shithouse crazy."

"Yes, I am shithouse crazy."

He leaves quickly. Drives away without pause. This is better. This is good. I walk back into my home where it smells of blood and sweat and piss and shit.

I have another drink. Light another cigarette and I sit down to my journal.

I will write no more. If all moments are the same moment, recounting each is the exercise of a lunatic. Individual lives are not worth documenting. Only the corpse registry and the carvers of stones care about names. My name is Ernst and I am meaningless.

Twenty-Eight: Sheriff Tom Rabbit

Tom rushed through his morning routine, forsaking time with Pilar and wolfing down his breakfast, suddenly uncomfortable under the watch of Estella's beautiful brown eyes. The city was quiet when he arrived, an hour earlier than was usual for him. In the office he met Walter, who told him the night had been uneventful, and Tom was grateful for it. He made it through most of the morning without interruption, reading reports and cross-referencing Ford vehicle registrations with a list of German names. He tried to keep Estella and Ernst Lang out of his thoughts as he poured over the documentation, attempting to see the Cowboy appear in the list. The change in his day came a few minutes after eleven when Gil limped into his office, wearing a frown.

"Those boys are here to see you," Gil said. "Burl Jones is with them."

"What do they want?"

"They want to change their statements."

The burn in Tom's stomach returned with a flash and he closed his eyes to keep his temper in check.

"Send them home," he said. "We already have their statements."

"They said we got it wrong."

"We got it wrong? All we've got is what they told us?"

"I'm just telling you what Burl told me."

"Son of a bitch," Tom muttered. "Send them in."

Burl Jones led his son and two of the other boys into the room. The Randall kid wasn't with them, but Ben Livingston and Austin Chitwood entered dressed like they were going to church, hair smoothed down to a shiny sheet with pomade, heads slightly bowed and hands crossed over their crotches like proper and respectful Christian boys. The display disgusted Tom.

Behind the boys, Burl Jones stood in his everyday suit, which had a smudge of dust on the left shoulder. He removed his hat and stood straight and said, "We just come from Buck Taylor's place."

Of the dozen or so lawyers in Barnard, Taylor was the only one that Tom couldn't stand the sight of. He was a pretentious old whale with white hair, yellowed at the temples. He walked around Barnard like he owned the sidewalks and was more than happy to chatter nonsense at a jury just to hear himself talk. But he won his cases, nearly all of them, and Tom didn't like receiving the information that Taylor was defending the little monsters standing before him.

"And where is Buck?" Tom asked.

"He'll be along," Burl said.

"He tried to touch us," Austin Chitwood announced with a voice that trembled so badly it sounded near to a giggle. "The German bastard tried to...."

Hugo shoved his friend to quiet him down.

"That's enough boys," Burl Jones said.

Tom examined the elder Jones's face, and what he encountered was a sorrowful and confounded expression, not the hard defiance he usually found there. The man chewed on serious thoughts and he stood distracted. Something had gotten into Burl's head and it was eating away like a worm through damp dirt.

No one spoke again until Buck Taylor walked into the office, wearing a lightweight, blue cotton suit. His full face shimmered with perspiration, and a smile as phony as a three-dollar bill showed rows of white teeth.

"Tom Rabbit," he said as if they were dear old friends, "it's been a long time."

"Yes, it has," Tom agreed. "What can I do for you, Buck?"

"It's a sad business," Taylor said. In a dramatic display the lawyer lost his smile and slapped a fat palm to the back of his neck. He looked at the floor, shaking his head slowly as if he was about to reveal a tragedy. "I think it would be best if my clients waited outside. Burl, why don't you take the boys down the street for some sodas? I'll be over directly."

Burl nodded. The boys filed out and the man followed them.

Tom recognized Taylor's ploy. Burl and those boys were just for show. The lawyer had wanted Tom to see the boys, the children of the community. Buck had told them to dress in their proper Sunday attire and instructed them in contrition and manners. Tom wondered if the lawyer would have gone to such trouble if he'd seen Ernst Lang bound to his bed, humiliated and bleeding. Tom figured the lawyer would.

"We already have the boys' statements," Tom said. "I'd imagine your discussion at this point should be with the judge."

"I'll be headed over to Jeff's when I'm finished up here," Taylor said, making sure Tom understood the lawyer's familiarity with the judge. "But we don't really need to involve him in this."

"I imagine he'll want to be involved, what with the trial and all."

"A trial isn't going to help anyone, and I would strongly suggest you listen to what I have to say, and then take the appropriate action." Buck took a deep breath, and Tom knew he was about to launch into a speech. "Those boys are the victims here, plain and simple. They were lured into the trap of a deviant with unnatural intentions. Plied with liquor. The great state of Texas has rather conclusive laws in regard to sodomy, Tom. They are not matters of etiquette or points of view, but concrete legislation meant to protect our children and our homes. To refute this legislation is to condone the most unnatural of acts including incest, bigamy, and bestiality, and succeeds in nothing but ignoring the moral sense of the people in your community and striking down the very foundations of the home. Furthermore...."

"Stop," Tom said. "Just cork it, Buck. I'm not a jury and I'm not one of your buddies from the Ranger Lodge, so just tell me what's on your mind and let me get back to work."

"Is it true you questioned one Ernst Lang in regard to the recent murders of Harold Ashton and David Williams?"

"Yes."

"And in the course of this questioning did Mr. Lang admit to being a homosexual?"

"He did, but...."

"Whoever has carnal copulation with a beast, or in an opening of the body, except sexual parts, with another human being for the purpose of having carnal copulation shall be guilty of sodomy. That is the law, Tom. It's as clear as the Good Book, and there you were with a confessed criminal, but you took no action."

"With what evidence?" Tom barked.

"You had an eyewitness account from Hugo Jones, and an admission of guilt. That man should not have been allowed to walk our streets like some wild boar seeking to devour the innocence of those fine young boys."

"They attacked Lang in his home and tied him to a bed and they burned him with cigarettes and they cut into him like a piece of barbecue."

"They acted in their own defense," Taylor said, nonplussed by Tom's irate tone. "All three of those boys were in the presence of a rattlesnake, and like all rattlesnakes it was only a matter of time before he struck. Austin Chitwood is ready to swear that Lang attempted to touch his privates, and both the Jones and Livingston boys will concur."

"There's nothing in those boy's statements about Lang attacking them. They got a bad idea and some juice in their balls and they decided Lang was a murderer, even though they didn't have a shred of proof. Then they knocked him cold, bound him and tortured him. So don't give me this horseshit. All of their statements match up."

"We'll be submitting new statements," Taylor said evenly.

"And they'll go in the trash."

The lawyer began walking past the front of Tom's desk the way he might pace before a jury box. His smile had returned and he slicked back a yellow wing of hair over his left ear.

"The initial statements are meaningless," he said. "As I noted to Burl, children enduring that level of trauma just want to pretend the incident never happened. This ridiculous talk about them ambushing Lang is clearly drivel. But in that version of the events, they remain unspoiled by lewd, unnatural, *and illegal* behavior. It's to be expected they would create a scenario that is less repugnant to them, even if it requires turning the guilt on themselves. I know a dozen doctors who'll support this theory should the case proceed to trial, but I strongly suggest you have this Lang man withdraw his charges so my clients – no, so this entire community – can avoid the humiliating stain of Lang's perverse carnal practices. Further, I suggest you press charges against the man and get him off the streets so he's not again tempted to act on his sickness."

"Here's what I think," Tom said. "I think your clients found out we were in pursuit of the Cowboy at exactly the same time they were torturing Lang, and they're changing their stories because the only thing that could have saved their asses here is the man's confession, which was extracted under duress and doesn't hold an ounce of credibility."

"And what do you think a jury will make of this?" Taylor asked. "Four upstanding young men, two of whom are only a year away from heading overseas to fight for their country, accosted in the most humiliating way any man might be by an admitted deviant?"

Taylor's logic was sinking in, but Tom struggled against it. Doc Randolph had said Lang suffered from a sickness, and though it may have been an unwholesome affliction, Tom didn't believe it constituted a valid excuse for four young men to all but murder him in his bed. He reached for the only light he could see.

"What about the Randall boy?" Tom asked. "I didn't notice him here this morning."

"Timothy Randall is still traumatized," Taylor explained.

Which meant the lawyer had not gotten to the boy, or the kid actually had a shred of integrity and would be sticking to his story. Still it would be Tim's word against the other three, and he was the youngest and by far the least credible to a jury.

"I highly suggest you consider these facts before proceeding against my clients. If Lang retracts his statement then the judge will have little choice but to throw the case out, and honestly, nothing would be better for this city than to have this wicked business packed away in the basement."

"You can go now," Tom said. "I'll take it under consideration."

"One more point," the fat lawyer said.

"No," Tom interrupted. "No more points. You can go now, Buck. I'll get back to you this evening."

⑂

Tom stewed in his office for an hour. He'd forgotten about his promise to Doc Randolph that they'd share lunch over at Bob's Stop, and he was surprised when the man appeared in his doorway, looking annoyed.

The sheriff apologized and rose from his chair. He led Doc Randolph back through the office and down the street to the restaurant. He looked around the room, grateful to find no signs of Buck Taylor, Burl Jones or the three boys. Noting his distraction, Doc Randolph asked what was on Tom's mind, and though he'd come to no conclusions of his own, he described Buck Taylor's visit and detailed the man's legal strategy to twist the blame for Ernst Lang's attack on Lang himself. The whole thing made a riot of Tom's gut and when he ordered his lunch, it consisted of four slices of toast and a glass of buttermilk.

"Taylor's a sharp one," the doctor said.

"He's a mosquito."

"He'll win, you know. There's not a man in this county that won't come down on the side of those boys."

"I know," Tom said. "If I hadn't been there with those little monsters, Buck's take on the situation would have carried some real weight."

"It's really for the best," Doc Randolph said. "For Lang I mean."

"How do you figure that?" Tom asked.

"Right now, between your office and those boys' families and a few of the hospital staff, very few people know about Lang. Gossip will get the word around, but it'll be nothing compared to what the newspapers will do with that trial. Lang is going to be vilified and condemned before this even reaches a court. Right now, he has the opportunity to recuperate from the attack and leave town quietly ahead of the mob. And you can keep your mind on our Cowboy."

"It sounds easy enough, but it doesn't sound right."

"Maybe not, but don't get overly defensive of Lang," the doctor said. "He's more than he lets on."

"How's that?"

"On the night I took Lang to the hospital, I stayed with him for a while. That place needs its forms and its questions, and I sat there while a nurse took down Lang's information. When she asked him his date of birth, do you know what he said?"

"You know I don't."

"He said eighteen eighty-seven, which would make him nearly sixty years old."

"For the love of Christ, Doc, he was delirious. If I went through what he did, I'd have a little trouble with dates myself. Hell, I probably wouldn't remember my own name."

"As a point of fact, he got that wrong, too."

"Come again?"

The doctor drank from his water glass and leaned back in his chair. "The first question they want answered is the patient's name, so I gave it to them when he was admitted, but the nurse asked for verification while she was taking down his medical history, and he said something like Roe. He wasn't speaking well, and most of what he said was in German or badly slurred, but when she asked his name, he said Ernst Roe. So while I can imagine that his advanced injuries contributed to delusional behavior, you might also want to consider the possibility that he's here under an assumed name, and if that is the case, why did he change it, and what is so interesting about Ernst Roe?"

"Or I can just leave the man alone," Tom said. "What I know is Lang is not the Cowboy, and he's been through enough. There's not a sentence a judge could pass for his crime that Hugo and his friends didn't mete out tenfold. So I'm going to go to his house and ask him to drop the charges, and I'll be choking on my tongue while I do it, and then as far as I'm concerned he can go wherever he pleases and be whoever he wants to be."

"He might go looking for revenge."

"And I wouldn't blame him," Tom said. "I'd arrest him in two seconds flat if he goes after those boys, but I wouldn't blame him one bit."

⫴

On his way out of the office to deliver his difficult request to Ernst Lang, Tom ran into Estella on the sidewalk. Her blue dress was buttoned up to her neck and the handle of a large basket looped over the crook of her elbow. In the basket she carried sundry vegetables and a tin of coffee. She stopped upon seeing Tom and smiled at him and wished the sheriff a "Good afternoon."

He still hadn't grown used to hearing her voice, and with everything else on his mind, he managed a simple parroting of her greeting and then stood there like a statue with a badly etched smile. Tom no longer knew how to behave with the girl. Estella averted her eyes and gazed at the sidewalk, and Tom felt like a fool for not being able to form a single pleasant word for her. He thought she looked particularly pretty today. Her cheeks seemed fuller and healthier, as did her figure, and he couldn't help but notice the way her breasts strained against the soft blue fabric, but the apparent physical changes brought shame fast as a flint spark, noticed but quickly snuffed as more pressing matters demanded his attention.

"You have a nice day," he said, tipping his hat.

"Sheriff Rabbit," Estella said, "may we talk? It is of great concern to my aunt that we talk."

"Of course," Tom said, "but I'm on my way out on business. We'll talk tonight at the house."

Estella dipped her chin in a nod and smiled at the sheriff, and then continued down the sidewalk.

Tom drove to Bennington and turned left, his sick belly and rapidly beating heart making poor passengers. On Dodd Street, he parked just beyond the Randall's driveway and crossed the street to knock on Lang's door.

The man opened the door and regarded the sheriff with half lidded eyes. He wore a loose-fitting green shirt and a pair of short pants the color of wheat. Two of the fingers on his left hand were bandaged and the knot above his eye still looked like a split plum, but his clothing hid the worst of the damage.

"How are you feeling?" Tom asked.

"What can I help you with, Sheriff?" Lang said, tersely. "I feel my company is less than pleasant just now, and since we are not friends, it would be best if you were direct."

"May I come in?"

"Yes, you may come in, but only for a minute. I need to rest."

Tom walked into the sparse living room and Lang closed the door behind him. He took a deep breath, hoping it would settle his nerves sufficiently for him to spit out what he had to say, but his throat had closed tight. He cleared his throat as quietly as he could.

"I don't know a good way to say this," Tom said, "but I need you to drop the charges against those boys."

The German made a growling sound low in his throat.

"Ernst, we can prosecute them, but it's not going to stick."

"So there is a good reason to be tied down and tortured? What reason is that?"

Tom closed his eyes and gave himself a moment to gather his thoughts. He thought through Buck Taylor's explanation and only succeeded in angering himself.

"After the boys heard that we were chasing a suspect – the real suspect – the same night they attacked you, they changed their stories and they're all saying the same thing."

"And what are they saying?"

"They're saying that you invited them in," Tom said. "They said you gave them whiskey and...." He grew frustrated at his inability to express the situation. "Ernst, they're saying you attacked them first, okay?"

The German nodded his head slowly, chewing over the information. "And they all say this? Even my neighbor?"

"No, Tim Randall is sticking to the original story."

"Then he will prove I am telling the truth."

"Jesus Christ, would you listen to me? You're a queer. A judge and jury are going to believe those boys because they want to believe them. They are going to crucify you. In school we picked on kids for being pansies. Somebody got the label and we'd beat the shit out of them in the playground. I didn't know why. I certainly never thought it through. Most of us didn't. It didn't fucking matter. And this is just another playground."

Lang stepped forward. His scarred cheeks flushed red.

"Do you want to know about my playground?" Lang shouted, sending Tom back a step. "At my school, I was the boy that decided which children bled and which children went unharmed. I grew up smart enough to know my place in the world and strong enough to defend it. And I became a soldier, and I became a captain, and men died because I told them to and men were killed because I ordered it and I have worn more blood than you can even imagine." The German paused. Spittle foamed at the corner of his mouth. His chest rose and fell like a bellows, and he winced from the pain to his broken ribs. When he spoke again, his fury was controlled, "And those bastards, those little shits humiliated me. *Me.* They made me lie in my own filth while they cut me and laughed at me. And you're telling me that if there is a trial, I will be defending myself?"

"Ernst," Tom said as evenly as he could manage, "right now, no one knows what happened that night. The newspapers are too caught up with the Cowboy, but if this goes to trial, every damn man in this county is going to know you're a queer, and your life is going to be ground down like a weed, and that's if one of those yahoos doesn't decide to blow your brains out over this."

"So now we know what the life of a German deviant is worth."

"I'm not saying it's right," Tom told him. "I'm just telling you the way it is. I could arrest you right now for what you've already admitted to me, but I figure you've been through enough."

"You are so kind," Lang said.

"Maybe you can find some help in one of the cities. If it's a sickness they might be able to treat you."

"That's enough, Sheriff," Lang said. His voice came across flat and weak. He walked to his front door and grasped the knob. "I am very tired now. Thank you for coming by."

"Think about what I said."

"I have spent a lifetime thinking about these very things," Lang replied. "Perhaps I will spend the next lifetime thinking about something else. Good afternoon, Sheriff."

Lang pulled open the front door. Burl Jones stood on the porch, holding a Colt revolver. Tom saw the man and the gun, but not before the German did. After a momentary pause, Lang turned in a precise, military step and faced Jones. He squared his shoulders and lifted his chin as if about to receive a medal.

Jones fired twice at point blank range. Blood blossomed on the back of the German's shirt like two great crimson eyes opening as the bullets passed through, and Lang shuffled back soundlessly. Then he crashed to the floor, his eyes gazing blankly at the ceiling, his mouth set in a defiant line.

Feeling stunned and off balance, Tom stared at the murdered man.

"He should'a stayed away from my boy," Jones said through a tight jaw. "You should'a arrested the faggot when I told you to."

Then Jones fired three more shots, each hitting Tom Rabbit in the chest. The sheriff died before he hit the German's floor.

Twenty-Nine: Tim Randall

I saw Burl Jones walk up to the German's house, and I saw him standing in front of the door, but I never saw the gun in his hand. For much of the afternoon, I'd taken frightened peeks through the living room window, certain that at any moment I would see the German stomping across the street and climbing the porch stairs to return the brutality I'd shown him. Ma had forbidden me to play in the front yard – partly as a punishment for my crime, and partly to protect me from my victim's retaliation. When I saw Mr. Jones walking down the sidewalk, I took a permanent place at the window, unease covering me like sweat. Sheriff Rabbit had relayed the lie Hugo Jones was telling, and I couldn't imagine how his father would react to it.

Then the gunshots. I heard five in all. The pops like firecrackers startled me and I pulled away from the glass, sank to my knees and peered over the windowsill at the street beyond. Burl Jones stepped into the afternoon light, head low with his hat brim pulled down, and returned the way he had come.

I shouted for Ma, and she rushed into the living room. Her eyes were again stained red from tears, but there wasn't time to entertain further guilt. I told her what I'd seen. She doubted me, and I couldn't blame her. I'd introduced her to as much violence as she'd ever known firsthand, and the idea that I was again its messenger seemed impossible and overwhelming, but I persisted until she called the sheriff's office, and I stayed close to her right up to the time Deputies Burns and Niall arrived, and I told them what I saw. Then my mother told me to go to my room and wait until she said I could come out. In my room, I went to my window and pressed against the frame, so that I could see the front of Mr. Lang's house. The deputies crossed the street and climbed into the shadows of the porch. My heart beat rapidly, unsure of what I expected to see. Then Deputy Burns came back out and he stood on the German's porch, looking upward with a wracked face and clenching his hat in his hands. Deputy Niall appeared behind Burns and put his hand on the distraught officer's shoulder and this seemed to anger Burns, who jerked his shoulder away from the touch and began shouting and waving his hat around like a bronco rider about to be tossed. Both men went back inside, and ten minutes later more police officers appeared and five minutes after that Doc Randolph walked up the porch steps to the German's house, and then an ambulance came, and a long time later two police officers carried out a stretcher covered in a white sheet, and two minutes after that, two different officers carried another stretcher with a bulkier cargo, and though he was covered in a white sheet, I knew the man on that stretcher was my neighbor, Mr. Lang, and I knew that he was dead.

Ma called me to come out of my room when Deputy Burns returned. The big man looked as miserable as any man I'd ever seen, except perhaps Mr. Lang near the end of his time with me and Hugo and the others. He asked me to slowly and with as much detail as I could muster tell him what I'd seen, and I did. Burl Jones went to the door of the German's house; there were five gunshots; and Mr. Jones walked away. Deputy Burns had to have asked me a dozen times if I was sure about who I'd seen. I was, and I told him so.

Then Deputy Burns left and the hearse pulled away and the police cars followed it, and in a matter of minutes, only Doc Randolph remained. He sat on the steps of the German's porch with his head down. I watched him until Ma told me to come away from the window.

That night my mother stayed home from work again. After supper she told me I could listen to the radio for an hour and then I was to go to bed. Rita Sherman didn't come over that night, and Ma, exhausted from so many days of strife, fell asleep at the kitchen table while she was writing a letter to my daddy, even though he was still missing.

I don't know why I went back to the German's house. Maybe I was still searching for clues, a piece of evidence that would link him to wrongdoing so that I could shrug off the repugnance I felt for my actions. If he were a criminal or connected to criminals, then my behavior might find justification and pardon.

Stepping into his dark living room, waiting for my eyes to adjust, I saw the two chalk sketches, outlining where the bodies had fallen. They were easy enough to identify from the shape, and I stood over the thicker, shorter drawing and looked down at the empty space between the lines where dark smudges stained the wooden floor, and the scent of rose water drifted into my nose. I thought about what this man was – not *who*, but *what*. Anger surged in to replace my grief and guilt, and I looked between the chalk lines and saw nothing but justice. The only thing left of the man was darkness and stains filling lines of white. He was a deviant. A faggot. A foreigner. He wasn't worth the half a penny the chalk had cost to draw him. These hateful thoughts were too brief, though, as the longer I gazed at the outline, the more my mind filled it in with specifics of my neighbor's appearance. For a moment he grinned at me from the floor, his terribly scarred face appearing playful and not frightening at all. Then the room fell away from me, because I'd finally learned the lesson the German had tried to teach me in this very room, and the weight of it struck my chest like a fist. If I thought of the man as a queer, or a Nazi, or "the German," or anything but my neighbor Ernst Lang, I could live with what I'd done. But the frame of chalk represented more than just a shape, a figure, a series of arcs and lines; it was where my good neighbor, a man who had done me no harm, took his last breath and where his final thoughts faded as his soul moved on. He had

been real, and he had been principled, and he had possessed a
life whether mundane or exceptional that I had helped end.

I don't know how long I remained in his house that night,
certainly not as long as it felt, and I don't know why I stole his
diary, but before I left Mr. Lang's house for the last time, I carried it securely under my arm.

That evening, Burl Jones was arrested for the murder of
Sheriff Rabbit and Ernst Lang. I never heard another word
about what we'd done to my neighbor, at least not outside my
own head. The matter was dropped and seemingly forgotten by
everyone in town as the focus shifted to the murder of the city's
respected sheriff. Rarely was Mr. Lang's name mentioned in the
newspaper articles, covering the crime. Often enough he was
referred to as "the other man," or "the second victim," or "a by-
stander."

Thirty: Tim Randall

Sleep provided my only sanctuary in the weeks following Mr. Lang's death. Dreams didn't invade my rest, and the sharp-nailed fingers of nightmares were spared me, and would have proved redundant considering the thoughts that haunted me during my waking hours. Unfortunately, my ability to sleep found considerable opposition in the racing thoughts given me by guilt.

Bum died the day after Mr. Lang. My best friend never woke up, so I never got the chance to apologize. I cried as much for him as I had for my missing father, but even the thin hope I held for my daddy's return was denied me with Bum. He was dead and he wasn't coming back, and his Spy Commander tin spyglass would rust away in a box in an attic as his sorrowful parents continued with their lives in the rooms below. Bum's ma spent the entire funeral looking around confused as if unable to understand why she sat in church on a Friday afternoon with so many other people – all staring at a minister and a polished box and a handful of flowers captured in a cheap glass vase. At the repast, she acted like she was the hostess of a fancy party, and her cheerful banter verged on hysteria until Clay Craddick led her upstairs so she could rest. Fatty appeared similarly confused on those occasions he stopped eating and actually lifted his head to observe the men and women in his daddy's living room. That night Ma told me Bum was at peace, and he was with God in

Heaven, and his soul would know eternal joy. I believed her, but only because I had to believe her, otherwise I could never have lived with what I had done.

Some nights when sleep eluded me, I would retrieve Mr. Lang's journal from under my mattress and I'd try to read what was written there, imagining that if I stared at the words hard enough and long enough they would resolve into recognizable phrases. They never did. The lines and swirls and dots remained meaningless.

The worst days of summer were on us and I spent my waking hours in a feverish lethargy, feeling nauseated and bone tired, and on the one afternoon I attempted to cool off in the lake, I slipped on a rock and went face down in the water, and instead of trying to right myself I swam deeper and further out and after a time I became so confused I didn't know which direction the surface was. Panic gripped me like the jaws of a coyote, and water trickled down the back of my throat and I spluttered, and for a moment, I looked to the green-tinged water engulfing me and saw innumerable dark shapes shifting and moving amid the gently waving fronds of plants, and I imagined the shapes were my daddy and Bum and Mr. Lang, but they were also Harold Ashton and David Williams, and maybe it would be better if I just stayed where I was and accepted their welcome because all that existed outside of the lake was scorching heat and pain. But I began floating upward, and with no conscious effort to fight my ascension, I surfaced, choking and rubbing my eyes to see the shore waiting only a handful of yards away.

As we entered September the promise of school loomed, and on the first Sunday afternoon of the month Ma suggested we go to the pictures at the Palace Theater, because they were playing a comedy with Bob Hope and Dorothy Lamour. Many of the faces at the theater were familiar. Not a single one of them meant a thing to me. I knew who they were, but I might as well have been looking over a field of pale gray flowers for all of the interest I took in the particulars of the population. Brett Fletcher had parked his wheelchair by an ashtray near the stairs. Austin Chitwood stood with a brown-haired girl and they both laughed like donkeys, and seeing him didn't so much as flick the numbing sickness in my belly. Estella Hernandez walked with her aunt across the lobby. Arm in arm with the ashen-haired woman, the girl's pregnancy was noticeable if not obvious. I saw friends from school but could barely work up a greeting for them, and they quickly returned to their parents and siblings, confounded by my reticence. Ma spoke to women from the factory, and they tried to cheer me up, but their voices raked across my ears like rusted blades, and their joyful laughter struck me as repulsive and inappropriate, though I couldn't expect them to share my list of regrets and losses. Rex Burns had Regina Mason on his arm. Maybe they were out celebrating Rex's appointment as Barnard's new sheriff, but he didn't look like he was in much of a celebrating mood. His frequent smiles failed to clear the clouds from his eyes. He noticed me at Ma's side and gave me a nod. He'd lost his best friend, too.

In the paper that morning he'd made a pledge to bring the Cowboy to justice within the month. It wouldn't take that long, but the Cowboy's apprehension would have nothing to do with the efforts of the Barnard Sheriff's Department.

Before the newsreel started Ma leaned over to tell me that Emily Owens's nephew would be coming home soon. She told me this because Dexter Owens had been reported missing in action back in April, and Ma took this as a promising sign that Daddy would also be found and sent home to us. The news seemed to cheer her, so I acted happy about it, but I didn't believe Fred Randall was going to be found or come home to his family. We weren't going to see him again. I could never tell Ma that I believed her husband was a hunk of rotting, punctured meat left in a field for the birds to pick over.

The features and cartoons and the Bob Hope film played out as smears of gray movement and random abrasive noises. When the audience laughed, it sounded like a thousand men screaming, and their applause cracked and popped like synchronized gunfire, and by the time the theater lights came back up, I felt like shouting at the smiling faces, wanting to know what right they had to be happy in this miserable, hateful world where a boy like Bum Craddick got his throat cut and my daddy lay dead in a field. And it wasn't their fault, and I knew it wasn't their fault, but they had no right to smile or laugh or feel anything but the full-of-empty nothing I felt.

That night I pulled the German's diary out from beneath my mattress and held it against my chest and prayed that when I opened it, the words would make sense. I couldn't help but think that something in Mr. Lang's journal would explain everything that had happened to me that summer. The book had to hold the answers. Things had to happen for a reason. If they didn't, then misery would always be a moment away.

∭

I spent much of the next day in my room, holding Mr. Lang's diary and casting furtive glances through my window at his now empty house. The sight of the house took only seconds to unnerve me, and I'd walk back to my bed and open the leather-bound enigma, reading the numbers and the occasional name. Eventually Ma came in and sat on the bed next to me, and she offered to stay home from the factory if I wanted her to, but I said no, and she offered to call her parents and have them come over, but I said no to that too. I received the usual instructions to keep the doors locked and ask who was there if anyone knocked at night while she was gone. Then she kissed me on the forehead and left.

Thirty minutes later, I carefully tied Mr. Lang's diary with my book strap and slung it over my back before retrieving my bicycle from the backyard. On Bennington Avenue, I turned north.

After another night of fleeting sleep, the cloak of exhaustion hung over my shoulders like a cape made of mud. The high heat of late afternoon worked into my skin and muscles and added further discomfort to the fatigue, gnawing at my muscles and joints. Already my vision blurred at the edges, and despite a bright and clear day, every house, tree, bush, and person seemed to exist beyond a sheet of old glass – colors deadened by a patina of dust. I pedaled all the way to the northern edge of the city, adjusting my book strap when it cut into my already pained muscles. At the farm road I stopped and wiped sweat from my neck and brow, and I looked to the west, knowing I'd reached the halfway mark of my journey, but feeling like the trek had already taken days.

I had to know what was in Mr. Lang's journal, and the only man I could think of to translate the volume was Brett Fletcher, who'd learned a fair amount of German while stationed overseas. If he couldn't do it, or wouldn't do it, I'd find one of the merchants in town – maybe Mr. Baker – to help.

The pedals fought my efforts, seeming to push back against the soles of my feet as I struggled to complete the ride out to the Fletcher place. When the house appeared on the right side of the road ahead, a fresh trickle of energy ran through me. The pedaling came easier and even the scratchy discomfort of my sweaty clothes seemed to ease, and I imagined this was the kind of relief a man in a desert felt upon seeing a distant oasis or mirage. My vision remained uncertain, though. The house and acreage beyond frayed at the edges like a watercolor landscape smeared at the edges.

I was surprised to find that none of the local kids had gathered on Brett's porch for an afternoon of storytelling. Likely, the heat had kept them all at home or had driven them to the lake.

Movement at the corner of my eye caused a reflexive turning of my head toward a low line of shrubs, and though the bushes carried the same feathery edges of everything else I viewed, I thought I saw someone crouching behind the shrubs, eyes fixed on me. Distracted by the certainty I was being watched, I wasn't paying attention to the ground. The front wheel of my bike went into a hole and I jerked forward and nearly fell off the seat completely before righting the handlebars and bringing the thing to a stop. When I looked back at the shrubs, no face hovered above the leafy mounds, so I convinced myself that my fatigued mind had drawn the face there in the first place. If I couldn't dream during my brief bouts of sleep, my mind seemed determined to deliver dreams while I was awake.

At the house, I leaned my bike against the railing of Brett's porch and then climbed the steps into the shadows, relieved to have the baking sun off of my neck. I rang the bell and as I waited, a shock of fear ran along my neck, causing my skin to pucker. The unexpected panic came from an image that presented itself without warning. A man had waited behind the low hedge and now raced across Brett's front yard, eyes wild and arms outstretched to scoop me up. The fancy struck my mind fully formed, and I spun on my heels to confront the man I expected to see racing up the porch steps to me, except no man attacked from the yard. I looked back at the row of shrubs and thought I saw a speck of white amid the green leaves, but upon focusing on the spot, I found nothing but a break in the foliage.

"Come on in if you're gonna," Brett called from the other side of the door.

I pulled back the screen and enjoyed a rush of cool air provided by a fan situated in the hallway ahead. Though gloomy, I could see dozens of framed pictures had been affixed to the hallway walls on either side of the fan, and a door stood open at the far end.

"This way, son," Brett said from my left.

He had parked his wheelchair in the middle of the living room, its tires making noticeable trenches in the soft carpet fabric. A brown sofa ran behind him. Large round doilies draped the back cushions and the arms. Light poured into the room from the picture windows on the south and west walls, and here again, I saw dozens of framed photographs. They all seemed to include a gaunt woman with a bun of snow white hair, and it occurred to me then, that for all of the times Bum and I had come out to hear Brett's stories, I'd never been in his house.

"What can I do for you?" Brett asked. He flicked his chin at me and said, "You got some homework you want me to look over?"

Confused I shook my head and then realized he had been indicating the book I carried over my shoulder. I removed the strap and held the journal for a moment, staring at its brown leather cover.

"You're the boy whose daddy went missing," Brett said.

"Yes, sir," I whispered, still entranced by lines of the leather's grain, etched like maps in the hide.

"I'm sorry for that, son," he said. "I truly am, but a war needs its heroes, and you can sleep proud knowing your daddy fought a good fight."

I wanted to tell him that my father wasn't dead. Daddy was still just missing. I didn't have the strength and instead of voicing what I had come to believe was a lie, I presented the book to Brett.

"What's that you've got?" he asked.

"It's a book. A diary, I think. It's got dates and stuff."

"Is this your daddy's journal?" Brett asked.

"No," I said, "It's in German."

"Really?" Brett said. His eyebrows arched and he ticked his head to the side, hands still grasping the rests of his chair. "And where did you come across this book?"

"Found it."

"Mmm," he hummed, unconvinced. "Found it, did you? Well maybe you better let me take a look at that."

I handed him the book, and Brett flipped it open, eyes moving rapidly as he absorbed the words on the page. He nodded and hummed and scratched his neck.

"There's a pad and pencil on that table." He pointed to his left. "Bring those here."

I did as he asked. He snatched up the pencil and returned his attention to the book, and then he closed it, setting the pad and pencil down on its cover. My heart sank as I took his dismissal of the journal as his inability to read it, but he wasn't interested in the book just then. He wanted to talk.

"You boys had the right idea," Brett said. "The only shame is that you stopped yourselves short. More folks should be following your example. Maybe soon enough they will." He scratched his ear and gave me a big smile. "What most folks don't understand is that evil runs in the blood. It passes down from father to son like the color of your eyes and the hair on your head. Now I don't claim to know all the scientific talk for such things, but those Germans come from rotten seeds, and their souls are sick with it from the moment they claw their way from between their mother's legs. Some of them learn to cover it up good and proper, but most are only one step away from demon. Burl Jones had the right idea, and instead of sitting in that jail, they ought to be throwing a parade in his honor, and you boys should be riding right up front with him."

"I don't know about that," I muttered. Brett's ideas made me uncomfortable because they reminded me of things Hugo had said.

"You're young yet," Brett said. "With a few more years under your belts, you boys would have done the right thing and seen to it that Nazi piece of filth never got out of his bed, but Hugo's daddy finished things up, so no harm done. We need more folks like Burl these days, a whole lot more. People need to understand that those bastards might have fled Germany, but that don't mean they left their evil behind. No, sir. They brought it with them, carrying the dark seeds like another piece of luggage. You move down the street, it don't change who you are, if you know what I mean."

"Yes, sir," I said.

Brett chuckled and slapped his thigh with a broad hand. "You do have some growing up to do yet. Maybe if you'd seen what I've seen you wouldn't be so shy. Now I told a story at the Fourth of July celebration, and I know you heard it because I saw you there. The thing is I didn't tell it right. I didn't tell it truthfully because I thought the truth of it might have been too grim for the youngsters. But I think you're man enough to hear it."

"Sir?" I asked. I didn't want to hear one of his stories. I wanted to know what the German had written in his journal.

"Before seeing the real action, I was stationed near Edinburgh, Scotland at a prisoner of war camp, where the English kept their German prisoners. Most of my day was spent speaking to that filth, trying to get information, but those fuckers just smiled at me and shrugged and acted like I'd asked them over for supper. I didn't blame them. They had it good. Truth is I've never seen the like of it. The military had commandeered a fine old hotel to use as the prison, and those Nazi sons of bitches slept on fine beds and ate the same rations as my squad. Why would they say one goddamned thing? They were practically on vacation.

"As for the girls, well I don't need to tell you how a lady is drawn to a uniformed man. No sir. The local women all but flocked to the edges of the camp to peer through the fences, and there were these two girls. Oh, they were the sweetest looking little things. Two sisters with the brightest eyes you've ever seen and pigtails, just as lovely as a spring morning. Many was the afternoon they'd stop by the hotel with a basket of cookies they'd spent all morning baking, and they thanked us for protecting their country. Maisie and Edeen. Those were their names. Well the security at this fancy prison wasn't good. In fact, many times I complained about the lax conditions but the commanding officer was a brittle twig of a man who didn't like his orders questioned so nothing was ever done about it. At least, not until he was forced to do something about it.

"I knew it would happen soon enough, and one day four of the Nazi bastards escaped into the hills. The commanding officer all but shrugged, certain his men would bring them back in no time at all, and I cursed up a storm, but the twig just sneered and dismissed me.

"His attitude changed fast enough when they found those two girls. A lot of attitudes changed because of that, I'll tell you.

"The girls had been strangled and opened up just like the Ashton boy, and there was this note, see. The note accused the girls of fraternizing with the enemy – which meant Allied soldiers, you understand – and it went on to say that the killers would murder every child in Edinburgh before they were through. Well, those four men were captured the next day, and I don't need to tell you things didn't go too well for our prisoners after that. That very night we took every one of the escapees into the hills and tied them to trees, and we showed them what we thought of their 'Master Race' by cutting off what made them men and letting them bleed out on the forest floor.

"I honestly thought we'd be seeing that same kind of justice after those boys were killed, but that's the difference, you see. Most men can be driven to kill if it's to defend themselves or their kin or if they get angry enough. The lousy Germans do it because they don't know anything else. Until folks realize that, they'll be in danger. Do you see what I mean?"

"I guess so," I told him, which brought another chuckle from my host.

"Well, whether you see now or not, you will soon enough." He slid the pad of paper to the side and opened the journal again. Lifting the pencil, he began whistling tunelessly, knocking the wooden pencil against his chin. He gazed into the journal for some time, writing nothing, before he said, "Why don't you go fetch us a couple of cold pops from the refrigerator? I know my whistle could use wetting."

Though thirsty myself, my first inclination was to decline the beverage and excuse myself from Brett's house, because the weird light in his eyes when he talked about those murdered girls and the Germans he'd helped tie to trees tightened my skin. He looked pleased about these things, as if he were describing a cool dip in the lake or a particularly good piece of barbecue. But I knew Brett often got lost in his stories, and he had trouble getting around, even his own house, so I agreed and followed the hall to the kitchen at the back of the house.

I pushed open the white door and stepped inside. To my right was the back door and through the glass I saw the polished black nose of a Ford jutting from a narrow stall in the yard. Next to the door a proper suit coat and a duster hung from pegs, and above this was a shelf. A gray Stetson sat on the projection, displayed like a trophy. But I wasn't thinking about the Cowboy. I don't know that I was thinking at all. I crossed the dirty wooden floor to the refrigerator, and I grabbed the handle. After opening the door it took me a moment to realize exactly what I was seeing, and once I did the blood fell out of my face, leaving my skin tingling with cold.

Ben Livingston stared back at me from the compartment. He'd been folded and tucked in tightly with his head against his knees, facing out. He was naked and dead and my mind took far too long to manage the sight.

I didn't hear Brett coming up behind me. My first warning of his presence was the rough cord he slipped over my head and wrapped around my neck. And just as I understood what was happening, the rope bit into my skin and compressed my windpipe, locking my last breath in my chest.

"You're doing your neighbors a service, Tim," Brett said. His hot breath covered my ear and neck like flowing blood. "After I collect the other two, I'm going to use you boys to create a monument to the German evil, and the people in this city will have no choice but to kill every Kraut motherfucker in sight."

I kicked my legs and scratched at the rope encircling my neck. My chest hitched violently, reflexively constricting to draw oxygen it would never receive. Brett's voice lowered to a rasping growl, his words punctuated by an animal's panting. Flecks of spit landed on my ear.

"You boys were heroes," Brett said. "Which is what makes your sacrifice so powerful. Because of you, we'll finally see the eradication of the...."

My head grew light. A high-pitched sound rang in my ears. The spasms in my chest became unbearable. Brett continued talking, but his voice faded to a buzzing in my ears, no more substantial than the beating of a mosquito's wings all but lost amid the shrill, persistent tone, and the louder the tone became the paler the world became until all was bleached and deafening.

⑃

The first thing I saw upon gaining consciousness was Brett Fletcher's face. He lay on the floor facing me. His eyes met mine, but there was nothing behind them. Blood dripped from his mouth and a small split high on his cheekbone. I tried to cry out, but the ache in my throat refused me this release. Instead

Lee Thomas

270

I choked on the sound and gasped harshly, drawing air over tender tissue. Still dizzy, I managed to roll across the floor, far enough from Brett so that his hands couldn't reach me on the chance that I'd misread his condition. I managed to stop gagging by taking shallow breaths through my nose, and a sweet, rich scent like roses tickled my nostrils.

The refrigerator door provided the leverage I needed to get to my feet. I closed it immediately to seal the terrible sight of Ben Livingston away. Then I returned my attention to my attacker. From this new angle, I saw the jagged knot below his ear, and though I didn't realize it then, someone had snapped his neck, and the days of the Cowboy had come to an end.

Confusion and fear sent me around in tiny circles as I tried to figure out what I should do. Eventually, the right answer came to me and I called the operator and asked her to connect me with the sheriff's office. It seemed as if I spent a very long time on the phone, and before I even hung up, I heard sirens squalling on the farm road. I wandered out of the kitchen, still too dazed to make sense of where I was or what had happened, and in the middle of the living room, I found Brett's empty wheelchair.

Except the chair wasn't empty. Mr. Lang's journal lay on the seat and a scrap of paper jutted from it like a bookmark. I lifted the journal and absently sat in Brett's chair before pulling the note from between the closed pages. I read the simple line of neatly printed words over and over and was still reading them when the police came in and started speaking to me, and again, even when they were grasping my shoulders and shaking me to get my attention. The note read:

Where will you go if not into flame or earth?

Thirty-One: Tim Randall

The week that followed became a series of twisted and blurred events. I spent those days mostly in bed accosted by recent, unpleasant memories and covered in a perpetual sheen of sweat. Ma put her hand to my brow a number of times and smiled, told me I wasn't feverish, but I thought she was wrong – the fever burned in my head and my chest; it simply hadn't surfaced to my skin. When I wasn't in bed, I lay curled on the sofa, hearing the radio but unable to listen to it as the stories became tedious and insignificant moments after they began. I had stories of my own, and they lacked the distant comforts of these fictions. Deputy Burns and other policemen came and went in a parade. They vacillated between extreme concern for my ordeal and joy for my having survived and admiration for my having stopped our city's monster, even though I had done nothing to subdue Brett Fletcher. They treated me like a hero, but I knew I was nothing more than an incomplete victim. Ma stayed home with me for the entire week and lost her job at the factory. Every morning she brought me a glass of milk and a copy of the *Barnard Register* to show me my name printed small and black on the page. She told me how proud she was of me; my crimes forgotten.

Brett Fletcher's story came out in bits and pieces over the next few months. His last name was really Fleischer, which his family – like many families – had changed when coming to America. When Brett was no older than I was that summer both of his parents succumbed to pneumonia, leaving him in the care of a stern – some said insane – old woman named Elsa: his grandmother. Many of the adults in Barnard knew these facts in the abstract way you know the family history of a neighbor, but he was never suspected of the Cowboy's crimes, not only because folks believed Brett had been crippled in battle and was confined to his chair, but also because he was a valued citizen, a true American, a patriot. Doc Randolph speculated that Brett's loathing of the German people was the result of the abuse he took from Elsa Fleischer, a woman who regularly beat the boy, humiliated him, and on occasion tied him to his bed and threaded a knitting needle through his urethra, leaving it there for hours at a time. As an adult, Brett was impotent and frustrated and hateful, believing it was his duty to turn the world against the men and women who shared his – and more specifically his grandmother's – heritage.

Of course his paralysis was a lie – in part. Brett had never spent a day near combat. There had been no mortar shell, no explosion. He'd run a Jeep off the road in Edinburgh while drunk, and the doctors had made a hasty diagnosis, taking Brett's temporary paralysis as a permanent affliction, and they'd filled out the reports to send him home, and no one had questioned Brett's story, because he hadn't served with any of the other men from Barnard, and since his grandmother's death, there had been no one at home to receive a telegram explaining the truth of his injury. He came home a fractured hero and had brought his war with him.

We know these things because the Cowboy kept a journal of his own. Deputy Burns found it in a trunk where Brett kept personal items, including an old dress, belonging to Elsa Fleischer, which Brett had shredded with a knife.

One morning while the glass of milk warmed on the table next to my bed, I read the *Register* and saw a passage attributed to Deputy Burns. He speculated that Barnard's Cowboy had died as the result of my struggles. Burns suggested that I'd thrown Brett off balance, causing him to fall backward, breaking his neck on the stove. It couldn't have happened that way, but since no one came forward to claim responsibility for saving me, and there was no hard evidence to prove a conflicting theory, that became the story. Like Brett Fletcher, a lie made me a hero.

I returned to school and suffered the accolades of my classmates. I didn't feel at ease with them, never knew what to say. Their faces and excited conversations were immature. Shallow. Bum was gone, and though I could call many of the boys and girls I shared classes with friends, I felt close to none of them.

If there was any light during this difficult time, it came in the form of a telegram. The note arrived on a Thursday afternoon and informed my mother and me that Daddy had been found alive and was in a French hospital and would return to us soon. My mother was ecstatic, sobbing and laughing and holding me every chance I would allow, but I remembered what my grandfather had told me. He'd said that the man who had left Barnard would never return. Whether the injuries he'd sustained were severe or minor, whether he'd seen the faces of the enemy or not, the experience would irrevocably alter Fred Randall.

Though happy for the news of my father's return, my grandfather's claims haunted me. I believed what he'd said because I'd been in battle myself. Young men – including my best friend – had died. I'd seen an innocent man tortured. The memories of his abuse and his subsequent murder fouled my body like a disease, eating away at my mind and muscles until sometimes I felt I should return to the lake and the black forms that swam beneath its surface. They waited for me there, people I had known and some that I had loved – phantoms of my guilt.

At night they emerge from the water, stalking over the grassy field, leaving bits of themselves on the ground. They gather at my bedside – Bum, Harold, David, the father I'd known before the war, and my neighbor Mr. Lang – and they gaze down on me, whispering revelations of who they were and who I am.

And the strongest voice belongs to the German, who looks upon me with concern and warmth, and he tells me, "If you can stand up, you'll live."

Epilogue: New York City

I go to school and then to college, and when it becomes clear that a wife is not in my future, I take Ernst Lang's example and let those who care to know that I am a certain kind of man: one no more or less important than any other man. As I grow older I move away from Texas and make a family of my own, finding love with a man named Charles who I meet in Central Park. We live in New York and watch the Civil Rights struggles and the Vietnam War and the Stonewall Riots, and I am struck by how similar all conflicts are, as if each generation must prove itself with fresh arguments and fresh blood, having learned nothing from the previous generation.

In time, Ma and Daddy die and then many years later Charles dies, leaving me alone, and I think it is greedy to mourn his death as we've shared so much, but I do mourn him because I'm human, and though life has given me a mile of gold, I want another inch of it, another foot. A second mile.

The millennium comes and goes. Sixty years pass since the events of that summer. One morning, I am watching the news, and a photograph appears on the television screen that chills me to my core.

Charges of misconduct are being filed against soldiers stationed in Baghdad. In a prisoner of war facility called Abu Ghraib, Americans are said to humiliate, sodomize, and torture a number of their Iraqi prisoners. Worse still, photographs of these soldiers show their great amusement at the dehumanizing tactics employed. Then a photograph of an inmate, standing on a box with his arms extended as if being crucified flashes on the television set. He wears a dark hood and a dark tunic that seems to have been made from a threadbare blanket. And suddenly I am again standing in a room on Dodd Street with my neighbor bound spread eagled on his bed, quaking in terror as the brown bedspread conceals his face so he cannot see the nature of his binding and those who have bound him.

It all comes back with such force, my breath locks in my throat. The odors of the room fill my nose, and the sounds of a desperate man wheezing and whispering harshly in German, and young men laughing ring in my ears, achingly like a saw on tin. Guilt resurfaces: a bloated corpse, frightening me with its ugliness. I cannot follow the story on the news because the pain it brings is personal and feels all too fresh, and though I turn the television off, the memories remain. I think of an innocent man whose face is smeared in blood and who will die a victim of ignorance and lies, and he stays with me throughout the day and into the weeks that follow, and I realize that he has always been with me, as is the case with anyone we have loved.

One afternoon, I leave the apartment on Broadway and begin walking in an attempt to dilute the memories with the city's sounds and motion. As I near Lincoln Center, I pass a restaurant's patio, where young and attractive people gather for expensive coffees and complicated pasta dishes, and I see a man sitting with his arm on the patio railing. He is speaking with a younger man who wears his hair in a nest of dark spikes. The younger man has his back to me, but he seems to be in the process of laughing, and the man I am facing smiles broadly, shrugs and continues speaking.

The man is thickly built with short brown hair and scars like a line across his nose and cheeks. In addition to the mustache I remember, he now wears a Van Dyke that is lightly salted with gray, and were it not for the miscellaneous impossibilities, I would swear this man once lived across the street from me in the city of Barnard, Texas. So great is this impression I feel a twinge of fear should he recognize me, but even if Ernst Lang had survived Burl Jones's bullets, he would be a hundred years old or more and certainly would not look so close to the way he had the last time I'd seen him.

Knowing I gaze on nothing more than a normal man, given attributes I ascribe to a long dead German – perhaps because of the hours I have spent thinking about him in the preceding months – I still cannot take my eyes off of him. His joy is palpable, and his eyes twinkle mischievously, the way they did when he climbed onto his sofa to explain the power of names to two little boys.

I stand there and smile. I want to approach him and even take a step forward before I stop myself. Then quickly I turn and hurry back the way I have come.

When I was a boy, I lived across the street from a German. His name was Ernst and he helped me once. He might have even saved my life, but that isn't something I will ever know for certain. If nothing else, I have tried to live an honest life because of what he taught me. There are many things I never told the German. So I will tell him now.

I am sorry, and I am grateful, and goodbye.

Wherever you are, live and rest in peace.

⑃

LEE THOMAS is the Lambda Literary Award and Bram Stoker Award-winning author of the novels *Stained, Damage,* and *The Dust of Wonderland,* and the critically-acclaimed short story collection *In the Closet, Under the Bed.* In addition to numerous magazines, his short fiction has appeared in the anthologies *Darkness of the Edge, Supernatural Noir, Horror Library, Vol. 4,* and *Inferno,* among others. Current and forthcoming titles include the novellas *The Black Sun Set, Crisis,* and *Focus* (co-written with Nate Southard). Lee lives in Austin, Texas, where he is working on a number of projects. Find him online at www.leethomasauthor.com.

LaVergne, TN USA
14 March 2011
220054LV00001B/71/P